Prodigal Son

Michelle Day

Reading order
1 - Prodigal Son
2 - Father + Son
3 - Wayward son
4 - Shattered son

Published by Michelle Day, 2013.

Also by Michelle Day

Prodigal Son
Book One of the Jensen Family Series
By Michelle Day

Disclaimer: This book contains sexually explicit material and profanity. Please do not read further if these things offend you.

This book is a work of fiction. The characters, events and places portrayed in this book are products of the author's imagination and are either fictitious or are used fictitiously. Any similarity to real persons, living or dead, is purely coincidental and not intentional.

In layman's terms, if you think you see yourself in this book, you don't.

To Yana and Stephen.
My life, my heart, my inspiration.

I am told that it is often the middle child that is the one who creates the problems in a family. This isn't the case in my family. My name is PAUL JENSEN and although I have a twin, I am the last fruit of my mothers' loins so to speak and therefore, the youngest which is exactly how my family view me.

You see, I am the proverbial black sheep; I don't seem to be able to put a foot right at least as far as my father is concerned. I share an acrimonious relationship with him and that is putting it mildly, it seems these days all I have to do is sneeze to have him lashing out, it's not all down to him however, I will admit that I do like to push his buttons and make him react, something I would never have attempted as a child but now, as I am growing in stature as well as confidence, I take a deep pleasure in it.

MICHAEL JENSEN, my father, developed his acerbic attitude towards me from the moment I was born. The reason for this being that all Jensen's, without exception are blue eyed blonds, he didn't take into account that when he married my Spanish mother MONICA, there was a chance that at least one of his offspring would take after her, I am said offspring.

Not to float my own boat you understand and I am simply stating facts, I am superb, I'm the epitome of tall, dark and handsome. My mother adores me which is just as well given my fathers' attitude. I adore women, they adore me and I fully intend to sample as many of them as I possibly can before I get caught up in that thing called love although at this point in my life I'm not sure if that woman would be the luckiest one in the world or the most unfortunate as fidelity isn't high on my list of priorities.

My relationship with my father isn't helped by the fact that we are a fairly prominent and wealthy family and my actions appear to have caught the attention of the paparazzi. I am a self confessed media whore, what can I say? It's good for business. The fact that it winds the old man up to epic proportions is just an added bonus.

This is the first part of my story, my early life, my trials, tribulations, loves, of which there are many and losses, thankfully only a few and an almighty scandal that would rock not only my world but all those involved.

MICHAEL JENSEN knows from the second MONICA PALOMA challenges him at the summer ball that he has to have her. Tall, handsome blond haired and blue eyed only child and heir to the Jensen fortune, he is used to getting what he wants by any means possible and is as shocked when she resists his usual tried and tested methods as he is to his actual attraction to her. He tended to be attracted to stick thin blond haired, blue eyed girls with the intent of keeping the Jensen gene pool alive and kicking when the time came to breed. Monica's dark eyes, hair and curvaceous figure captured his imagination and wetted his appetite. His sights set firmly on her; he wouldn't stop until she wore his wedding ring and took his last name.

Of Spanish decent, Monica lives at home with her parents and older brother. Strong willed but kind and loving, she detests the way her classmate Michael Jensen treats women as if they were mere playthings put on this earth solely for his amusement and is appalled that she finds herself attracted to him, even more starling had been the glint in his eyes when she stood up to him, looked him squarely in the eyes whilst putting him firmly in his place. While his efforts to capture her attention after the ball amused her, she steeled herself against the thoughtful gifts that arrived on her doorstep with regularity, if he wanted her as much as he professed, he'd damn well have to work harder to get her.

By the end of the following summer, the unlikely pair are married and expecting their first child. TESSA JENSEN is born, the apple of her father's eye if only for the fact that her appearance made her every bit a Jensen. Michael proved himself an attentive husband and father, surprising both his parents and hers with his loving manner towards his wife and daughter.

Two and a half years on after a difficult pregnancy which put her on bed rest, Monica gave birth to twin boys MATTHEW and PAUL. Both boys were healthy, taking characteristics and colouring from each parent. Although Michael was in raptures that he now had sons and professed his love for his wife and the beautiful, blond haired baby that was Matthew, his joy soon turned sour when he turned his attention to the younger of the twins.

Having taken on his mothers' colouring of olive skin and dark hair, Paul was nothing like the son Michael had expected his wife to produce, his dislike for the darker baby only heightened by the fact that he would squall each and every time Michael approached his crib. It was only a matter of hours after the birth that Michael announced his rejection of the child based solely on the fact that he wasn't a true Jensen due to his colouring. After only four years of marriage, where his children were concerned Michael returned to being the stubborn, hard headed man he had been at school and Monica knew she had a battle on her hands.

She didn't count on the battle being a lifelong thing for as Paul grew he began to exhibit her own stubborn nature and would challenge his father at every available instance leading to violent clashes between the pair.

Monica guided her children through their childhood and was proud of them as they progressed into adulthood. All three showed kind and thoughtful tendencies and although Tessa had given her relatively few problems, her sons Matthew and Paul more than made up for it. Her sons were stunning in appearance and used their looks to their full advantage with Matthew being the more subtle of the two, she only every got to hear of Paul's exploits which would put him directly in the firing line of his father's temper.

Not one to back down and severely lacking the skills to bring his better judgement into play, Paul used the legendary Jensen temper to full advantage against the man he considered his sperm donor and would proceed to do things that put him firmly in the public's eye. His affair with his teacher and the subsequent pregnancy was the straw that broke the camel's back in forcing Monica to step back from her position of keeping the peace between father and son. As much as she loved him, where the teacher and pregnancy were concerned, Paul was on his own.

Prodigal Son

Chapter One

"I now pronounce you Man and Wife", the Vicar closed his Bible and smiled at the two young people before him.

Two families cheered as the Groom took a step towards his Bride and kissed her. Charles Jensen was especially proud of his only son Michael, he had chosen well from the previous year's crop of society debutants. Monica Paloma, his new daughter in law, was beautiful with her dark hair, huge brown eyes and olive skin; she complemented his son's blonde hair and blue eyes perfectly.

The wedding had made society news. Charles Jensen was well known in London's financial circle as account and financial advisor to the rich and famous, his son Michael was being groomed to take over the company within the next two years as Charles planned to retire early along with his wife Penelope who had been his loving and faithful companion for the past twenty five years.

Jackson Paloma and his wife Paula had moved to England from Spain with their baby son Juan (who re-named himself John) many years before their lovely daughter was born. Jackson had a talent for making one of a kind ladies shoes and had begged and borrowed enough money to start his own business, with Paula working by his side and attending night school in order to better her English and subsequently his, they had hit the jackpot when one of the mother's at John's school had noticed Paula's unique pumps, commissions followed and their success grew as the mother's discussed their quaint little shoe maker at coffee mornings and bridge games.

So, two, rich, successful families were joined by the marriage of their children and while the Jensen family were more than satisfied with their child's choice, the Paloma family had reservations.

"Are you sure Monica?" Paula had asked at the fitting of her daughter's wedding dress

"Of course I'm sure." Monica had replied, "I love him, he loves me, and there is nothing to be unsure about. Why do you hate him so much?"

"I wouldn't say I hate him exactly, it's just that he seems so cold Monica, he keeps you at arms length and that temper." Paula shrugged.

"He is uneasy around you and Dad that's all; he is very sweet to me when we are alone." Monica reassured her mother for what seemed like the hundredth time, "I do admit that he has a temper though, but really Mum, its nothing I can't handle and so far it hasn't been directed at me."

"But sweetheart, you are so bright, you could achieve so much before you settle into a marriage with a man who has already made it more than clear that he expects his wife to remain at home."

"I want to stay at home, be a homemaker, have children, if I do all that when I'm young, I can still pursue any interests I develop after the children have grown."

"I'm not going to be able to talk you out of this am I?"

Monica shook her head "He's a good man, he will take care of me and more than anything, I want to be with him."

Michael guided his bride down the aisle and out of the church, holding her hand tightly and grinning broadly, he had just married the girl who had made it impossibly hard for him to date her, she frustrated the hell out of him with her sly grin and the reply of "Maybe" when he asked her to date him.

Her dark looks hadn't immediately attracted him, he preferred skinny blondes who had air in their heads and who would let him go further than just kissing on the promise of a second date.

Monica had told him to get over himself when she had walked past him loudly bragging to a bunch of airhead blondes of his achievements at college and his first successful client win at work, he had been furious that a woman had dared to speak to him in such a tone, he had spun away from the blondes and grabbed her arm, turning her towards him.

"How dare you speak to me that way." he fumed, "Don't you know who I am?"

"I'm more than aware of who you are Michael Jensen," She blazed at him and instead of trying to free herself from his grasp she stepped closer "And I strongly suggest that you take your hands off me before I have you singing soprano for the rest of your life." she looked down as she finished speaking. It was Michael who stepped back when he noticed her sharp nails about to dig into his crotch.

"You're supposed to be a lady." He spat.

"I will behave like a lady when you can prove you can be a gentleman." she replied then flipped him a sideways grin as she slid from his grasp.

Michael gawped after her, angry beyond belief but recognising that this woman was the one he would marry.

"Who is she?" he asked his select group of friends

"You mean the hot little brunette who had you by the balls?" Ray, his best friend and future best man asked "Monica Paloma, she's way too smart for you Michael, I'd give it a miss."

Michael smiled, he had no intention what so ever of letting this one get away, no woman had ever spoken to him that way or even dared to stand up to him. He watched the gentle sway of her hips as she walked away noticing the way most of the men in the room turned to watch her walk by and although she wasn't what he would class as his usual type, he did recognise her classic beauty and felt challenged by her fearless confrontation with him. He was prepared to be impossibly persistent in wooing this woman; she would be his before the end of the summer.

And so it began, first the delivery of fresh flowers every day which Monica would refuse to accept, sending the florist away. Then the gifts started to arrive, Michael started with simple things like chocolates and fruit baskets and moved onto more expensive gifts of jewellery all of which returned to him within the day.

Michael found himself pacing his office daily in a white hot rage over Monica's refusal of his gifts, what the hell was wrong with her? Didn't she realise the gifts were his way of asking his permission to court her. He decided to confront her and took a day out of his busy schedule to pay her a visit.

Sitting across the street in his sleek blue Mercedes, Michael watched as Monica's parents left the house. He waited for their Range Rover to turn off onto the main road before leaving his car and approaching the house. It seemed to take an eternity for her to answer the door but when she did, she took his breath away. Her thick dark hair was tied back in a pony tail, she was wearing incredibly tight cropped, red gingham trousers and a pretty white blouse that did nothing to hide her shapely figure.

"Michael Jensen." she said crossing her arms and leaning against the door frame "To what do I owe the somewhat dubious pleasure of this visit?"

Michael did not reply immediately, he looked at her, smiled then offered her the transparent box he held, the note inside the box read Return to sender.

"I thought, as you have returned my gifts, that I would deliver this one in person, or would you like to return this one too?"

Monica glanced at the box, tutted then replied "It takes more than fancy gifts to impress this girl, you need to try harder." she moved to close the door.

"Monica" Michael stepped forward and put his hand on the door "Won't you even give me one chance to prove myself?"

"Maybe." she grinned and dropped her head, glancing up at him though her dark lashes.

"May I take you out one evening?" he asked, feeling silly with the formality of his request.

"You may. Pick me up tomorrow at eight and we will take it from there." she stepped back and closed the door in his face.

The following evening, Michael rang the doorbell of the Paloma household, he smiled at Monica when she opened the door.

Monica pointedly looked at her wristwatch "You're late, it's a minute past."

Michael opened his mouth to speak but then thought the better of it, Monica laughed

"I'm only teasing, come on in." she guided him to a tastefully furnished sitting room where her family were waiting to receive him.

The courtship began with Michael wrongly thinking her Latin blood would have her all hot and steamy at his advances. She never let on just how aroused she was by his touch, he clearly knew which buttons to press but she was determined to wait until her wedding night, a fact she reminded him of each and every time he tried to push her further than she was willing to go.

For his own sanity, Michael slowed things down a little, deciding that trying to push her into bed with him was not the way to go and recognising that her will was far stronger than his and that she would ultimately win in a battle of wills.

Within the month he had asked her to marry him, she completely captivated him and although at first she was reluctant to accept his proposal, when he told her "I can't breathe without you" she realised that this outwardly arrogant, cold man, did have a heart and it belonged to her. Within moments of accepting his marriage proposal, she had on her hand the biggest diamond ring she had ever seen.

Michael didn't want a long engagement, he insisted that they were married as soon as possible and so the mad rush of wedding planning began.

Within weeks of returning from their honeymoon and moving into their beautiful detached house, a joint wedding present from their parents, Monica discovered she was pregnant. She couldn't contain herself long enough for Michael to return home from work so she caught a taxi to the offices of Jensen Incorporated and waited for her husband outside.

Michael spotted Monica the moment he stepped onto the street, he frowned, thinking that perhaps something was wrong, knowing Monica would never come to the office on a trivial matter but she smiled as he went towards her then she reached out to touch his forehead.

"Don't frown Michael, you'll get wrinkles."

He smiled, she was always telling him not to frown "Is that better?" he asked.

"Yes" she took his hand as they began to walk towards his car.

"Are you going to tell me why you are here?"

"Do you love me Michael? She countered his question.

"You know I do." he answered, truthfully, he loved this woman deeply.

"How much do you love me?"

"More than the moon and stars," he replied, knowing this was the answer she wanted. He stopped by his car, unlocked the passenger side and opened the door for her.

"Would you love me even more if I told you that I am going to make you a daddy?" She asked smiling sweetly, the smile turning to a laugh as his stunned expression changed to a huge grin as he dropped his briefcase, picked her up and swung her around in a circle.

"You clever girl," he whispered in her ear, "I will get you the best possible care, you wont want for anything ever again." he promised.

"I know."

Daughter Tessa was born on a hot July day in 1974 after a near perfect pregnancy and a long but pain controlled labour.

Tessa Marie Jensen weighed in at a hefty eight pounds and apart from the occasional grizzle, was a model baby, heart stoppingly adorable having inherited her fathers blond curls and blue eyes and a hint of her mothers' olive skin.

She began sleeping through the night at just six weeks old leaving Monica free to once again pursue her husband in her quest for a big family.

Michael had wanted to wait at least until Tessa was attending nursery, grumpily admitting that he didn't really want to share his wife with any more children just yet. Monica pointed out that she kept the house and child spotless, had his meal ready for him when he returned from work and still had more than enough energy to fulfil his healthy sexual appetite and that more babies wouldn't make a difference, then, soon after Tessa began nursery school she fell pregnant again.

The sickness started almost immediately as well as feeling feint and constantly tired. Jackson and Paula Paloma began to spend a lot of time with their daughter much to Michael's annoyance as he feared they would interfere. He changed his attitude when his wife unexpectedly collapsed when four months pregnant while making lunch for Tessa, she would have remained that way until he returned home had his in-laws not been there.

Monica woke in a private room of a prestigious Harley Street hospital, wired up to monitors with the anxious faces of her husband and parents peering at her.

"Where's Tessa?" she asked, struggling to sit up.

"She's with my parents, you need to lay flat." Michael answered.

"What happened?"

"You passed out, you have started to bleed, the doctor has put you on complete bed rest in an effort to preserve the pregnancy." Michael told her, he was tired, it had been almost twenty hours since he had slept, he was sick with worry for his wife and found he simply couldn't leave her side.

Monica passed her hand over her stomach, feeling the unusually large bump of her early pregnancy "Is the baby ok?"

"You have had an Ultra sound scan, it would appear that you are carrying twins, they both seem fine." Paula leaned over her daughter.

Monica frowned "Is that why I'm so big, twins?" she paused "I need to see a doctor; I'm not ready for this."

Moments later, Michael and his in-laws left Monica with her doctor, he explained to her that her twins were not identical but fraternal; each baby had its own placenta. He continued by telling her that the smaller twins' placenta had detached slightly and there was a possibility, even with complete bed rest, that she would lose that baby, he told her to try not to worry, she must relax as much as she could and that he would monitor her closely and tell her of any changes, good or bad.

Monica stayed on bed rest for the remainder of her pregnancy. The bleeding stopped and both twins appeared to be developing well. Tessa's care was taken over by Monica's parents and they handed over to Michael who had proved himself a loving, caring father, when he returned from his nightly visit to his wife.

Monica's consultant decided it would not be possible for her to attempt to give birth normally as the smaller twin was in the breach position. Several fruitless attempts had been made to turn the baby but it had stubbornly returned to its preferred position after a matter of only a few hours. A caesarean section was planned and Michael arranged extended leave from work.

Matthew Charles Jensen was born at midday on 17th October 1977, a robust 7lb in weight with light blond hair, his brother, Paul Nicholas Jensen reluctantly entered the world at twelve fifteen on the same day, smaller than the older twin, only weighing 5lb 6oz but giving the appearance of being exceptionally laid back, his breach position in the womb had meant he was born with his legs straight. He had caused the delivering consultant to swear under his breath as he struggled to deliver the second twin, he could have sworn the baby was clinging to its mother's womb in its struggle to remain within the secure environment. This tiny baby had darker skin than his fair haired brother and a thick mop of dark hair.

Monica felt an instant rush of love for her baby boys once she was allowed to see them, her joy was short lived however when Michael visited her shortly after she had been introduced to her twins.

Looking into the cot nearest to him, Michael smiled when he saw the pale skin and blond hair of the eldest twin, reaching into the cot he picked up the small bundle of baby and held it to his chest. He moved to the other side of Monica's bed and the second cot, peering over the edge, he breathed in sharply

"What on earth is that?" he asked upon seeing the olive skin and dark hair of the youngest twin.

"That is your son Michael." Monica answered, a cold edge to her tone.

"Impossible, all Jensen's are blond haired and fair skinned, there have never been any exceptions."

"Has it crossed your mind that perhaps he takes after my family?"

Michael ignored the comment and handed the blond bundle to her, he stepped closer to the second cot, reaching in for the baby. As his hand went behind the baby's head to support it, it let out an ear piercing scream.

"How can something so small make such a racket?" he asked holding the infant at arms' length.

"Take Matthew and give Paul to me." Monica spoke above the howls of her son. No sooner was Paul in his mothers' arms when he stopped screaming, his small mouth searching for her breast "He's hungry." she told Michael "Give Matthew a bottle would you?" she gestured to the small bottles of formula milk "I'll feed Paul."

"Why should my son have to be fed second rate formula when that runt gets all the goodness of your breast milk?"

"Paul is also your son and as he is the smaller of the two he needs the extra nutrients and protection my milk gives him. Just because he isn't blond doesn't make him any less of a Jensen." she scowled.

"You can sugar coat it all you want Monica, Matthew is my son, you can do what you like with Paul."

Monica found it hard to believe that her husband would reject his child simply for the colour of his hair but knowing how stubborn and pig headed Michael could be, she knew his opinion wouldn't change in the slightest unless this child proved himself to be something outstanding, then Michael would welcome him with open arms.

Two weeks after the birth, Monica and her twin boys were allowed home. Michael had returned to work so Paula moved in to help her daughter. During the day everything went swimmingly, both boys were fairly content and were growing well. Tessa was enthralled with her new brothers, spending hours playing with them and whining when it was time for her to nap.

Paula didn't quite believe her daughter when she told her of Michael's attitude towards the beautiful dark haired baby. Michael so far had been a wonderful father; it wasn't until she saw it for herself that she, along with Monica decided that this little boy would need all their love and attention as he clearly wasn't going to get it from Michael.

When the twins were a little over two months old, Paula returned home. Michael would leave early for work so that he would be home in the early evening to help his wife with the children. The routine was always the same, Michael would come home, put his briefcase in the hall and his keys on the hook by the front door, he would then stroll through to the kitchen where he would inevitably find his wife and offspring. After kissing Monica, he would turn to his daughter and kiss her fondly on the cheek then reach for Matthew and lift him out of the pram he shared with Paul who generally got ignored. Paul didn't help his own cause by bursting into gusty wails every time Michael got near him.

The years seemed to fly by, before Monica knew it, she was preparing Tessa for Primary School and the boys for nursery. Tessa had developed a sunny personality and was eager to please her parents and teachers; she had a few close friends who, unbeknown to her parents, would remain close her entire life.

Matthew and Paul were a handful, always getting into mischief. They had both developed into robust two year olds with a terrible sweet tooth which Monica had to admit she did indulge them with sweets and tempting desserts causing both boys to be slightly rotund. Starting out as the smaller twin didn't seem to have affected Paul's development in any way; he was already taller than his brother and far more active.

Matthew, although having developed the blond hair and blue eyes of a typical Jensen, he had the Paloma body shape being fairly short and squat with broad shoulders and a barrel chest, he had also inherited his nose and chin shape from Monica's family. Paul was the opposite of his sibling possessing the Paloma dark hair, olive skin and deep brown eyes that caused his father to reject him, he had many of the Jensen traits which showed themselves in Paul's long body and limbs. The straight nose and almond shaped eyes came straight from Michael's gene pool as did his temper.

Dropping Tessa off to her second day at Primary school, Monica then took her boys around the side of the school to the nursery unit. She had been preparing them for this day and was absolutely dreading it even though the boys were familiar with the nursery building as they had been regular visitors during Tessa's time there.

Matthew dashed into the nursery playground, always the more outgoing of the two boys, he wasn't shy and made friends easily, he had been so overwhelmed with the sight of outdoor oversized building blocks that he hadn't given his mother or brother a second glance before running into the playground and immersing himself in the blocks.

Paul watched his brother from behind Monica's skirt, he desperately wanted to go and play but was so afraid that his mother would leave he was pinned to the spot with fear.

"Mrs Jensen, we've so been looking forward to the boys joining our little group." Katherine Bates, the senior teacher greeted Monica.

"I'm afraid someone isn't too keen." Monica greeted the teacher while stroking her son's dark hair.

"I'm sure we can persuade him." she knelt down in front of Paul "Hi Paul, I'm Kat, I have some lovely things for you to do, why don't you come with me and see what you would like to do." she smiled into the huge dark brown eyes and wasn't discouraged when the child simply shook his head and buried himself further into his mothers' skirt. "Ok, I'll just have a chat with your Mummy then." she came to her feet "Has he always been this shy?"

"He's fine around people he knows, he doesn't like change or new situations, he lacks confidence." Monica explained "He will come around, it's just going to take some time, perhaps I should take him home and try again tomorrow."

"I really think that would be the worst thing you could do." Kat replied, she continued to talk to Monica, encouraging her to come into the playground so that the child was surrounded by happy children having oodles of fun in the hope of encouraging him.

From Paul's point of view, for now, he was quite happy where he was, safely close to his mother but this new lady smelled nice, like Monica did when she had been baking, a smell he would later recognise as Cinnamon. He watched the lady with growing interest as she talked to his mother noticing that she would glance down at him and smile every now and then. He became distracted when a helicopter cruised low overhead and stepped away from Monica's protection to get a better look. Kat picked up on the boy's interest immediately and once more came down to his level.

"You like helicopters?" she asked.

Caught unaware and at least three feet away from Monica, Paul initially froze when the teacher spoke to him, his attention was drawn once more to the helicopter as it circled and began another slow pass.

"That's an Apache helicopter, I have a book on helicopters in the class room if you would like to see it, I bet Mummy would love you to draw her a picture of it."

Paul looked at Monica who nodded encouragement at her son. He turned back to the teacher, looking at her outstretched hand; he took a hesitant step towards her and placed his small hand in hers.

Kat smiled "I'm so glad you have come to our school, I really need someone to help me with the milk and fruit for the other children, do you think you could be my helper?" she kept up the constant stream of chatter all the way into the classroom while behind her back she was waving goodbye to Monica.

Much to Monica's surprise, Paul was all smiles when she returned to the nursery at midday to collect her sons,

"Both boys have been an absolute pleasure." Kat smiled warmly as the Jensen twins ran to their mother, "I think Paul will be just fine and Matthew is such a sociable little thing that I can't see him ever having any problems."

"I can't thank you enough for persuading Paul into school, he's such a Mummy's boy that it worries me sometimes."

"Perhaps he could spend some more time with Mr Jensen?"

"Michael and Paul tend to avoid each other, Michael never did take to him and I probably over compensate for the attention Paul doesn't get from his father."

"Is there another male role model Paul could spend time with, a Grandparent perhaps?"

"Yes, he has two doting Grandfathers'; I will have to talk to them about it."

"I really do think it would do him the world of good. I'll see you tomorrow Mrs Jensen."

Monica and the boys stopped to get ice cream on the way home much to the boys delight. Once they arrived home, Matthew pulled out his building bricks while Paul watched cartoons, within half an hour both boys were sound asleep leaving Monica free to have a chat and a coffee with her neighbour who stayed with the boys while Monica went to collect Tessa later that afternoon.

The following weekend the entire family descended on Michael's parents. Charles and Penelope Jensen were besotted with their three grand children and both had witnessed their son's rejection of the youngest twin, it troubled them greatly.

"Look at the boy Michael, he's pure Jensen, he has our nose and eyes and I've seen his little temper in full force, I don't understand why you won't have anything to do with him." Charles frowned at his son while bouncing Paul on his lap.

"I don't understand how you say he's pure Jensen, look at him, he's nothing like us." Michael protested "Plus the little runt hates me, he either screams at me or just stares, he doesn't interact with me at all."

"That's more to do with the negative attitude you project towards him than his attitude towards you, he's two years old and he hasn't done anything to deserve this attitude from you." Charles warned.

"The only thing he has inherited from our family is his temper; everything else is from Monica's side."

"He is still the fruit of your loin's son."

"You can talk at me about it all you want, I don't want to know." Michael insisted.

"The boy needs a male role model Michael and so far you aren't doing a very good job."

"Then you take over that role, between you and Jackson he should have all the male role models he needs." Michael spat then left to join his other two children.

Michael hadn't been aware that Monica had been listening in on the conversation with Charles; she went to sit by her father in law when Michael left.

"What am I going to do?" she asked Charles.

"You are going to carry on as normal, between myself and your father; we will make sure this little boy has his father figure. I can only apologise for my sons' bigoted attitude Monica, he certainly wasn't raised that way" Charles turned the dark haired boy towards him "You are destined for great things young man, I can feel it in my bones." he smiled at the child who reached out and pulled at his Grand Fathers' nose.

As the years progressed, the Jensen children each developed their individual personalities. Tessa was a happy sunny girl who loved to help anyone or anything that needed her; she remained charmingly pretty with large, clear blue eyes and long blond hair. Matthew was a bouncy, loud individual, he loved to play football and tennis and when he wasn't with his brother was more often than not surrounded by friends, his golden halo of hair, steel blue eyes and easy going nature afforded him many female admirers in his teenage years. Paul liked to be at home, he spent a lot of time playing video games and loud, loud music, and he had two very close friends who would follow him through to adulthood. He was a watchful child and would often stand at the side lines summing up the situation while his brother dived straight in. Quietly confident with a sharp wit and intelligence, he became easily bored at school and started to misbehave half way through primary school, he would also lash out if anyone tried to pick on either of his siblings not caring about the consequences at school or home.

By the time Tessa was seventeen and the boys almost fourteen, Paul had been suspended from school three times, his expulsion coming shortly before the summer holidays and the family's annual pilgrimage to Spain.

Monica and Michael had been called to the school where it was explained to them that Paul was being expelled as he had viciously attacked another boy and broken his nose, when asked why he had done this Paul had remained stoically silent until he saw that Monica had arrived with Michael in tow. Paul had been standing in the corner of the head teachers' office while the explanation of his expulsion had been explained to his parents.

Monica turned to her son "What do you have to say for yourself?"

Paul took a step towards his mother, he hated upsetting her and could see that she was cross with him "I only hit him once Mum" he shrugged.

"Why did you hit him?"

"He was teasing one of the girls in my class, I told him to leave her alone but he wouldn't, he was calling her names because she has to wear braces, when I took her hand and tried to pull her away, he grabbed her hair and pulled a big chunk of it out of her head, she started to cry and I just hit him." he explained.

Monica turned to the Head Teacher, "I trust the other boy will be receiving a similar punishment?"

"He has been dealt with."

"My son was after all, defending a class mate, it would appear he didn't start the attack." Monica persisted.

"The boy in question has received a suspension."

"Only a suspension? Why isn't he being expelled?" Monica demanded.

"It's the first time this particular boy has been in trouble whereas we have been here before with Paul, he's a regular visitor to my office as you are well aware Mrs Jensen, I would say it's a jolly good job that you intend sending both boys to boarding school next term, I feel the added discipline will be advantageous to both of them although in my experience, some schools are more interested in receiving their fees than the behaviour of their students."

Leaving the school with their disgraced son, Michael was fuming;

"Who does he think he is to lecture me on Boarding Schools?" he growled

"He's just jealous because he doesn't earn as much as you." Paul commented.

"I don't want to hear another word from you boy." Michael rounded on his son, "Get in the car and keep your mouth shut, I will deal with you when we get home."

Climbing out of the car once they reached home, Monica stroked her son's dark hair as he passed her "Go to your room son, I'll be up in a bit." she told him, she put her bag on the kitchen table and turned to switch on the kettle,

"Why do you mollycoddle him so much? He's in the wrong and still you protect him." Michael asked her.

"Michael, he was defending a girl, I find that quite honourable."

"He just likes the attention getting into trouble gives him."

"Don't be ridiculous Michael, he was doing what he thought was right."

"Stop defending him woman." Michael bellowed "He's a trouble maker, he always has been, he's the one who knocked Matthew's teeth out last summer and cost me a fortune in dental bills and you defended him then, he thinks he can do as he pleases because you pander to his every whim, I'm sick of it, it stops now."

"Don't shout at Mum." Paul's voice from the kitchen door "She hasn't done anything to deserve that."

"Paul be quiet." Monica warned but she wasn't quick enough to stop Michael as he lunged at the boy and she felt physically sick as she heard the awful thud of Michael's fist connecting with Paul's face.

The beating continued for a good five minutes with Monica vainly trying to pull Michael off the boy now crouched on the floor. Michael, his anger finally spent, grabbed his car keys and sped away from the house.

Guiding Paul to the bathroom, she sat him on the edge of the bath and began to clean the bruised and bloodied face, pushing Paul's fringe off his face, she encouraged him to look at her "You mustn't come between your father and me." she told him "I can handle him, you are still a boy, he will lash out at you not me."

"I hate him." was all Paul replied.

Monica decided it would be best for Paul if he stayed out of Michael's way until their flight to Spain and after a brief discussion with her parents, Paul was moved to his Grandparents home for the next two weeks.

Paul immensely enjoyed spending time with Monica's parents, through them he had learned to speak Spanish and was as fluent as they were, his Grandmother, Paula had begun to teach him everything he would need to know to run a business, something he had expressed an interest in as he desperately didn't want to work for Michael when he was older but recognised that he would probably have to do a short spell at Jensen Incorporated in order to earn the money he would require to set up on his own.

Grandfather Jackson and Uncle John would take him fishing on their boat, teaching him that he didn't always need to be tense. Between them they were also the ones responsible for Paul's future love of cars, Jackson being the proud owner of a Silver Aston Martin DB5 and Uncle John had recently purchased an E-Type Jaguar.

Paul was a welcome addition at the small factory the Paloma family owned to step up the production of their now designer shoes. He learned almost every aspect of the shoe making process and while it wasn't something he wanted to pursue, he found it immensely interesting and would spend a lot of time with the workers, learning their jobs or even making cups of tea when they were up against a deadline and wouldn't leave their work stations. His down to earth attitude and fantastic smile coupled with the fact that he would speak their native tongue all day, every day won him the hearts of the Paloma employees.

"He really is one of us." Jackson commented as he watched his Grandson carry a pile of souls from one work bench to another, laughing and joking with the workers as he went. Jackson's office was the floor above the factory, glass walled, he was able to survey his empire just by glancing up.

"He is a natural leader; do you see the way the workers respond to him? He does genuinely show an interest in each and every one of them, the fact that he has learnt our language and speaks to them in Spanish has won them all over, he works hard too, Michael should be proud of the boy instead of beating him and suppressing his good nature." Paula agreed.

"He doesn't need Michael, he has us and Monica and I have to admit, Charles and Penny have been very supportive of him, I'm sure Michael hates that." Jackson smiled "We'll see how they get on when we return home to Spain, then we will decide if Paul should return home or live with us permanently."

"I know you love the boy Jackson but he isn't our son, I'm sure Monica doesn't see this as a permanent arrangement and she will want Paul home before the start of the school year, she'll want to spend some time with him before he goes to Boarding School."

"That's another thing I disagree with, why send the boys away? Paul's happier here. Look at him, he smiles, laughs and is relaxed around us, do you see him behave like that in his own home?" Jackson protested, he adored all his grandchildren but recognised that Paul needed a little more attention than the others and he didn't like to think of the boy being suppressed by his father.

"I know how you feel honey." Paula came to hug her husband "But we can only guide him, he has to make his own path, he knows he can come to us if he needs help and we have a month in Spain to look forward to, Paul loves it out there, he'll have time to find himself and it means that Michael won't put a foot wrong all the time we are out there plus Paul will speak Spanish all the time which irritates Michael no end."

Paul travelled with his Grandparents to the airport where he was reunited with his siblings and Monica who wrapped her arms around her son and held him tightly.

"Can't breathe Mum." Paul laughed when Monica refused to let him go then when she finally released him "Are you ok?"

"I'm fine, I've missed you so much." she kissed his cheek.

"I missed you too, bet it's been quiet at home without me." he grinned.

"Understatement of the year dude" Matthew came over and slapped his brother on the back "I've missed listening to you fart all night."

"Matthew!" Monica exclaimed.

"Sorry Mum." Matthew led his brother away leaving Monica to greet her parents "Seriously dude, you really wound Dad up this time, what did you do?"

"I told him not to shout at Mum and he spazzed out." Paul replied "He has a mean right hook on him, still, I had a great time with Grandma and Gramps while you were slaving away at school, even earned a bit of money so all's good." Paul grinned at his brother then noticed his sister and her best friend "Things have just got considerably better." he finished.

Matthew turned to see what his brother was looking at "Oh yeah, Mum said Tessa could bring a friend as she gets left out when you and I go off."

"I love my sister." Paul said "She has the best friends."

"Suzanne's way out of your league bro, there's no way she's going to be interested in you virgin boy." Matt mocked.

"And you have loads of experience I take it? Do you think I care if she's in my league or not? She's just so nice to look at; I think this holiday is going to be awesome."

"I have more experience than you, lost my cherry last week actually" Matt boasted.

"Nice one Matt." Paul gawped at his brother "Always thought I would be first."

"You have some catching up to do brother."

Chapter Two

Suzanne Smith, Tessa's best friend was a petite blond who had developed early and had an absolutely stunning figure, the perfect hour glass. She had known Tessa since nursery school and subsequently the twins. She had watched the boys grow into tubby toddlers and then teenagers.

The teenage years had been kind to the Jensen twins. Matt had remained stocky and the shorter of the two boys , his love of sport had toned his puppy fat into rippling muscle while his blond hair had been allowed to grow from its normal tight crop and was showing signs of beginning to curl in a most endearing manner. Matt was quick to smile and treated her as a sister making an effort to include both girls in many of his activities when they appeared to be at a loose end but she had caught his appreciative glances when the weather allowed her to wear tiny skirts and even tinier tops.

Paul had grown tall and lean with a naturally athletic body which he had no problem displaying as he would quite often appear in the family kitchen or living room in just a pair of jeans or boxers while seeking Monica to find out where a certain top or other garment would be. He was the quieter of the twins but equally the more confident of the two, he wouldn't get embarrassed when Suzanne caught him on more than one occasion looking at her breasts encased in one of her tight tops and he would meet her eyes with a cocky grin twitching at the corner of his mouth. Paul had also noticed that she had a particular fancy for dark haired men, recognising that he was exactly her type boosted his confidence immensely. She had no doubt what so ever that Paul had already had the pleasure of exploring at least one of the many females that flocked around him at school. His dark good looks and volatile nature made him her perfect match; she was looking forward to this holiday and seeing just how far she would be able to push him.

PRODIGAL SON

In recent years Michael had purchased a private plane, mainly for business use but it came in handy for group holidays such as this and was so much nicer than standard first class. The previous two weeks since he had laid into Paul had been peaceful with the removal of what he considered to be his wayward son from the house. He felt a flash of anger upon seeing the boy now and the way the rest of the family welcomed him back into the fold and he just knew the boy would spend the next month mocking him in Spanish and he wouldn't be able to do a damn thing about it.

Tessa, Suzanne, Matt and Paul commandeered the seats at the rear of the cabin away from the adults. Sinking into the lush white leather seats to await take off and the customary snack provided by the small, highly paid staff, Suzanne noticed that Paul had turned a most unattractive shade of green.

"What's up with your brother?" she leaned closer to Tessa.

"He doesn't like to fly." Tessa replied surveying her younger sibling "It's not that bad Paul." she teased "Statistics say that we probably won't crash", the plane had begun to taxi along the runway.

"Shut up." he murmured gripping the arms of his seat as the plane began to speed up.

"Anyway, if we did crash, the plane would just explode into a huge fire ball in a matter of seconds, we wouldn't know what hit us." Tessa continued as the plane completed it's take off.

Paul unfastened his seatbelt and bolted for the bathroom at the back of the plane.

"That was uncalled for" Matt told his sister.

"It was a little mean" Suzanne agreed.

"Oh give up you two, he teases me about everything, this is the only thing that I have to get back at him."

Monica has also left her seat, chatting with her parents and brother as she made her way to the galley to check their food was being prepared before heading back to check on her children. Noticing the empty seat, she asked.

"Is Paul in the bathroom?"

"Yeah, he went a fantastic shade of green before he took off." Matt told her.

Monica made her way through the small games room and to the planes luxurious bathrooms, knocking on the only locked door, she called her son's name. Paul appeared shortly after her knock looking pale and most unwell.

"Come back to you seat son, you'll feel better when you have eaten."

She walked with him back to his seat;

"Dude, do you want to sit by the window? The view is awesome and it might take your mind off feeling sick." Matt offered.

"Because looking at the ground hundreds of miles below is going to make the sickness and my fear of flying any better?" Paul snapped at his brother.

"It was only a suggestion." Matt huffed.

"Be nice." Monica warned "I'll get you all something to eat, try to do something to take your mind off the flight."

Monica was right of course, Paul did feel better after he had eaten and although it was only a short flight, he decided the best way to pass it would be to sleep. He reclined his chair, turned onto his right side and was asleep in moments leaving the other teenagers to amuse themselves.

He slept so soundly that he didn't even wake when the plane landed. He was shaken awake by Suzanne and was pleasantly surprised to find that he was eye level with her breasts as she leant over him to nudge him awake.

"That's a nice sight to be woken up to." he stretched and met her pale brown eyes.

"You have no shame" she told him.

"Not when you wear tops like that." he answered, his eyes dropping once more to her breasts wishing they could stay as they were right now so that he could reach into her top and guide the delightful orbs between his lips, he began to smile as he noticed her nipples hardening and once more looked into her eyes "One day." he said allowing his seat to glide into the upright position, unclipping his seat belt, coming to his feet and enjoying the flush that spread over her cheeks.

Suzanne composed herself, she had known volunteering to wake him up was a mistake but she hadn't been able to stop herself, she had become so attracted to this boy over the past few months that she had simply needed to wake him just to see the look on his face as he registered her presence. He confirmed his attraction to her by his last comment. As the blush left her cheeks, she turned to face him. "We have a month here, that one day may come sooner than you think."

A short ride in the fleet of air conditioned Mercedes and the family were at Jackson's parents' substantial villa, a gift to them from him once he had made his first million. Matt used to hate the initial meeting of families as Paul was the child that usually got all the attention, his colouring and fluency in the language displaying his more than obvious Spanish heritage this was until Monica had pointed out that the resentment and jealousy Matt felt at these meetings was how his brother felt all the time as Matt was the one who received all the attention from their father.

Once the various family members had found their rooms, the Paloma and Jensen families settled down to an opulent meal followed by a long stroll on the beach, Matt and Paul leading the way throwing a rugby ball to each other. On these occasions Michael felt somewhat left out, he had never bothered to learn Spanish and the Paloma family would gabble constantly in their native tongue with Monica only pausing occasionally to translate for him.

Paul loved it here, the freedom he had was endless, he was popular with the locals and had to admit that he would be happy to live here permanently, if he never spoke English again it wouldn't bother him. He felt relaxed and calm around these friendly, social people, their sense of family appealed to him as did their unconditional love for their children coupled with the fact that he would be able to wind Michael up to the hilt and wouldn't have to face the consequences until they got home, he now also had the added attraction of Suzanne and had every intention of pursuing her.

For the first few days, the brothers spent most of their time either on the beach or in the sea while Tessa and Suzanne worked on their tans only occasionally joining them in the water causing Paul to swim further out to sea as the sight of Suzanne dripping wet in a thin swimsuit turned him on immensely.

Around midday every day, the family would disappear into the villa for their Siesta much to Paul's irritation as he didn't like to sleep through the day. While the family slept he would swim or sit in the shade out of the midday sun listening to music or reading. By the fourth day of the holiday, he noticed that Suzanne had also stopped taking her siesta, using the time to hunt for unusual shells in and around the rock pools.

Suzanne and Tessa had drawn quite a lot of attention from the local boys both being fair skinned blondes, they stood out like a sore thumb amongst the curvaceous dark haired girls that frequented the beach and had spent these early days of their holiday fending off over amorous Latin advances.

Glancing up from his book as Suzanne passed him on her way to the beach, Paul paused in his reading to watch the gentle sway of her hips as she walked away, sitting up a little straighter to get a better view as she removed her sarong, dropped it on one of the sun beds and carried on towards the sea. Once she had submerged herself in the water and had settled into a steady swimming pattern, he went back to his book, glancing up now and then to see if she was still in sight.

Getting engrossed in a fast paced chapter of his book, he realised he hadn't checked on Suzanne in at least fifteen minutes, looking up, he surveyed the beach and then the sea. Nothing! Her sarong was still on the sun bed but she was nowhere to be seen. Coming to his feet, he dropped his book and headed down the beach, by the time he reached the waters' edge he was beginning to worry, he still couldn't see her. Wading into the sea up to his waist, he leapt forward and swam in the direction he'd seen her heading in.

He'd reached the small cove before he spotted her standing in the shallows, arms folded across her chest, back ram rod straight as she tried to extract herself from the group of Spanish boys surrounding her. Swimming until his feet touched the sandy floor of the cove, he was by her side in moments, his hand sliding across her back as he drew level with her to confront the boys "Hey, you ok?" he asked .

"Yes, I'm so pleased to see you, these guys don't seem to get the idea that I'm not interested." she had jumped as he touched her but was now so grateful to see a familiar face that his warm hand on her back didn't bother her in the slightest.

"¿qué hace usted a tipos?" he addressed the boys in Spanish, translation "What are you doing guys?" he received a loud gabbled response asking him what business was it of his and where did he come from. He pointed to the clearly visible villa and told them "It's my business because she's mine - esto es mi negocio porque ella es la mía" and "derribe y déjela en paz – back off and leave her alone."

The boys turned to look at the villa "¿usted es la familia Paloma? – You're Paloma family?"

"Sí" he pulled Suzanne into his side and began to back away, the rabble of local boys knew better than to upset a member of the affluent Paloma family, most of their families were employed by them, muttering apologies they headed back up the beach away from the couple.

"You can let go now." Suzanne said as Paul continued to glare after the boys.

"I kind of like you this close." he answered tightening his grasp and turning to face her, both arms now around her waist, he leaned down to her "You shouldn't go off on your own." he gently admonished softly pressing his lips to hers and pulling her body against his.

With her hands resting on his biceps, she allowed him to kiss her responding in kind to the hesitant searching of his tongue.

"You do know I could have taken care of those boys on my own right?" she asked, her lips still only centimetres from his.

"Of course you could." he replied kissing her again. When she sucked his full lower lip into her mouth it felt like his temperature soared, his skin tingled where her hands touched him and his heart began to race, he tightened his grip on her as his body responded to her stimulus. Embarrassed by his complete and obvious arousal at her hands, he pushed her away a little too roughly and headed out to sea.

Once submerged up to his neck, he turned to face her still standing in the shallows. She was obviously more than a little aggravated, her hands on her hips until he looked at her then she threw her hands in the air and yelled "What the hell was that?" at him before wading out to where he bobbed just out of her depth. Standing on tip toes, she held out her hand to him and pulled him closer to her when he took it. "Don't be embarrassed, just find us somewhere to go." she whispered once more finding herself in his arms. Unable to reach the sea floor, she wrapped her legs around him, flattening her body against his, completely surrounding him with the cage of her limbs.

"I will find us somewhere but it won't be today." he glanced at his watch over her shoulder. "Everyone will be awake soon, we should get back." for all his bravado in flirting with her and initiating the first kiss, the way she had responded to him told him that she had far more experience than he did and he felt a little intimidated. His sister had hinted that her best friend had had one or more sexual partners leaving Paul the inexperienced second baser virgin. As Suzanne unwrapped herself from his highly aroused body he grinned to himself, nothing was going to stop him being with this gorgeous girl, he'd just have to man up a bit and swallow his nerves.

The following day Paul was up early scouting around looking for somewhere where he could, quite literally, take possession of Suzanne. He found just what he was looking for in the small cottage in the villa's grounds that was set aside for the housekeeper who was yet to join the family as she was supervising the closing up of the main house for the summer.

Circling back to the villa, he came across his Grandfather who had just been for his morning swim, greeting the older man; they made their way into the kitchen for breakfast deep in conversation. For the benefit of Michael and Tessa, meals were mainly conducted in English, Paul and Jackson however had continued their conversation in Spanish. Michael looked up when he heard Paul say his name; he frowned when his son continued to gabble to Jackson in Spanish glancing up occasionally to sneer in his fathers' direction.

With breakfast over, the four youngsters were left to clean the dishes as the adults set about organising their day. With the hated task over, they headed out to the shaded pergola and sat exchanging friendly banter while they digested the more than ample breakfast they had just eaten. Paul was leaning over yesterday's newspaper spread out on the table discussing a story about one of his and Matt's favourite actors when Michael appeared at one end of the table,

"What were you saying to Jackson?" he addressed Paul, the boys' mocking smirk at the breakfast table had got under his skin and he had decided to confront his son while Monica was busy packing a bag for their intended day trip..

Paul looked up at his father and leaned back in his seat "Nothing." he replied, his arms folding defensively across his chest.

"You said my name more than once boy, I suggest you tell me what it is you think I have done to you now." Michael demanded.

"I wasn't saying that you had done anything to me. I was simply telling Gramps that one day, everything you have will be mine." Paul answered, mocking smile and all.

"You have some front boy; do you seriously think I will be leaving you anything in my will?" Michael fumed.

"I don't need you to leave me anything Dad, you have misunderstood, I meant that one day, in the near future , I am going to take everything you own because I will be rich enough to do so and there won't be a damn thing you can do about it."

"In your dreams, you will never be in a position to take anything from me, I am the one who will do the taking and you needn't think I will let this insubordination slip just because we are here." Michael lent on the table to get closer to his son "We will be re-visiting this conversation when we get home."

"You can threaten all you like Dad and you can do to me whatever you want, I don't care, I'm not scared of you anymore." Paul had leant forward in his seat and had made to stand when Matt placed a restraining hand on his arm.

Michael's face went beetroot red, he snarled "We'll see." before leaving.

It was a few moments before the stunned silence was broken;

"That was brave." Suzanne murmured.

"That was stupid." Matt countered "He'll beat the shit out of you when we get home."

"No he won't, he can't risk sending me to boarding school with bruises, anyway, I don't care if he does hit me, like I said, I'm not scared of him anymore." Paul answered.

"You are insane." Matt told his brother.

"I don't know why you two talk about Daddy like that, he has never raised a hand to any of us." Tessa cut in.

"He has never raised a hand to you Tessa," Paul replied "Matt's had a few back hander's and he seems to take great delight in punishing me for the slightest mistake."

"You go out of your way to wind him up." Tessa protested.

"Uhuh, and you wear blinkers." Paul snapped "He has a go at me at every available opportunity, you just witnessed this last bit, he'll find any excuse possible to give me a beating, you need to wise up Sis and stop defending him."

"Have you ever stopped to consider that perhaps he does these things you say he does to get some attention from Mum, she's so wrapped up in you that the rest of us don't get a look in and that includes Dad."

Paul got to his feet "You're deluded," he glared at his sister "I'm going to take the boat out for a bit." he squeezed past Matt's chair and headed into the villa to get the keys for his Grandparents boat managing to sneak the keys for the housekeeper's cottage at the same time.

Jackson stopped him on his way out of the villa; he had noticed his grandson's scowl and wanted to check that everything was alright with the boy. When Paul told him he planned on taking the boat out, Jackson handed him a wad of notes and told him to fuel it up while he was out he then informed Paul that the adults would be out for the entire day and as Tessa was the eldest, she was in charge and would be seeing to the youngsters food for the day.

Paul spent the majority of the morning on the boat, doing a little unsuccessful fishing. Pulling up alongside the family's private dock, he secured the boat then erected the hood over the wheelhouse so that the interior of the boat would remain dry should it rain and therefore be ready for use when Jackson or anyone else needed it. He noticed that no one was outside when he came up the beach from the dock and so made a quick detour to unlock the housekeepers' cottage before going to the villa to find his siblings.

"Hey." he said upon entering the kitchen and finding Matt cutting up tomatoes

"You were gone a long time." Matt glanced at his brother before turning back to the chopping board

"Yeah, had to go and get fuel then I thought I'd do some fishing."

"Catch anything?"

"Nothing." Paul answered "I thought Tessa was doing lunch?"

"She pulled the big sister card and told me to do it; she and Suzanne wanted to take showers before lunch to wash off their sun cream, you can give me a hand now you're here."

"Oh hell no, I'm not interfering, I've been sweating on the boat all morning, I need a shower too, anyway, I'm not hungry so you only need to make enough for three." he slipped out of the kitchen and up the stairs, as he reached the first floor he could hear a hairdryer and the two girls having a shouted conversation over the noise. He continued on up to the second floor where his room and bathroom were, closing the door and stripping off, he stepped into the shower, holding his face up to the warm water, trying not to think about Suzanne and the things they would hopefully get up to later that afternoon.

After vainly trying to take his time in the shower, thinking on his way down the stairs "Seriously, what takes girls so long in the shower?" he walked through the kitchen, grabbed an apple and went to sit in the pergola while he waited for Matt and Tessa to finish their lunch and go off for their siesta. He was sorely disappointed when all three teenagers stretched out on the sun beds after lunch. He decided to join them;

"What was the point of you two taking showers if you are just going to sit in the sun again?" he asked sitting astride the vacant sun bed.

"We aren't in the sun and we get a breeze here, it gets far too stuffy in the villa for a decent siesta." Tessa replied.

Paul shrugged and lay back on the sun bed next to Suzanne, he stretched out his hand to touch her arm knowing from this position neither of his siblings would see the movement. Suzanne turned her head in his direction, lowering her shades to look at him; she smiled when he held up a set of keys and raised a questioning eyebrow.

"Be patient." she mouthed at him, smiling again when he let out a theatrical sigh and folded his arms over his chest. Suzanne had picked her bikini carefully when she stepped out of the shower choosing one with easily releasable tie up straps on both the top and bottom, one tug on the loosely tied bows and she would be fully exposed.

Turning onto her left side therefore presenting her back to Tessa, not only did Suzanne have the lovely view of Paul's tanned, sleek body but it also gave the message to her friend that she didn't want to talk, she just wanted to sleep. It didn't take long before she heard light snores from Matt and, glancing over her shoulder, she saw that Tessa was curled up in a ball, also sound asleep. She touched Paul's hand as she came to her feet; he glanced at his siblings, got to his feet and preceded her to the footpath that led around the villa. As he walked, he felt his nerves kick in, his stomach felt like lead and his hands began to get clammy;

"Come on Paul." he talked to himself in his head "You can do this, you want this, find some balls and for God's sake don't let her see how nervous you are, it's not like you're a total novice after all." Paul had had various experiences with some of the older girls at school and he was more than adept and using his hands and mouth to give pleasure and enjoyed it immensely but not one of the girls had been willing to let him get past what he saw as second base.

Suzanne watched Paul as he walked ahead of her, his smooth, tanned back was tense and he wasn't walking with the graceful fluid movements of his natural pace. With a jolt, she realised he was nervous and was puzzled as to why. He had a reputation at school as a ladies' man; the girls would literally climb over each other to get some attention from him and she'd heard reports from the luckier ones that he knew what he was doing. She shrugged; perhaps it was just the fear of getting caught that was making him nervous.

"What is this place?" Suzanne asked as they reached the cottage

"It's the housekeepers' summer place, she won't be here until the end of the week." he replied as he opened the door and stood aside to let her in.

"Lucky housekeeper." Suzanne commented as she surveyed the plush but simple decorations, she heard the door click shut "You'd better lock that." she advised.

"Can I get you anything? A drink maybe?" he asked, stalling.

"You can come here." she smiled and reached up to tie her long blond hair into a pony tail, his hands were on her waist, his mouth pressed to hers before she had finished, dropping her hands to his shoulders, she kissed him back, hard. She felt the strap around her ribs loosen followed swiftly by the one around her neck then felt his warm hands on the pale skin of her breasts.

Paul had to stoop for his mouth to reach her breasts, he felt awkward and uncomfortable like this. As he moved to stand straight, his hands grasped her behind and he hoisted her up against his body, she responded by wrapping her legs around him and planting another kiss on his wonderfully full lips. Paul backed up into the bedroom and gently laid her across the bed leaning over her to pay her breasts the proper attention they deserved as her hands grasped his hair and guided his movements.

Letting his hips rest on hers he felt her begin to grind against him heightening his arousal to epic proportions. He lifted himself off her, looking at her luscious body then having to close his eyes, blocking the sight, calming himself but not succeeding as her hands were roaming his body.

Suzanne felt herself becoming impatient, she didn't want the niceties this time around, she didn't want him to be gentle and had fully expected for him to have her naked and be pounding away by now but he seemed determined to take his time which only served to increase her frustration. She reached for his loose fitting shorts and swiftly dealt with pushing them off his hips exposing him in his full glory to her, she used her feet to push the shorts down his legs while reaching for him and holding the hot hard flesh in her tiny hand, she heard him gasp as she began to stroke him, making him harder if that was possible.

Paul plucked at the bows either side of her hips, once undone, he grasped the scrap of material and whipped it out from under her and she was now as naked as he was. His hand spread out over her mound, the skin was amazingly soft and she was shaved clean fulfilling one of Paul's fantasies. Turning his hand and once again leaning over her, he kissed her deeply, sliding a finger along her slit at the same time as his tongue slid into her mouth.

Her hips bucked against his hand and she reached down and covered his hand with hers, pushing his fingers harder onto and into her, a brief thought of "Wow he's good at this." flitted through her brain moments before he slid another finger into her and kissed his way down her body. He paused for just a moment before leaning forward and tasting her, she moaned and pushed her hips toward his mouth, removing his fingers from her to concentrate on sucking her sex into his mouth, clamping his hands on her hips preventing her from moving and giving him total control as he began to drink her in.

Suzanne began to breathe quicker, she had grasped a handful of his dark hair and hung on for dear life silently thanking the powers above that he hadn't just pushed his way into her for a quick fuck, she gave herself over to his tongue and lips, relishing in his obvious enjoyment of the act. She felt the familiar tingling and pushing sensation that marked the start of her orgasm hoping frantically that he wouldn't stop now,

"Don't stop." she gasped, pushing against his restraining hands "Don't stop, yes there, stay there......I'm going to cum." throwing one leg over his shoulder, the force of her orgasm finally freeing her hips from the cage of his hands as she rode the final waves of her orgasm on his persistent tongue. With her clitoris now super sensitive, she pulled his head away from her by his hair, hooking her heels behind his legs, she guided him up the bed and into her, kissing him and tasting herself as he eased his ample appendage into her, feeling him open her with each movement.

Paul's head was reeling, she had tasted so good, he could have stayed there for a good while longer but she obviously had other ideas. He had to admit, he was slightly impressed with himself, he'd been immensely worried about cumming too soon but as that so far hadn't happened he figured he was good to go the whole way, he hadn't even considered that the intense feelings around the head of his penis as he entered would very nearly push him over the edge.

He paused as the head of his penis slid past her lips, holding his breath frantically thinking of things that would normally turn him off. Succeeding in keeping his cool, he edged a little further into her feeling her slick inner walls stretch to accommodated him, this is the feeling he'd been waiting for, he could honestly say he had never felt anything quite as good. He planned to savour every moment, to slowly inch his way into her up to the hilt but Suzanne didn't allow that, when he paused for the third time, she took matters into her own hands and thrust her hips up to meet his forcing him into her, she then began to gyrate against him, relieved when he took up the rhythm and began to fuck her how she really wanted him to.

Suzanne kept gasping "Harder." at him and slamming her hips up to his.

"I don't want to hurt you." he whispered.

"On your back." she ordered, she was overly aroused now, she had come once and wanted to again, she wasted no time in straddling him as he turned onto his back digging her fingers into his chest, she began to ride him in earnest delighting in the size of him and how deep inside he was.

Paul watched as this petite blond lowered herself onto him, he watched as he disappeared inside her, had he known sex felt this good, he would have done it long before now. Suzanne was riding him like she was in a rodeo, he felt her juices on his stomach and running between his legs as she brought herself to orgasm twice before he'd even gathered his thoughts, he reached up to roll her erect nipples between his fingers then gently but firmly pulled her down to him so that he could once more pull the delicious orbs into his mouth.

She came again as he gently bit down on her nipple, her whole body shaking, her vagina having spasms around his penis, his hands left her breasts to grab her hips as he too reached a long awaited orgasm. Suzanne collapsed onto his chest, they were both breathing heavily. She snuggled closer into him as he wrapped his arms around her wanting to stay this way. She raised her head to kiss him;

"When does the house keeper arrive?" she asked.

"She'll be here by the end of the week."

"Cool, same time tomorrow then?"

Paul nodded but in his head he was shouting and punching the air "Score, I didn't mess up, she wants to do it again."

Paul encouraged Suzanne to leave the cottage before him to make it less obvious to Matt and Tessa that they had spent the siesta together; it also gave him time to gloat over his performance.

Locking the cottage and dropping the keys into his pocket, he found he couldn't wipe the smile from his face; he was a very happy boy.

Matt was setting up the volley ball net when he reached the beach. Paul gave his brother a hand then went to find the ball from the stores under the villa. Suzanne saw Paul disappear under the house and joined him on the pretence of helping to find the ball.

"Can't get enough?" he grinned.

"You weren't that good." she mocked "I just wanted to get a couple of things straight." she continued "Tessa doesn't find out about us and just so you know, we aren't dating, you are far too young."

"I'm too young to date but not to fuck?" he asked "That's rich but ok, I'll go along with that, I'm all for Tessa not finding out. So, this means I can chat up some of those stunning brunettes that swan around the beach?"

"Yes, so can I, in case you hadn't noticed, this entire place is filled with tall, dark, handsome men, just my type."

"Ok, don't you go getting jealous though." he threw the volley ball at her and stepped towards her his arm whipping around her waist before she could back away, his lips planting themselves on her lips "Just leave yourself with enough energy for me." he whispered in her ear before leaving the store room.

Suzanne stood breathless in the doorway for quite some time, she liked masterful men and Paul seemed more than happy to take the lead, unbeknown to her, she had been the key to unlocking his voracious sexual appetite.

The volleyball game started out with the girls versus the boys, the boys destroying the girls easily. To even things up, Suzanne joined

Paul on his side of the net, Matt joined his sister much to Paul's relief, he had missed a couple of easy shots having been distracted by Suzanne's breasts bobbing opposite him as she jumped for the ball, he really didn't understand why Matt wasn't as distracted as he was by his sister's friend.

The adults returned while their young charges were still involved in their game and slowly, one by one, they drifted over to join in. By the time the game ended, each team had an inordinate amount of people and had deteriorated from Volley ball to just trying to get the ball over the net by any means possible amid much laughter.

Chapter Three

The following morning dragged for Paul, he kept glancing at his watch certain the damn thing had stopped. He took himself for a long swim hoping it would ease his frustration with time standing still, all that happened was he swam as far as he could before returning to shore only to discover that not only had he only killed an hour but now his legs felt like lead. He was hungry but found he couldn't eat; his stomach was churning far too much. He ended up helping his Grandfather set up the fishing equipment on the boat for the trip Jackson had planned the following day, one which he would have to find an excuse to get out of.

Finally the family showed signs of going to lunch and subsequently siesta. Paul jogged to the cottage to unlock it before putting in an appearance at the villa and picking at his lunch.

Suzanne beat him to the cottage as he had decided to have a shower to wash off the salt water from his swim; she was waiting for him in the bedroom already naked and stroking herself, she giggled when she saw Paul's hungry gaze travel over her body and stop at her hand watching her fingers slid into her secret folds.

In the blink of an eye he was naked and beside her on the bed his fingers joining hers. Laying on his right side, he moved a little closer nudging her leg with his knee so that she would rest her leg over his opening her further to him. He slid two fingers inside her while she toyed with her outer lips and clit, occasionally delving inside to gather more of her wetness. She began to moan and ride his hand when he inserted a third finger then a forth her own fingers now flying with amazing speed bringing her closer to climax.

Paul was dumbstruck, he hadn't imagined in a million years that girls masturbated in front of guys outside of porn films, he had four fingers inside and she was humping his hand like no tomorrow. He was so incredibly turned on by this girl and her confidence, not one of his friends would believe him if he told them a girl had brought herself off in front of him. Too late he realised that the throbbing in his groin was warning of imminent orgasm, he tensed, held his breath then let the breath out as he exploded.

"What the fuck?" Suzanne shouted.

"Shit." Paul murmured, too embarrassed to look at her, he glanced down at the part of his body that had betrayed him. "I'm so sorry."

She pushed his hand from her and wriggled away from him and off the bed grabbing a handful of tissues to mop up the fluid that had hit her side.

"Look at the state of me."

"I said I'm sorry." he said but thinking. "I think you look amazing."

"What's up with you? You weren't so easy to please yesterday."

"That was beginners luck and basically Suzie, if I walk into a room and see you fiddling with yourself it's going to get me off ok?"

"You need to learn a little control" she fumed, then his words hit her "What did you just say?"

"You fiddling with yourself is going to get me off" he repeated.

"No, the other bit."

"Beginners luck." he mumbled.

"Do not tell me yesterday was your first time, no, it can't have been, you are far too good with your mouth for it to have been your first time."

"It wasn't my first time as far as the oral bit goes but when it comes to actual sex then yes, it was my first time." He admitted.

"You should have told me."

"Would it have made a difference?"

"No, I'd still have fucked you, I would've just tortured the shit out of you first" she gave him a wicked grin.

"You did." he confirmed "Are you going to let me make this up to you?" he glanced at his watch. "We have time for a quickie."

She walked over to the bed and stood in front of him still sitting on the bed, twining her fingers in his hair and pulling his face to her breast "Make it good boy." she told him as she lowered herself onto him.

They continued this way throughout the week, meeting up at the cottage then going their separate ways as siesta ended. It became such a routine that they began to get careless, forgetting to lock the door after them.

Jackson had charged his son John with the care of the Housekeepers cottage, telling him to stock it with food for the arrival of the loyal, long serving member of staff.

John had been puzzled when he couldn't find the keys to the cottage but figured his father had probably opened it up to air and left the keys there. Armed with a large bag of groceries, John made his way to the cottage not at all surprised to find the door unlocked. He had arrived home with the shopping just as the rest of the family went for their afternoon nap and had planned to stock the cupboards and fridge before going to the villa for his own siesta.

He was stocking the fridge when he thought he heard a noise, standing still he listened but all he could hear were the birds singing outside, he went back to his task. No sooner had he turned back to the fridge when he heard the noise again, this time he knew he had heard it and that it was coming from inside the cottage. Closing the fridge, he moved into the living room, empty, then the noise again, a very distinctive noise, one that John recognised well but who the hell was in here? His entire family was asleep.

Going to the bedroom, he peered around the open door, catching sight of his nephew; he grinned and backed silently out of the room. Going to the kitchen, he grabbed the grocery bag and left the cottage. From the image he'd seen he figured the two youngsters wouldn't be long before they were spent, he decided to wait for his nephew and took a seat in a secluded corner of the small garden that afforded him a clear view of the cottage door.

Sure enough, within ten minutes, a flushed and dishevelled Suzanne stepped out of the cottage and quickly made her way towards the villa. John waited for Paul to open the door before he made his move.

Paul had locked the door and was sauntering down the path when he saw his Uncle;

"Oh, hi, I was just......".he stammered.

"Coming with me." John finished for him "Keys please." he held out his hand and led his somewhat embarrassed nephew back to the cottage. Once inside and placing the groceries on the kitchen table, he turned to the boy. "I'll do the kitchen, you can change the bed."

Paul scurried to do his Uncle's bidding knowing he'd been caught and wondering as he stripped the bed what would happen now. With the dirty bed linen bundled in his arms, he rejoined John in the kitchen and stuffed the linen in the now empty grocery bags.

"You have good taste." his Uncle started "Suzanne's a stunner, bit risky playing this close to home though don't you think?"

"Yeah, Tessa will flip if she ever finds out but I can't help myself, there's just something about her that draws me in." Paul mumbled.

"Don't be embarrassed mate, it's a perfectly natural thing. How long did you think you'd get away with using this place though? Very, very risky, anyone could have walked in, you were lucky it was me and that I'm the perfect open minded Uncle." John laughed "Your face was a picture when you realised you'd been rumbled."

Paul relaxed and laughed with his Uncle "I thought you were going to go nuts."

"Hey, I have a different girl on my arm every time you see me, who am I to lecture anyone about what they do and who they do it with, we can't help it, it's our Latin blood, you really are a chip off the old block."

"Thanks, I think."

"Come on, we'd better get this dirty laundry back to the villa and washed before anyone starts asking why it needed washing in the first place."

"Thanks John, for understanding." Paul told the older man as he locked the door.

"Not a problem. You are a fool though, you have the only room at the top of the villa, it used to be mine, I know from experience that no-one can hear you scream up there."

"Awesome. Why didn't I think of that?"

"I'm guessing you aren't doing a lot of thinking with your head right now." John grinned and ruffled the boys hair. "A little tip though, lock your door, I've already seen far too much of you." he shuddered in mock disgust "Not a sight I want to see again and definitely one I could do without in my head."

"You didn't have to watch." Paul countered.

"True. The housekeeper will be here in the morning so the cottage is out of bounds from now on ok?"

"Yeah. You er, won't tell anyone will you?"

"And risk arguments and repercussions? God no. Plus, if your Dad decided to wade in and tear a strip off you, I think I'd have to deck him."

"Now that I'd like to see." Paul commented.

"It's not my place to do it Paul. I can see him pushing you too far one day; you'll get your chance."

"I hope so. He only treats me this way because I don't look like him, it's so pathetic."

"If he looked a little closer he'd see that you do look remarkably like him you just have our colouring. Paul, you can come to me at any time if you need to talk or need help with anything, you do know that right?"

"I know, you and Gramps and Gran have been great, I love spending time with you. It's almost worth pissing Dad off so that I get banished to Gran's."

"Almost? Ah, you miss your Mum?"

"I do, that's kinda pathetic too."

"Not at all. I don't know what I would do without my Mum even at my age. How are you going to manage at boarding school?"

Paul smiled "I don't plan on being there very long."

"Michael will go ballistic if you get kicked out."

"Don't care, I'm not ready to stay away from home, I recognise that, I don't see why he can't. I'm going to do everything I can to get expelled from that place but I don't want to think about it now, I have another three weeks of sun and sand to enjoy."

"Not to mention the lovely Suzanne."

"Your right, not to mention her this close to the house." Paul warned.

"Your secret is safe with me young Casanova." John laughed.

The clandestine meetings were moved to Paul's bedroom from the very next day thus further allowing Paul to experiment and learn what would turn into considerable self control. He would leave the more experienced Suzanne panting at the end of each session as he stepped into the shower and she dressed and left.

Suzanne watched as Paul slid from the bed and walked naked to the shower. His skin had turned a deep brown except for the part where his trunks had been which always made her chuckle. Deciding that she hadn't quite had enough, she followed him through to his bathroom and stood silently watching as he rinsed the shampoo from his hair, the lather cascading down his firm young body, before he had a chance to reach for the shower gel, she stepped into the shower and with one hand in the centre of his chest, pushed him back against the tiles and moved in to kiss him.

As expected, he responded to her, grabbing a fistful of her long blond hair, he pulled her back under the jets of water, soaking her then pulled her into his arms, kissing her roughly before turning her away from him and telling her to bend over.

Bracing her hands on the tiled wall in front of her and spreading her legs a little wider she waited for him to come to her. She felt the warm water falling on her back move to her bottom then heard the jets become more vigorous as Paul changed the setting, the next thing she knew, the warm water on the most powerful setting was between her legs, Paul's fingers holding her lips apart and positioning it on her clitoris.

Paul saw the shudder travel all the way down her spine, she had her head thrown back and was gasping and groaning, he reached forward and grabbed her right hand, bringing it back to hold the shower head in position as he bent his knees and powered into her revelling in the tightness of her and the slickness her orgasm added to his motion.

During the day Paul and Suzanne took great pleasure in antagonising each other. She would surround herself with handsome young men laughing and flirting outrageously whenever Paul's gaze ventured in her direction. He would do the same, pushing it further by kissing and outright groping the local girls causing them to squeal and vie harder for his attention.

Monica had asked her sons to walk into town for a few bits; both boys were more than happy to do so, taking the circuitous route along the beach. They hadn't gone far when they were joined by the two girls they had spent the previous evening with, petite curvy Maria had a short bob haircut and a innocently sweet smile, she greeted Matt with a knowing grin causing Paul to chuckle as his brother had told him in graphic detail what he had done with the girl last night. Taller and with most impressive breasts, Catalina had attached herself to Paul and while he enjoyed her company, she hadn't managed to arouse him in the same way Suzanne could just yet but he'd kissed her and they had had more than an over the clothes fumble on the way back from town last night.

Suzanne had decided to walk into town with the boys as Tessa was busy helping her mother and she was just getting in the way, she strolled after them, walking at the waters edge looking all the time for shells and stones. Glancing up, she saw Paul and Matt talking to two positively stunning local girls; she speeded up and slipped her arms through theirs as she reached them putting her self between the two boys. Paul had been about to pull Catalina into a kiss when Suzanne's cool hand slid onto his arm, her familiar touch and the way his skin responded to it suddenly had him irked.

"Hi boys, mind if I come with you?" she asked.

"Sure." Matt replied.

"Actually." Paul answered, "We're a little busy, maybe you should go back to the villa"

"I'm fine here" she replied frowning at him "You're mum said I should hurry you along. You'd better say goodbye to the girls so we can get a move on."

Paul extracted his arm from hers and mumbled something to Catalina, then he bent and picked Suzanne up, marched waist deep into the water and unceremoniously dumped her in the sea. As she came spluttering to her feet, he leant over her and growled.

"We aren't dating remember." before turning away and joining his brother and two Spanish girls on the beach, he glanced back at Suzanne as he wrapped an arm around Catalina's waist .

"I'm not even going to ask what that was about." Matt commented.

For two days following the incident on the beach Suzanne didn't show up in his room during siesta and Paul hadn't had the opportunity to get her alone and question her about it. On the third day, half an hour after his family were happily snoozing, Paul decided to go to Suzanne's room and have it out with her, he wrenched open his door and almost walked straight into her, her first reaction was to slap him hard across the face, he stepped back away from her;

"What was that for?"

Suzanne stepped into his room, closed and locked the door "You threw me in the sea and completely humiliated me."

"You're still cross about that?"

"Fuming."

"So that's why you haven't been to see me in two days." Paul sat on the edge of his bed "I was just making a point Suzie, it was you who said we weren't dating after all but it's also you who has a problem with me being close to another girl."

"Fair point I guess." she sat beside him "I do hate seeing you with those girls."

"How do you think I feel when I see the guys pawing at you?" Paul nudged her "It drives me crazy; I want to rip their hands off."

"Ok, I promise I won't do any more flirting with the boys if you back off from the girls."

"Deal, we're still not dating thought right?"

"Right. It's a pity you have to go to boarding school; we could have continued this when we got home."

"Erm, no time like the present." he gestured around his room "We appear to be alone."

"I can't, I got my period."

Paul shuddered involuntarily, the female monthly cycle hadn't bothered him until Tessa has neglected to flush her tampon away properly. "Shame."

"There is something I can do though." Suzanne grinned "Do you trust me?"

"Yes."

Suzanne pushed him back onto the bed "Just relax and let me do this ok?" she didn't wait for an answer. She began to kiss him, stroking his body; she winced as his fingers pinched her nipples, they were tender and she gently moved his hands away and held them at his sides as she continued to kiss him, moving occasionally to nip his chest and collar bone.

She loved the way he responded to her and also, apart from the occasional softly spoken instruction the way he remained silent just regulating his breathing and giving himself over to her, she kissed him again, biting his lip hearing his sharp intake of breath;

"Te amo" he whispered as she sat back and slid his shorts off his hips.

"What? Speak English." she told him.

"Look it up." he answered then his whole body tensed as she lowered her mouth over him caressing his length with her tongue, another first for him.

She had let go of his hands and was using her own to heighten his arousal, dragging her nails gently over his scrotum and up his inner thigh towards his genitals, she paused, glancing up at him, his entire body was tense, his breathing shallow, his hands grasping the bedclothes but for all this, his face was relaxed, lips slightly parted, eyes closed. She continued to pleasure him, taking it first fast then slow, she felt him hold his breath and one hand softly stroked her hair.

Suzanne let her hands take over for a while, letting her jaw rest but planting tiny wet kisses on his lower stomach, when he held his breath, she closed her mouth around him once more and together with her hands, bought him to climax.

Paul released his breath, opened his eyes and swallowed hard. His body was still reeling from her touch, he'd never imagined her mouth on him could feel so damn good, so consuming.

"Hey." Suzanne appeared in front of him "You ok?"

He nodded and smiled opening his mouth to receive her kiss, tasting his own juices in her mouth.

"Another first I'm guessing?"

"Yeah." he found his voice "Holy shit that was good."

"I aim to please." she laughed.

"You do that very well." he confirmed "I wish I knew more, could do more to you."

"You do pretty well, give it time Paul, you'll gain experience as you get older."

"But by then you will be long gone."

"I'll always be around, we're friends too you know, not just fuck buddies."

Before they knew it, the month was at an end and they were once again in the air conditioned Mercedes being dropped off at the airport.

"I hate this bit." Paul moaned.

"Dude, it's going to be fine." Matt assured "Give me your bags, I'll get them over to the baggage cart, you sit and chill."

Paul sank down into one of the opulent leather couches in the VIP lounge, rested his head against the high back and closed his eyes.

"I bet I can give you something to keep your mind off flying." Suzanne whispered in his ear before sitting beside him.

Turning his head to face her he half smiled, half frowned "I thought you were cursed."

"Not any more, meet me at the back of the games room after take off." she told him.

Gripping the arms of the chair and keeping his eyes closed during take off, Paul could feel himself turning green and wasn't sure he would be able to stomach whatever it was that Suzanne had in mind. He heard the seatbelt sign ping off and opened his eyes in time to see Suzanne leave her seat. Leaning over the edge of his seat, he gauged what the adults were doing before checking out his siblings, Tessa was engrossed in a fashion magazine, Matt had his headphones on and was deeply involved in the hand held video game he'd purchased in Spain.

Coming somewhat unsteadily to his feet, Paul wasn't surprised when neither of his siblings glanced up; they were more than used to his customary dash for the bathrooms after take off. Suzanne was waiting for him; she grabbed his hand and pulled him into the bathroom furthest away from the main cabin.

"Strip." she said, pinning him against the sink.

"Completely?" he asked beginning to unbutton his shirt. As this was a private plane, the bathrooms were larger than normal giving them plenty of room.

"Yes." she unbuckled his belt and pushed his jeans and underwear to the floor. Going down onto her knees, she took his semi erect penis into her mouth her hand snaking around his hip, pulling him to her, once she had him fully erect she came to her feet and removed her clothes amidst much slapping of his hands as he tried to grope each newly exposed piece of skin.

Pulling him away from perching against the sink, she swapped places with him, hopped up onto the worktop, opened her legs and beckoned to him.

He grinned "You aren't even going to make me work for this are you?"

"Not at all, fuck me now, fuck me hard."

Stepping between her legs, he positioned himself, savouring the moment. Suzanne wrapped her legs around him loosely only tightening her grip when he entered her in once swift and forceful movement. They ground against each other until they were both spent. Paul held her to his chest, calming his breathing and stroking her hair.

"We should get back." she whispered.

"Hmm, in a minute." he replied prising himself from her grasp, he dropped to his knees and began to eat her.

"Oh." she gasped sliding her fingers into his hair holding him to her as he once again successfully brought her to orgasm.

Wiping the excess fluid on the back of his hand, Paul stepped into Suzanne's embrace,

"Want to know what we taste like?" he asked as he lowered his head to kiss her.

Leaving Suzanne to compose herself, Paul made a quiet exit from the bathroom and bumped into Matt on his way through the games room.

"You don't look as green as normal." Matt commented as he set up the air hockey table "Fancy a game? He asked regarding his brother "In fact, you look rather pleased with yourself."

Paul grinned and turned on the table, making the small puck float "I just joined the mile high club." he told Matt.

"Oh really, which one of the stewardesses did you jump on?" Matt asked, then quieter as Suzanne walked past. "Was it that smoking redhead?"

"It wasn't a stewardess." Paul answered.

"Paul, whacking off in the bog isn't considered joining the mile high club." Matt said.

"I wasn't alone, I was with Suzanne."

"No!" Matt gasped.

"Yes and I have been for most of the holiday."

"You jammy bugger! Dude, Tessa is going to freak." Matt laughed.

"She isn't going to find out; you and John are the only ones who know, I'd like it to stay that way."

"You know I won't say a word. How does John know?"

"He caught us." Paul shrugged "Says the image will stay with him for a very long time." he grinned "Good times."

Chapter Four

When the family arrived home, Monica switched into fifth gear ordering both boys to the barbers for haircuts while organising the washing and the final fitting of their new school uniforms. Three days later, cases and trunks jammed in the back of Michael's car, they dropped Tessa off at Suzanne's house while the rest of the family made the long journey to Lincolnshire and the boys' new school.

Matt remained silent on the journey, he had already argued with his parents about being sent away for school and had clearly lost that battle, now his twin took up the argument and didn't let up for the entire four hour journey.

On arrival at the school, the family were greeted by the deputy head and one of the science teachers, the deputy head escorted Monica and Michael to the Principal's office after insisting that the boys say their goodbyes to their parents. Matt and Paul were taken to the infirmary where they underwent a medical examination and also where Paul received his first punishment in the form of a cane across his hands for stating rather loudly whilst standing in nothing other than his shorts.

"This is bullshit."

Monica and Michael were treated to an informal meeting with the Principle, the finest bone china had been bought out of storage for the occasion, Michael, after all, took care of the school's accounts.

"Your boys will receive the highest standard of education." the Principle assured "We also teach respect and discipline."

"Judging from their performance on the way here, both boys could use a little more discipline." Michael gruffed "I'd like them placed in separate dorms and kept apart as much as possible, they egg each other on and are very protective of each other, I feel you will have fewer problems with them if they spend the majority of their time apart."

Monica was flabbergasted, she hadn't agreed with sending the boys away to school but had given in under Michael's insistence but now he wanted them kept apart, she knew neither boy would take kindly to this and expected to receive calls from the school on a regular basis lamenting her sons' behaviour.

When Paul realised he was to be separated from his brother he knew he'd have to find a way to get out of this school and quick. He didn't want to be away from home but had counted himself lucky that he had his brother to lean on, now that crutch had been taken away and he was completely alone he knew he wouldn't survive here on his own.

Matt was stunned that he had been placed in a different dorm to Paul, he was sharing a room with a large, friendly boy named Cameron but that didn't mean he wouldn't rather be sharing with Paul, he knew his brothers' habits and flash points and now he would have to learn this other boys' foibles, he didn't want to be here but his placid, laid back nature wouldn't allow him to rebel.

During supper the first night, Paul had tried to sit with his brother but was firmly directed to the table his dorm mates occupied, placing his tray on the table in front of him, he folded his arms across his chest and resolutely refused to eat resulting in him being sent for an early shower and the removal of his television privileges.

The following day Paul had hoped to see his brother during lessons but soon learned they had been put on a vastly differing timetable. At morning break, he took himself to the far edge of the quad and sank down against the chain link fence close to some boys from an older year. He hadn't intentionally listened to their conversation but happened to overhear one of the star rugby players complaining that he wasn't allowed to play as his science work wasn't up to scratch. Paul caught the boys' eye and offered to do the work for him in return for cigarettes and the occasional message passed to his brother. It was also during that first break that he discovered his all boys boarding school was situated right next to an all girls comprehensive, his squeaky clean uniform marked him as a new boy and the girls on the other side of the fence soon discovered the newcomer was strikingly good looking, positively charming and an incorrigible flirt.

By the third day Paul had come up with the plan that the best way to get out of the school would be to go through the rule book and systematically break each and every rule. He had already managed to break the no fraternising with girls rule, that one was easy and also the highlight of his day. He stopped working in lessons and refused outright to do homework which earned him a trip to the Principles office and a stern talking to as did his loud and raucous conversations with the girls each morning.

Sitting on his bed the following evening, rule book in hand, he discovered that refusal to attend lessons was a major misdemeanour as was smoking, he'd already figured that one out and he just needed to get caught in the act. The very next morning, he refused to get out of bed and ended up being dragged out of bed by his head of year marched to the Principles office, caned across the hands and doing his days lessons in his pyjamas at a desk outside the Principles inner sanctum. That evening, he hit the rule book again.

Standing on the headboard of his bed, he opened the window and lit a cigarette, well aware that he could be seen by the teachers outside, he took a deep drag and, resisting the urge to cough up his lungs and vomit, blew the smoke out of the window, as soon as he got the attention he desired, he stubbed out the disgusting cigarette, jumped down off his bed and went to sit at the small desk in the corner of his room only seconds before two teachers burst into the room dragged him to his feet and once again marched him to the Principles office.

"This is becoming a habit Mr Jensen" the Principle said as he came around his desk "Let's see if we can discourage further visits shall we?"

Paul didn't answer, he recognised the rhetorical question.

"Drop your trousers boy and lean over the chair." the Principle told him, he didn't move, the Principle nodded to the two teachers who had brought him to the office who leaped into action, wrenching Paul's trousers down to his ankles and holding him over the arm of the leather chair, he soon learnt that it was useless to struggle against the two teachers holding him and was completely unprepared for the sting of the cane as it hit his backside, he cried out in pain and shock at the first blow but bit his lip and remained silent during the next nine lashes. "I do not expect to see you in here again. What do you have to say to me?"

Paul was thinking "Sadistic bastard." but as the school rules stated, he said "Thank you Sir." and was marched back to his room. Sneaking to the bathroom during the night, he pulled down his boxers and surveyed his backside, he saw the red welts in his flesh and he still felt the pain but boy was it worth it. Having checked the school rules again, he noticed that boys were required to wear pyjamas to bed, as he usually only wore his boxers at home, he had found the bedtime garments uncomfortable and restrictive and after today's punishment decided that sleeping naked, refusing to go to lessons and smoking should put him well and truly in the bad boy books.

He received twenty strokes the following morning after being forcibly dressed by the house master and again spent his day at the desk outside the Principles office, shifting from one cheek to the other to alleviate the pain along with two other boys from his dorm who also seemed to have a knack for getting into trouble. He was allowed out to his morning break which he spent flirting with the girls, he received a further five strokes for this.

That night, he stayed up late, much to the annoyance of his room mate who had begged him to tow the line, studying the rule book one again. He smiled to himself before he turned out the light and whispered to his roommate that he should get up early and get out of the room so that he didn't get caught up in Paul's plans.

"What are you going to do?"

"I can't tell you Louis, if you don't know what I'm up to then you can't take any of the blame, I'll be out of here soon and hopefully you will get a decent roommate."

He heard Louis leave the room an hour before breakfast and quickly stripped off his boxer shorts before sliding back under the covers. He had discovered that a major infraction of the school rules was masturbation, hugely frowned upon in this institution, he realised he may have hit upon the one thing that would indeed get him expelled. As the bell for breakfast sounded, Paul lay back in his bed and turned his thoughts to Suzanne and all the things she had taught him in their month together.

"We'd better get the Jensen boy up." Mr. Roberts, Paul's science teacher said to his colleague, Games Master Shore, a large brute of a man. He felt for the boy and hated that the task of getting Paul out of bed and dressed had fallen to him, having been sent to boarding school himself he knew what the boy was going through, he despised himself for working here but needs must, a wife, child, another on the way and a hefty mortgage had necessitated him taking this job.

Opening the door to the room that Paul and Louis shared he couldn't believe that this boy appeared to be breaking each rule in order.

Paul had kicked off the covers as his thoughts of Suzanne aroused him beyond belief, he didn't realise at first that he wasn't alone until the Games Master growled and hauled him out of the bed by his hair screaming at him to cover himself up.

Paul shook off the hand holding his hair and stood up straight both hands at his sides making no attempt what so ever to cover his engorged penis. He knew the kind natured Mr Roberts wouldn't do a thing about this but he hadn't counted on Games Master Shore being his back up that morning. Realising he had made a huge error in not checking the duty rota, Paul had two choices, cow tow to this man, apologise and cover up or tough it out. His need to be at home in his normal surroundings gave him the courage he needed to keep his hands at his sides and his gaze fixed on the large man screaming at him.

Mr Roberts was sent to get the Principle while the Games Master continued his tirade of insults. Principle Baxter listened to his teachers' accounts of what they had caught Paul doing as he surveyed the still naked boy in front of him;

"I have dealt with boys like you before and broke every single one of them, what makes you think you are any different? I will tear you from your mothers apron strings if it's the last thing I do." he hissed in Paul's face, turning to his staff he said "Seclude him."

Wrapping a sheet around him, the two teachers led Paul to a small cell with no furniture and a tiny window, before locking him in, the sheet was taken from him, leaving him naked and alone for the rest of the day.

As night fell Mr Roberts unlocked the door to the cell and came to stand in front of Paul. Handing him his boxer shorts, he glanced over his shoulder to make sure they were alone then spoke quietly to the boy

"What are you trying to achieve Paul?"

"I want to go home Sir." Paul replied, he couldn't help but like this man, he was the only one who used the boys' Christian names and always treated them fairly

"All that's going to happen to you is endless beatings, you've put yourself on the Principles hit list and he won't stop until you obey the rules and start to work."

"He's going to have to step up the punishment a bit then, so far he hasn't even hit the level that my father is at." Paul told him.

"This is a battle you can't win."

"There are only so many rules I can break before I get kicked out, a few beatings aren't going to stop me."

"Paul, he will never expel you because he knows that's what you want. Why not just tow the line and get through this as painlessly as possible?"

"Because that would be giving in and that's not something I'm willing to do."

"I wish you would apply the same determination to your studies." Mr Roberts sighed.

"It's nothing against you Sir, you're the only decent teacher here, I just want to go home"

"I appreciate your words and under different circumstances, in a different school, maybe I would be able to help you but my hands are tied, I have a family to support, just know that I wholeheartedly disagree with what comes next and I urge you to reconsider your actions."

Paul felt the first tingle of fear "What's going to happen to me?"

"I can't tell you, I think it's unjust and that you should be given the chance to apologise and turn yourself around but the faculty has cast a majority vote on your punishment, I was sent to get you as I'm the only teacher you haven't presented any problems to, I'm so sorry."

"Sir..."

"Bring him out" Games Master Shore bellowed.

"Come on." Mr Roberts urged.

"No." Paul shrunk back into the corner of the cell.

"Don't make this worse than it has to be, please Paul just come with me."

Paul stepped forward and felt the trembling grasp of his science teacher around his wrist. He was led to the common room for his dorm where the two other boys who had a habit of getting into trouble were standing, also only in their underwear, in front of the vaulting horses that had been brought up from the gym, a hefty sixth former on either side of the boys, two more stepped forward to grasp Paul's arms and lead him to the centre vault horse.

At a nod from the Principle, all three boys were turned to face the horses, their arms stretched out to their sides; they were pulled so that their chests rested against the gym equipment, their backs to the room. Each boys' crime was read out along with the number of lashes he would receive, Paul's head began to swim as he heard his punishment would be forty lashes, considerably less than the boy either side of him, he could feel the sting of the cane on his backside even before the punishment began not realising that now most of the lashes would be aimed at his back.

He looked up into the eyes of Mr Roberts as Principle Baxter asked each boy in turn if they would like to make amends for their crimes, only one boy caved in order to receive less lashes,

"This is barbaric." Paul snarled at the teacher "It needs to be stopped."

"I can't." the teacher replied looking away from the boy's furious face.

Paul bit down on his lip as the first lash hit him across the shoulders, with his eyes screwed tight shut; he refused to cry out in pain. He woke in the infirmary, the other two boys whimpering in the beds opposite him, he had to find a way out of this school, breaking the rules obviously wasn't going to achieve that, he'd have to run away. Gasping in pain as he tried to sit, he bit down on any further noise escaping from him when he saw the matron at the end of the ward, looking around, he saw the other entrance to the ward was unmanned, if he was going to get out of the school, escaping from the infirmary would be his best bet as it was away from the main school building, lightly staffed and close to the Comprehensive school next door, he was sure the chain link fence was climbable if taken at speed. He noticed his school uniform neatly folded on the chair beside his bed, his stay in the infirmary would clearly only be a short lived one. He lay back in the bed and feigned sleep waiting for the Matron to go off duty, leaving the ward unattended. As soon as she was gone, Paul was out of bed and pulling on his clothes.

"What are you doing? Get back into bed, we'll all get punished again." One of the boys pleaded with him.

"Sorry guys." he whispered "I'm going, you didn't see anything ok?" he slipped from the ward and began his journey to the quad. He was halfway across the tarmac when the security lights came on; stranding him like a deer caught in car headlights "Shit." he cursed as he heard his name being called. He turned his back to the school and regarded the chain link fence, a little higher than he had imagined and topped with barbed wire, he hesitated, how the hell had he missed the barbed wire? Running footsteps behind him galvanised him into action, going from a standstill to a sprint in a matter of a few paces, he hit the fence and scrambled up it, flinging his body clear of the barbed wire he thought he had cleared the fence until he felt the flesh on the inside of his right arm tear, the barbs ripped into his skin and held fast causing his body to slam into the fence on the opposite side to the boarding school. He felt his blood pour from the wounds on his inner arms soaking his shirt and trousers then his vision began to fade, he was vaguely aware of someone supporting his weight by grasping his legs and raising him up while someone else shouted to call an ambulance before he passed out.

He came to in the ambulance; his arm heavily bandaged and elevated trying to prevent further blood loss.

"Back with us hey, what were you thinking kid?" the paramedic asked.

"I thought the fence was lower than it was, I forgot about the barbed wire." he smiled weakly "Am I going to be ok?"

"Looks like it, you may need surgery though, school can't be that bad can it?"

"It's worse than bad." Paul swallowed "I think I'm gonna be sick."

The first Monica heard of Paul's indiscretions was the phone call from the hospital asking for her permission to take him into surgery. After a detailed conversation with the doctor in charge of Paul's case in which said doctor voiced his concerns of the treatment the boy had been receiving at the hands of the school, he made light of the swollen red welts on Paul's back over the phone, preferring the child's parents to see them with their own eyes.

Finishing the conversation with the doctor, Monica then dialled Michael's private office line, something she rarely did and had a very curt conversation with her husband telling him in no uncertain terms that a plane had better be waiting for her at London City Airport by the time she got there, she then told him to call Suzanne's parents, explain the situation and ask them to have Tessa for the night,

"When you've done that, you'd better get yourself up to the hospital. This is your fault Michael, you'd better pray that Paul is going to be alright." she didn't wait for his reply, she slammed the phone down, marched out of the house and made the airport in record time.

Paul was out of surgery but still drowsy when Monica arrived. She got taken to the head surgeons' office where the extent of damage to Paul's arm was explained to her.

"He's going to make a full recovery Mrs Jensen, he didn't damage any nerves and we managed to repair the damage to his veins and muscle, his arm is swollen however and he may experience some tingling in his fingers for some time and he's going to have two rather large scars, he did lose quite a bit of blood so we are having to transfuse him at the moment but I'll take you to see him, he may still be slightly groggy." the doctor held open the door to his office and followed Monica through.

"You mentioned he had other injuries unrelated to his accident?" Monica asked.

"Yes, we had to cut his uniform off him I'm afraid, he was in no fit state to remove it himself and it was covered in blood. When we rolled him to remove his shirt we discovered that his back is covered with deep welts consistent with being beaten, two of the welts have actually split his skin, not badly, and we have closed those wounds with temporary stitches, there appear to be older welts across his buttocks as well. We have questioned the school about these wounds who deny all knowledge of them, as yet we have been unable to ask Paul how he got them." he opened the door to Paul's room. "Go on in, I'll get his nurse and we will show you his wounds."

Paul was asleep, flat on his back, the sheet pulled up under his arms, a bag of blood suspended above him and his right arm heavily bandaged. Monica stepped up to the side of his bed and pushed the thick black fringe from his forehead bending to kiss him there and gaze on her son's sleeping face. She looked up as the doctor returned with a nurse and between them they turned the sleeping boy onto his right side.

Monica gasped when she saw the wounds, reaching out, she tugged the sheet lower, regarding the older welts and bruises covering Paul's backside. "I've seen enough." she stepped away "How long until he wakes up?" she asked.

"I should be able to wake him." the nurse replied "He's just drowsy from the anaesthetic." she reached over and lightly shook Paul's shoulder saying his name as she did, Paul reacted slowly, swallowing then opening his eyes "Hi" the nurse smiled "You have a visitor." she stepped back and allowed Monica next to the bed while she busied herself checking his bandages and pulse and marking her findings on her chart.

Paul regarded his mother silently, he was relieved to see her but at the same time incredibly angry that she had left him at the school; he turned his face away from her and closed his eyes causing both the nurse and Monica to frown.

"Paul, I know you've been through a rough time sweetie, look at me, we need to talk about what happened." Monica spoke softly and slowly Paul turned to face her. Using his uninjured arm, he tried to push himself into a sitting position; the nurse was at his side in an instant helping him.

"If you start to feel dizzy just lay back down ok?"

Paul nodded at the nurse and gave her a weak smile then once again turned to his mother.

Monica stepped back from the look of pure hatred her son shot at her; he'd never looked at her like that before. Not caring that the doctor and nurse were still in the room, he took a deep breath.

"You left us there." he accused.

"I had no choice, it wasn't my decision to make." Monica replied.

"You could have put your foot down, you do it enough with Matt and me, you are after all, the one who takes care of us most of the time."

"I'm sorry, I wish I had refused to let you go, I can't say anymore than that. I'm here now, tell me what happened."

"Isn't it obvious? I was beaten, several times, the last time put me in the infirmary, that's when I decided I was going to try and get home."

"Did you do anything to deserve punishment?" Monica asked even though she really. didn't need to, she knew her son and should have taken his threat of getting expelled from the school seriously.

Paul chuckled. "Yeah, course I did", his answer causing his nurse to smile.

"What exactly did you do?"

"I'm not sure you really want to know the details Mum," Paul answered "Some of them aren't for your ears."

Monica shook her head, what was she going to do with this boy? She loved him dearly and was relieved that he was going to be fine; she was more relieved that the look of hatred had left his face, now he just looked tired, she bent and kissed his forehead again.

"How long before I can take him home?" she asked the doctor.

"It'll be a couple of days yet Mrs Jensen, I want to make sure his arm begins to heal properly and that he doesn't get an infection."

"In that case, I'd better find a hotel and wait for your father."

"Dad's coming?" Paul asked "Oh."

"It'll be alright, he'll be fine and I need him to confront the school with me when I go to get Matthew."

"You're taking us home?"

"Absolutely, you won't be going back to that place and neither will your brother after today. I suppose I should let you rest."

"I'll take good care of him Mrs Jensen." the nurse assured her "I'm on the night shift so I'll keep an eye on him."

"Thank you my dear. What is your name, it just sounds so terribly formal to keep calling you Nurse."

"I'm Cindy" the girl smiled.

"Well, Cindy, thank you for your obvious concern for my son, I'll leave him in your more than capable hands. I'll see you in the morning Paul, try to get some sleep."

Monica left the hospital but only got as far as the car park where she waited in her rented car for Michael, she left her car as soon as she saw the dark blue Mercedes enter the car park and waved to get her husband's attention.

"How is he?" his first words.

"He's going to be fine Michael but he's been beaten to within an inch of his life. We will have to get Matthew out of there, today, and I want answers from the Principle about Paul's wounds."

"Can I see him?"

"Not today, he's resting, he told me he did break some rules and did deserve to be punished but Michael, you should see the state of his back, it looks like he's been flogged." her composure broke and her voice began to tremble.

"Monica, I can only apologise, I should have listened when you told me boarding school wasn't a good idea for our boys." he wrapped his arms around his wife.

"Yes you should have and I hope from now on you will listen to me when it comes to the welfare of our children."

"Without question." He assured "When can we take Paul home?"

"The doctor said a couple of days, the staff in there are all very nice, we'll have to find a hotel, after we've had it out with the school."

Chapter Five

Turning up at the boarding school unannounced really wasn't the norm but given the circumstances, the faculty had been warned to look out for the Jensen's and direct them to Principle Baxter's office where the best bone china was once again waiting for them.

"Mr and Mrs Jensen, I have to say, I wasn't expecting to see you quite so soon."

"I'll bet you weren't, tell me why I had to hear my son was injured from the hospital and have yet to hear from the school?" Monica waded in.

"Monica!" Michael was shocked at his wife's out right attack.

"No Michael, I'm not going to sit here and let this sycophant sugar coat what has happened to Paul."

"You're son is no angel Mrs Jensen."

"I'm well aware of that and having spoken to him I understand that he did indeed expect to get punished, the extent of his injuries are unacceptable and I would like them explained" Monica turned once again on the Principle.

"Surely Mr Jensen, you aren't going to let your wife speak to me this way?" Principle Baxter turned to Michael, immediately undermining Monica's authority.

"Actually, given the circumstances, I think my wife's tone and questions are spot on, I'm more than happy for her to continue." Michael replied, Monica had become somewhat subservient over the years, nothing like the feisty Latina who had stood up to him at the Debutants ball, he should have known that anything to do with their children would cause her temper to stir and he liked it.

"I want answers." Monica demanded.

Furious at having to deal with a woman, Principle Baxter decided not to spare any details,

"Paul began by fraternising with the girls at the adjoining Comprehensive School which he followed swiftly by smoking in his room, refusing to wear nightclothes and sleeping naked, refusing to attend lessons and when we did get him to lessons, refusing to work or take part in any way, he was rude to staff members and we finally caught him masturbating yesterday morning, all of the aforementioned misdemeanours are against school rules and all are punishable."

"I agree he should have been punished but the skin on his back has been ripped to shreds, explain that."

"He was punished in line with recommendations and with two other boys who received considerably more lashes than your son, both of whom are fine and back in lessons, I would suggest that Paul worsened his own injuries and that perhaps his lifestyle up until now has caused him to become a little soft."

"My son would never have knowingly caused himself further pain." Michael stepped in "And I cannot believe that he would be outright rude to anyone, he simply isn't that kind of boy, as for sleeping naked, well, that is personal preference and, in my opinion shouldn't be imposed."

"What about his repeated fraternising with the girls and masturbation?" Principle Baxter snarled.

"He's fourteen years old, those things are a natural part of growing up, and surely you aren't so old as to remember what it was like to be a teenage boy?" Michael mocked.

"I stand firm to my belief that he was punished accordingly."

"Would you like to see his wounds for yourself?" Monica now, the man nodded "Then I suggest you meet us at the hospital tomorrow where these matters can be discussed with Paul, his doctors and social services, in the meantime, I suggest you send someone to fetch Matthew and have both of my son's things ready for collection in the morning, Matthew will be coming with us now."

"I really don't recommend removing either boy from the school, while Paul has certainly challenged us, Matthew has been a model student, I would suggest keeping them here but putting them in the same dorm and on corresponding timetables."

"I have no interest in your suggestions, now are you going to get my son or do I have to walk through the school shouting his name?" Monica raised a questioning eyebrow.

"Very well, I will have Matthew summoned here, you are making a rod for your own back Mrs Jensen, your boys will become unruly hooligans."

"That's quite enough." Michael's stern tone stopped the teacher dead "Kindly wait outside until our son is returned to us."

Once Principle Baxter had left the office Monica turned to her husband.

"Thank you for sticking up for Paul."

"I may not see eye to eye with the boy Monica but he is my flesh and blood, I won't allow him to be mistreated. I dish out the punishment in our family; this institution has gone way too far."

"You aren't going to punish him further are you?"

"No, I think he may have learnt his lesson."

The following morning, the three members of the Jensen family and Principle Baxter met at the hospital to discuss Paul's injuries. Matt was banished from the doctor's office when a representative from Social Services arrived to question the Principle further.

Nurse Cindy was doing her final checks before handing over to the day shift when Matt entered Paul's room.

"Hey Matt." Paul grinned at his brother. His blood transfusion complete, he was feeling stronger and was sitting on the edge of his bed in a pair of pyjama trousers while Cindy applied ointment to his back and re-fixed the temporary stitches.

"Dude" Matt grabbed Paul's outstretched hand and they bumped shoulders "You are a fucking legend at the school."

Paul laughed "I didn't do it for the notoriety; I just wanted to get home."

"I owe you; we've been pulled from the school, we'll be going home and back to normality when you get out of here." Matt looked at the nurse "Hi, I'm Matt, Paul's brother."

"Hello Matt, I'm Cindy." she smiled at the cute blonde boy then turned back to her patient "I'll change the dressing on your arm before I go." she gestured for Paul to stretch his arm over the small treatment table she had rolled over to his bed and cut the bandage off.

"Ah cool, you are going to have some awesome scars." Matt said as Cindy peeled the bandage away to reveal two lines of stitches stretching from the inside of Paul's elbow to his wrist. Cindy tutted and proceeded to clean the wound.

"Let me know if I hurt you."

"It's fine, just a little sore." Paul answered her "I did a good job of ripping my arm up didn't I?"

"You certainly did, you have dissolvable stitches holding the muscle layers together, the one's closing your skin will only stay in about ten days, you are very lucky you didn't damage any nerves."

"Yeah, I was stupid; I can't believe I forgot about the barbed wire."

"Apparently, the vault you did over the fence was impressive until you got hung up, the whole school is talking about it. Mum and Dad are going nuts at the school; they have social services involved, the whole shebang."

"And so they should," Cindy put in "No one should be beaten like this, the practices at that school need a close looking at." She gestured to Paul's back, Matt walked around the bed to see for himself.

"Holy shit, I didn't know they did that to you."

"They held me down Matt otherwise I would never had stood still long enough to take a beating like this, there were two other boys who got more lashes than I did yet I seem to have come off worse than them."

"You need to tell social services about the other boys, they may well need treatment and aren't getting it." Cindy told him "Right, that's you done, take it easy today, no dancing in the hallways ok? I'll see you tonight."

"Thanks Cindy, see you later."

Paul spent a further five days in hospital as infection raged through his body and his temperature soared. The wound on his arm had become so swollen that it threatened to burst the stitches leaving the doctors no choice but to re-open it and clean it further, letting the swelling subside before replacing the stitches.

Monica sent Michael and Matthew home as there was little point in them all sitting in the hospital especially as Paul spent most of his time asleep.

With the school under investigation and the other two boys who had also been beaten at the same time as her son now receiving treatment, Monica had time to meet with the families of those boys and together they were pursuing the school and the local education authority causing the school to be closed temporarily while the investigation took place.

The doctors meanwhile, assured Monica that allowing Paul to sleep was a good thing and she really needn't worry, her son was young and strong and would make a full recovery. The nurses were in regular attendance, waking Paul in the morning to change his sheets then carrying out their observations every half hour along with regular sponge baths to keep the sweat from his body.

Cindy was surprised to find that Paul was still her patient when she returned from her two day break. She took over Paul's care from her colleagues and encouraged Monica to take some time away from the hospital assuring her that she would take good care of her son.

Over the next few days Paul's temperature started to come down as the antibiotics began to fight the infection and he began to spend more time awake.

"Hey, you're awake." Cindy smiled as she put the bowl she was carrying on the table. She came to Paul's side and took his temperature. "And your temperature is almost back to normal."

"I feel fine." he told her "Do you know when I'll be able to go home?"

"Well, you've had a few bad days." she soaked the sponge "Now that you are over the worst, I expect we will let you home by the end of the week." she had folded the sheet down to his waist and now picked up the sponge.

"What are you planning to do with that?" he asked.

"You've spent the last three days bathed in sweat, we've had to wash you every couple of hours."

"I'm probably capable of getting to the bathroom and washing myself." he told her.

"Don't be daft." Cindy laughed "You haven't eaten for three days either and you do still have a slight temperature so you are not getting out of bed, besides, you haven't got anything I haven't seen a hundred times before."

"You may have seen hundreds Cindy but you haven't seen mine."

Cindy slapped the sponge onto his chest "Think again. Look, to save your blushes, I'll let you wash yourself but just so you know I have been the one washing you for the past few days" she patted his shoulder. "Boy, you are going to be a lady killer when you get older" she winked.

"Maybe I already am." he grinned.

"Please you are just a boy, you know nothing."

"I'm a quick learner."

Cindy laughed "Shut up and get washed, I'm going to get some clean sheets and some PJ bottoms. I want you clean by the time I get back."

Paul was released from hospital three days later. By the time he left the hospital, the scandal of the school had hit the papers and the youngest member of the Jensen family had his first encounter with the press in the hospital car park.

"Mrs Jensen, would you care to comment on the role you have played in the closure of the school."

Paul stopped a couple of paces behind his mother as she turned her brilliant smile on the journalist.

"As you are well aware the investigation is ongoing and as such I am unable to comment at this time."

"Paul, how are you doing?" a female journalist jostled through her male colleagues.

"I'm fine, pretty much healed" he replied after glancing at Monica for guidance.

"Looking forward to going home?"

"Absolutely, I've missed my brother and sister and it will be nice to sleep in my own bed." he answered honestly.

"Have all your injuries healed?" Sadly Monica and Michael hadn't been able to stop the publication of the goings on at the school or the information of their son's injuries from reaching the papers.

"I still have stitches in my arm but only for another few days, once they come out I should be able to go back to school." his confidence growing, he stepped around Monica to get closer to the female journalist as trying to hear her soft voice over that of her male counterparts was difficult.

"You had us all worried when the infection set in and your temperature went up" speaking quietly now, twenty four year old

Antoinette Savage was taken with the boys dark good looks and the attention he paid her.

Paul smiled "It's run its course now, as you can see I'm back on my feet, thank you for your concern." he grinned.

"No problem." she blushed, he really was breathtaking.

"What's your name?" he asked.

"I'm sorry, I should have introduced myself, I am Antoinette Savage."

"Right name for your career choice" he commented, Monica touched his arm, it was time to go "It was lovely meeting you Antoinette, I plan to keep my name in the headlines so I expect we'll meet again" he winked then followed his mother to the car.

Paul was quiet during the journey home, very unusual for him when he was alone with his mother. When Monica questioned him on his silence, he pointed out that he had been stuck in a hospital bed for the last week and didn't actually have anything to talk about.

"Your old school agreed to take you back if you promise not to fight." she told him.

"I'll behave." he answered "Matt's more than capable of taking care of himself and Tessa's left now, I have no reason to fight."

"Actually, Tessa is re-sitting her A levels so she will be there for the next year."

"She failed?" Paul asked stifling a smile.

"She got lower grades than expected even after a re-mark so your father and I have insisted that she re-sit them. She'll only be doing three days at school, the other two day she will be doing work experience with your father."

"Huh, sitting in his office reading magazines all day." he commented.

"Paul" Monica warned "You just said you would behave."

"Sorry, can we stop for something to eat? I'm starving."

Paul was to start school after his stitches were removed. Matt had already joined Tessa at their previous Secondary School and been reunited with his friends.

Monica was pleased with Paul's new attitude but couldn't help but wonder how long it would last, even Michael was for the first time enjoying his son's company, expressing his appreciation for the boys quick sense of humour and take on life.

Paul personally was going stir crazy being stuck in the house, his only trips out so far had been to have his stitches removed and a visit to a physiotherapist who gave him a list of exercises to do to prevent the damaged muscles from becoming atrophied. He did the exercises religiously as his right arm had started to look weedy in comparison to his left through lack of use.

Midweek and only a few more days until the weekend and then returning to school. Monica had readied herself for her weekly shopping trip to the supermarket giving Paul the choice of accompanying her and meeting with her friends for coffee and a gossip before doing the shopping. The thought horrified Paul so much that he opted to stay at home and even offered to make a start on dinner.

The doorbell rang as he tipped pasta into a colander. Leaving the pasta to drain, he went to open the door.

"Hi."

Paul smiled and stepped aside. "Hey Suzie;"

"I'm meeting Tessa here when she gets home from school, thought I'd drop by early and keep you company." She strolled by him and made her way to the kitchen then hopped up onto one of the stools at the breakfast bar.

"It's good to see you." He told her, turning back to the pasta and continuing the dinner preparations, "Are you staying for dinner?"

"Yep, you'd better do some more pasta." She watched him as he worked, she could watch him for hours. Already tall and broad shouldered although nowhere near as developed as he would become a few short years from now, his movements were fluid and graceful.

"When do you go back to school?" She asked.

"Monday," he answered "Tessa said you'd left."

"Yeah, got the results I expected so figured it was time to move on. I think I'm going to have to start looking for a job soon though, Mum and Dad are really pissed off that I don't want to go to college."

"So what will you do?" He asked as he leant on the breakfast bar beside her.

"I don't know. Personal shopper would be my ideal job right now, you know, getting paid to do someone else's shopping and spend their money. Hell yeah" she laughed.

"You don't actually plan on working then?" he grinned.

"Cheeky," she nudged him "Let me see your arm", she reached for his hand as he pulled the sleeve of his sweatshirt up past his elbow and turned the inside of his arm towards her revealing the raised red scars.

Suzanne bent her head and pressed her lips to the top of the scar on the inside of his elbow then she moved to kiss its end at his wrist. She heard his sharp intake of breath and tightened her grip on his hand as she pulled him towards her lifting her lips from his wrist and raised her face to him. He didn't hesitate to kiss her, moving closer to cup her face and slide his tongue along hers.

As quickly as it started, the kiss was over, Pauls released his grip on her and stepped back;

"I can't." He shook his head.

"Why not?" she asked "We're alone."

"I told Mum I'd behave, Tessa's due home within the hour and I don't know when Mum will get back."

"It'll be fine, come on Paul." she moved towards him.

"Suzie, no, I have to at least try to make an effort after all the trouble I've caused."

"So I was just a holiday fuck?" she demanded, hands on hips.

"No!" he frowned "Not at all, I just need some time Suzie, all eyes are on me at the moment, they are all watching to see what I'll do next, getting caught with my pants down buried in you isn't a good move right now."

"By the time you've finished justifying yourself we could have had a full on session, be dressed and decent before anyone came home. Why don't you just admit that you used me and don't want me anymore?" she shouted.

"I didn't use you, I wouldn't. I can't tell you how much I want you, not a day goes by without me thinking about you, just having you this close is torture but things are good right now, I have the opportunity to do the right thing, please just let me do it." He thrust his hands into his pockets and looked at her through his eyelashes.

Suzanne melted, the puppy dog look had worked, she huffed "Don't take too long to do the right thing." She softened "I won't wait forever and you will have a whole lot of making up to do." She warned.

A slow smile spread across Paul's face as his mind played all the possible scenarios of making up with her "I'm sure trying to be good is just a temporary condition, once that's over I will do whatever you ask of me."

Paul had his final physio session on Friday then spent most of the weekend with Matt and his friends playing video games, swimming and hanging around in the local park watching girls and kicking a ball around.

As soon as the Jensen twins walked onto the school grounds on Monday morning, Paul was summoned to the head teachers' office for a pep talk on the behaviour expected from him. He agreed to all the terms implied and gratefully accepted the late note he was handed for his History teacher.

Paul received somewhat of a heroes' welcome from his friends and a fair few of the other students as Matt had loudly told the tale of his brothers' rule breaking and daring escape. He found himself surrounded by people waiting to see what he would do next which he found largely irritating, the up side being lots of attention from some very pretty girls.

By his third day back at school, he was becoming more than a little irked by the group of students following him around watching his every move. He removed himself from his friends and sought the company of his sister who wholly disapproved of his actions and would make a welcome change from the fawning adoration he currently received from a majority of the student body.

Sitting opposite his sister and moaning about his supposed heroics he actually felt better when she laughed and said:

"Not so much a rebel without a cause, more like a rebel without a clue."

"Exactly," he replied "I could smack Matt for opening his mouth but as I'm being a good boy I'll just give him an evil stare instead." He grinned at his sister.

"You aren't fooling anyone with this good boy act you know. You are one of those people who will always do things your own way Paul, you might give the impression of towing the line but I know you, I can see your thoughts turning to just how much you can get away with." She chided.

Paul was about to reply when an older boy sat next to Tessa "Hi Tess," he smiled at her "How're things?"

Tessa sighed and made the introductions between the two boys, explaining to Paul that the newcomer, Carl had transferred from another school about a month ago.

"How come I don't know you?" Carl asked.

"I started Monday and I'm a lower year than you," he gestured to his uniform. As sixth formers Tessa and Carl were allowed to wear their own clothes.

"Ah, so you had better go back to people in your own year." Carl dismissed him and turned to Tessa.

"Actually, I'm quite comfortable here." Paul replied, smirk fixed firmly in place.

"Well, just be quiet, Tess and I are still trying to get to know each other."

"I already know her." Paul answered folding his arms across his chest, he smiled and leant back in his chair.

"Oh really?" Carl rounded on him "How do you figure that out, you only started Monday?"

"I started Monday this time around, I've been to this school before so therefore, I know Tessa better than you do."

"I doubt that very much." Carl scoffed.

"I guarantee it." Paul glanced at his sister, she was smiling, enjoying the exchange.

"With the obvious age gap and knowing which particular type of company Tess likes to keep, I am certain you are just being juvenile and trying to create a scene." Carl lent forward to impress his point.

"Ok," Paul leaned in too "For starters, she hates to be called Tess, her name is Tessa and that's how she likes to be addressed. I also know the type of people she likes to surround herself with and am in fact good friends with several of her girlfriends. I know where she lives and where she works, I also know the person she works for exceptionally well. So you see, quite clearly, I know her better than you." he finished.

"You're bluffing." Carl challenged.

Paul shook his head "Nope, I know her better because I'm her brother." He grinned then held out his hand, "Paul Jensen, nice to meet you." He dropped his hand when Carl didn't move, he turned to his sister. "Tessa, that was a little sneaky of you not to introduce me properly." He admonished her.

"You only have one brother." Carl blustered.

"I have two, Matt and Paul are twins." Tessa said firmly "Now if you don't mind Carl, Paul and I would like to get back to our conversation" she waited for him to leave before turning back to her brother "See you don't have to use your fists, thanks for that though, he's been on my case since he started here, perhaps he'll back off a bit now."

Everyone was quietly amazed that Paul appeared to be behaving himself and even though his relationship with Michael had once again begun to deteriorate, school and home life seemed fine.

The twins turned fifteen in the October half term, as both of them had expressed an interest in the newly opened leisure centre and gym, Monica presented her sons with fully paid up gym memberships which went down a storm with both boys spending a majority of their free time there.

Matt managed to get himself a Saturday job at a local bakers who would find work for him during the school holidays as well, he also started doing a little work for Michael, spending his Sunday's in his father's study going through the accounts of Jensen Incorporated's smaller customers, something he showed a natural aptitude for and receiving a small wage from Michael.

Getting fed up of being woken early every Saturday, Paul thought perhaps he should look into getting some weekend work as he hated it when Matt would pay when they teamed up with their friends in the evenings, lack of money was seriously cramping his style.

Monica mentioned to him that her good friend's gardener was on extended leave and she had offered Paul's services on the weekend to mow the extensive lawns, do a bit of weeding, clean the pool as well as a little maintenance work around the house for which he would receive a reasonable wage and use of the pool any time he pleased.

Kay Morello had been Monica's friend since primary school; she had been Monica's maid of honour and was Tessa's god mother. She had been invaluable when the twins were born, stepping in to babysit at a moment's notice, she had watched her friends children turn into stunning teenagers and loved them all dearly. She was more than happy to have Paul helping around the house and garden and pay him well for the work he did.

Kay had married well and had had a deeply loving relationship with her husband, she had been devastated when he had died suddenly and would be forever grateful for the support Monica had given her. Her husband had left her well provided for and she lived her life comfortably, filling her days with coffee mornings and various sporting activities. Having no children of her own, she had taken an active role in the raising of her friends children and had remained close to all three throughout the years even having her say about the boys being sent to boarding school much to Michael's annoyance even though she had agreed with him that it would be good for them.

Paul arrived with Monica just after nine the following Saturday morning. Kay set him to work on the lawn, not a difficult task as she had recently invested in a ride on lawn mower for her regular ageing gardener and Paul had lots of fun on the machine, whizzing up and down the huge expanse of grass while Kay entertained his mother and another friend with tea and toast on the patio.

Having finished the lawn, Paul set to work on the pool, looking forward to having a swim once he'd finished cleaning it.

"I may have a few jobs Paul could do." Edwina, Kay's other breakfast guest and mutual friend told Monica.

"I'll let him know." Monica replied, she would have to keep a sharp eye on Edwina, a divorcé with a penchant for younger men,

Monica was more than aware that her sons' physical appearance would appeal to her friend.

"If he could do a couple of hours one evening a week or something, my window frames are badly in need of painting and I would rather pay Paul than someone I don't know." Edwina pressed her case.

"I'm sure he will be delighted" Monica agreed.

"For Gods' sake Monica, when will you stop being so polite?" Kay asked "We all know Edwina's preference for young men, this coupled with the fact that Paul is an incorrigible flirt should have alarm bells ringing in your head and would make him working for her disastrous as well as scandalous if either of them lose what little sense they have and heaven forbid start something." She finished.

"Kay! You are awful." Monica giggled at her forthright friend.

"He is rather eye catching." Edwina admitted "And yes, I can't deny that I will flirt with him but he's your boy Monica, it would never go any further."

"I have your word on that?" Monica asked.

"Absolutely. I promise." Edwina made the motion of crossing her heart.

And so it began. Paul would work for Kay at the weekends and every other night after school he would be at Edwina's house painting her windows and flirting with the attractive forty-something woman as he did so, thoroughly enjoying Edwina's sense of humour and her tainted view on life.

Word of mouth soon spread and Paul found he had a healthy list of clients requiring his skills and the quality work he provided.

Working hard between rigorous work out sessions at the gym left him more often than not, over tired and his school work began to suffer mainly because his attention span had shrunk to that of a gnat and he would occasionally nod off in lessons bringing him to the attention of his teachers and subsequently Michael who wasted no time in dishing out a suitable punishment.

During the six months since his fifteenth birthday Paul had had several liaisons with girls in the year above him most memorably getting caught in the act one Sunday afternoon when his parents unexpectedly returned from visiting friends resulting in Paul being dragged from his bed by his hair by a furious Michael. He acted as if the blow to his abdomen that Michael delivered had hurt him but in reality the hours he spent in the gym had honed his stomach muscles and he barely felt it.

During science Matt and Paul shared a bench and had proved themselves to be efficient lab partners among a class of reprobates who had caused their lab assistant to walk out of her job within six weeks of the new term starting.

Matt glanced across at his brother. Paul was slumped over leaning on his arms exhausted from working the previous evening after school and a very late but rewarding night with one of his girlfriends. For the time being he had escaped the teachers notice as she was currently shouting at a bunch of girls at the back of the room.

A knock at the door made Matt look away from his slumbering sibling but he reached over to nudge him awake as the new teaching assistant walked into the room.

At Matt's persistent nudging Paul dragged himself from sleep, ran his hands over his face and through his hair and sat up looking straight into the eyes of the most beautiful woman he had ever seen. He straightened his now crumpled shirt and sat up straighter taking a deep breath as she glided by, breathing in her scent, his eyes followed her as she passed and placed the armful of folders she was carrying on her new desk and then reached for her lab coat.

Matt recognised his brothers' attraction to the newcomer, he was well tuned in to Paul's subtle movements and posture when he was in the presence of an attractive female, he shook his head half in sorrow and half in begrudging admiration of his brothers' aspirations.

Paul caught Matt's slight shake of the head and frowned at his twin asking "What?" Matt leant closer to him.

"She's way out of your league dude."

"Didn't you say that about Suzanne? Haven't I been banging her for the last year? You've just made this a challenge." Paul whispered.

"If you don't start improving your grades you are going to get kicked out of school which is going to put a definite kink in your style." Matt warned.

Both boys turned to the front of the class as their teacher cleared her throat and introduced the new teaching assistant.

"Class, this is my new assistant Miss Scott, let's treat her a little better than her predecessor."

That was it, Paul knew he had to have her. He cut back on his work load and got some more sleep in order to be more alert at school much to the pleasure of his teachers.

Normally a vocally inspiring student, Paul became dumbstruck in the presence of the teaching assistant and only verbally contributed in class when she wasn't there. Matt took to teasing his brother about his lack of action and his inability to speak when the woman of his dreams was in the same room.

Galvanised into action by his brothers' cruel jokes, Paul remained behind after several classes asking for help on the current subject.

Carmen Scott had been at the school for three weeks. Originally from Gloucester, she had moved to London five years ago with her boyfriend. The relationship had deteriorated rapidly after the move and the couple had gone their separate ways but both remained in London. She had noticed Paul's silence every time she was in the room and the way he would remain after class and realised the teenager had a huge crush on her and that she would have to handle him carefully.

Turning from her work station to begin tidying up the lab, she was wholly unsurprised to find Paul sitting at his bench.

"This is becoming a habit." she said as she sat beside him "What's the problem now?"

Paul smiled, he knew he'd been rumbled "No problem other than the fact that you can't see past my age." He told her.

"You are my student, even if I was attracted to you, this would never happen."

"Yeah, I thought about that, technically as you aren't a teacher, I'm not your student" his smile widened.

"You think you have it all worked out don't you?" She couldn't help but smile "However, besides the fact that technically you are my student you are also legally underage and I do have to say, you are certainly not my type, sorry."

Paul looked down at his hands momentarily then he turned back to her "Normally a comment such as that would wound me deeply but in your case I'm prepared to forgive you and continue to be impossibly persistent." He grinned.

"You can be as persistent as you like young man, it is never going to happen." she warned.

Paul rose from his seat grabbing his bag and heaving it up on to his shoulder before facing her again "You keep telling yourself that Miss Scott, you will change your mind eventually, I can wait, after all it's not like I don't have other things to keep me distracted while I work on you." He smiled "See you tomorrow", he left the room without a backwards glance and walked straight into the arms of an attractive red headed sixth former.

Carmen had been in this situation before where students had expressed feelings for her and she had managed to extract herself from their affections with a few choice phrases, this boy however was different. Mature for his age, charming, funny and incredibly good looking, she had the feeling that he was used to getting his own way and believed him when he said he would be persistent. She tried to tell herself that she wasn't flattered by his attention or that she wasn't just the slightest bit attracted to him to no avail even though her morals screamed at her that her feelings were wrong and the more attention he paid her the more she felt the fringes of jealousy tugging at her when she saw him with one of the many girls that flocked around him. He obviously preferred older girls but she still considered herself way beyond his reach.

Paul continued to worm his way into her affections, he was always polite and smelled so good each and every time he stood that little too close to her when returning books and equipment to her work station.

School ended at three thirty five each day with the sound of pounding feet and the loud chatter of relieved students. Carmen usually waited until the students had left before venturing out to her car, this particular day she had to leave shortly after the final bell for a doctors' appointment.

There were still students milling around when she reached her car. She saw Paul wearing jeans, trainers and his white school shirt standing in the staff car park, he had obviously changed before leaving the building. She took her time loading the students' exercise books into the boot of her car, keeping an eye on him, wondering what he was up to. A white Volkswagen Beetle pulled into the car park and pulled haphazardly into a space. Tessa Jensen got out of the drivers' side and approached her brother, a t-shirt in her hand.

"Thanks for this." Carmen heard Paul greet his sister.

"That's ok, I'm going into town to pick up Suzanne anyway so I had to pass here."

Paul unbuttoned his shirt and handed it to Tessa. Carmen gulped, the boy had a body to die for; smooth olive skin covered toned muscles. She closed the boot on her car as Paul reached for his t-shirt, he heard the noise and turned to face her a smile spreading across his face as he noticed her flush at getting caught gawping at him, pausing before sliding the shirt over his head, he called to her;

"Hi Miss, you're leaving early."

"Er yeah, must dash." She jumped into her car, not daring to look in his direction as she drove by "Shit" she cursed, he had caught her looking at him, now he would double his efforts to get her attention.

"You are such a show off." Tessa admonished.

"What? She looked at me, can't say I blame her though, I do look good." he laughed, he'd won, he had her attention now, time to back off and let her come to him.

"Huh" Tessa gruffed "Do you want a lift?"

"Nah, I'm heading in the opposite direction to you, you could take my bag home though." He dropped his bag into the back seat of her car said his goodbyes and headed off to Edwina's house as he was now working inside repairing her banisters amidst much laughter as she told him the tale of how they had managed to get broken in the first place.

Edwina was cooking dinner for them when Paul arrived. She was an excellent cook and also loved to bake, something she had little reason to do since her children had gone to university. Paul had a very healthy appetite and his presence in her house had given her the opportunity to break out her cake tins once again.

Edwina thoroughly enjoyed Paul's visits, she paid him well and was more than pleased with his work, noticing that he was a perfectionist and wouldn't be happy with his work until it was spot on.

They had many long and involved conversations about Paul's relationship with his father. Edwina wholeheartedly disapproved of Michael and his treatment of this charming boy but couldn't deny that he provided well for his family and for all Paul's gripes, he rarely went without. She found herself living vicariously through Paul's many conquests and he had actually had her crying with laughter at the description of exactly what he had been doing when Michael had grasped a handful of his hair and pulled him not only out of his bed but also out of the girl he had been buried inside of at the time.

"Michael must have been furious." Edwina laughed.

"Understatement." Paul replied "He almost had steam coming out of his ears."

"You really are a bit of a whore aren't you?"

"Hey, if girls want to prostrate themselves in front of me, I'm going to take advantage, I'm only human, I have needs and desires." He protested.

"Lucky girls." Edwina commented.

"You know I think you and I would have loads of fun together Edwina but I honestly think Mum would castrate me and I'm far more afraid of her than I am Dad."

"Sweet little Monica would never do anything to you."

"She doesn't have to, it's the way she looks at me when I do something wrong, it kills me to know I've hurt her or done something she disapproves of." He answered.

"I know what you mean, my mother had one of those looks" she chuckled "And as much as I'd like to mess around with you, my friendship with Monica is far more important to me."

"And as I'm finding out, the fantasy is often better than the reality anyway" he added.

"How very true" she agreed "You are wise beyond your years."

Chapter Six

For the rest of the term until the Easter holidays Paul made every effort to ignore Carmen in class and stopped remaining behind after class. At first Carmen was relieved that he appeared to be over his crush but every now and then she would catch him looking at her, he would quickly look away on the odd occasion but generally he would meet her gaze, his eyes twinkling as he recognised her confusion, this coupled with the fact that she never saw him with the same girl twice began to irritate her.

Easter holidays proved to be a busy time for Paul, gardens were beginning to come to life again and he found himself much in demand from clients old and new, he was raking in money hand over fist and eventually persuaded Matt to give up his bakery job and work alongside him.

Kay Morello had informed Paul that her regular gardener had decided to retire after a long illness and she asked if he would consider taking over her garden and property maintenance on a permanent basis to which Paul readily agreed.

Paul always set aside a full day for Kay's garden as her grounds were extensive and now that he was officially her maintenance man, he needed to ensure everything was just how she liked it. Taking Matt with him, he set his brother to work weeding the patio area and rockeries as well as leaving him to clean the pool while he began on the lawns.

Kay called both boys over to her mosaic tiled garden table for lunch where Paul stayed with her when Matt went back to work.

"Business is good?" she asked him.

"Yeah, so good that it has me questioning my decision to stay on at school."

"Surely it will be difficult to run a business full time when you can't drive?"

"That's what I was thinking but I have looked into buying a van and hiring someone who can drive for the times when I'm at school, it's not like I can't afford it, the downside would be not being able to keep an eye on the quality of the work unless I leave school."

"You have given this some thought haven't you? You just need to hire someone you can trust, you'll also need to invest in some tools, not everyone is as well equipped as me" she smiled.

"I have to admit, taking care of your property is one of my favourite jobs, you do make it easy for me as everything I need is here."

"I'm only one of your favourite jobs?" she chided "Let me guess, Edwina is your other favourite."

"Yep." Paul laughed "I have a lot of fun working for her."

"Please tell me it's just banter."

"Of course it is. Although, Edwina is a very attractive woman." he admitted.

"Paul" Kay warned.

"It'll never go any further than flirting honestly, the connection she has with Mum is way more important to her, having said that, if she wasn't Mum's friend, there wouldn't be anything to stop us."

Kay gasped "I'm shocked, she's old enough to be your mother."

"I know but credit where it's due, she keeps herself in fantastic shape and like she says, I'm a bit of a whore, if it's got a pulse I'm generally there." He grinned.

"I'd have to agree with her there. The accounts of your exploits I've heard from your mother are quite eye opening, you should be careful, you will get caught big time one day"

"I already have been, didn't Mum tell you? They keep catching me; apparently discretion isn't in my nature."

"I don't mean caught in that sense, I mean babies and infections."

"Nah." He shook his head "I'm far too careful for that."

"I hope you are, Monica keeps saying to me that for the first time in your life she wishes you were more like Matt."

"What? He was at it before I was and he's with more girls than me, he just doesn't bring them home" Paul said "Me getting caught in the act just keeps the heat off him the snidey git."

"In that case, you both need to be careful."

"We will be" Paul told her "I'd better get back to work."

"Yes you should. I'm popping out to pick up my niece, I won't be long."

"Ok, thanks for lunch."

Kay returned an hour later to find the Jensen twins fooling around in the pool. A quick survey of her garden revealed it in excellent shape and all the equipment had been put away, she was sure, knowing Paul that all her tools would have been cleaned; letting the boys use the pool was a perk she gladly allowed them.

"I've put my things in my room" Hayley Simms, Kay's twenty year old niece stepped onto the patio.

"Good, have a seat, I'll make you a sandwich."

"Cool. Who are they?" she asked pointing to the pool.

"You remember Monica and Michael Jensen don't you?"

"Yes."

"They are the twins, Matt and Paul."

"Oh, they were babies last time I saw them." Hayley's parents, Kay's sister and brother in law were in the process of moving home to England from South Africa, Hayley had been sent ahead of them to be able to receive their worldly possessions as they arrived. An unfortunate economical downturn had caused the family to be forced into bankruptcy and necessitated their move home. Kay had insisted the family move into her spacious home, she would enjoy their company and it would give them a chance to get back on their feet without added financial burden.

Hayley watched the boys splashing in the pool; they hadn't noticed either her or her Aunt and were happily entertaining themselves in the water. The darker of the two boys pulled himself out of the deep end of the pool, picked up his towel and wrapped it around his hips, with his back to her she was able to get a good look at the firm back and long muscled legs, he turned and said something to his brother and that was when he saw her, he smiled and began a slow saunter down the side of the pool, she heard him tell the other boy to get out.

Hayley's eyes almost popped out of their sockets when Matt hauled his stocky frame out of the pool, the water cascading down over his massive shoulders and wide chest, his blond hair slicked back from his face. He stood up and wiped the water from his body then caught the towel the dark haired boy threw at him. She noticed the darker one incline his head towards her which caused the blond boy to look in her direction just as her Aunt placed a mug of tea and a plate of sandwiches in front of her.

"Boys, come over here." Kay called.

Still dripping from their swim, both boys checked their towels were securely fastened and made their way to the patio. Hayley found that her throat was dry and her stomach churning, she couldn't keep her eyes off the shorter, stockier twin, a sentiment clearly reflected in his eyes as they didn't waver from hers during the walk over.

Kay made the introductions and announced that she was holding a barbeque that evening to welcome her niece, the entire Jensen clan were attending and Kay had asked Tessa to bring some friends and introduce them so that Hayley would have some people of her own age to talk to and hopefully make friends with.

Returning to Kay's that evening, Matt, unaccustomed to a girl obviously finding him more attractive than his brother fully intended to make the most of this and had harassed his parents into hurrying out of the house and into their car shortly after Tessa had left to collect her friends much to Monica's surprise as she usually had to drag Matt to these sort of occasions.

All became clear when she caught sight of Hayley. The girl could be a model with her brown highlighted hair, large dark blue eyes and lips in full pout, it would appear both her sons had an eye for a pretty face.

Paul found Matt's immediate obsession with the girl most amusing and was prepared to tease him mercilessly about it, he hadn't seen Matt this enthusiastic about a girl before and felt it was the brotherly thing to do by winding him up about it as much as he could.

After a brief circuit of the guests, Matt subtly made his way to Hayley's side and slid into the seat next to hers.

"I hate these do's." She blurted as he sat beside her.

"Me too," He replied.

"And to make it worse, I'm told I have to spend the day shopping tomorrow with your sister and her friends."

"That won't be so bad; Tessa and her friends are good fun to be around."

"The point is, I have no money. How much fun is shopping when you're skint?

"You honestly think Kay will send you out without money? She's not like that."

"You obviously know my Aunt better than I do." Hayley replied. Wow, she loved his eyes, blue with flecks of brown and green, his presence dominated her just from his size and she was a sucker for blond hair and while he wasn't as obviously good looking as his brother, she noticed his face was well proportioned, his eyes twinkled when he talked and he used hand gestures to emphasise his point, his laugh was a deep rumble and the attention he paid her was unwavering.

"I could always show you around town when you tire of shopping." He offered.

"I'd like that. Aunt Kay said I can borrow her car anytime, maybe we could catch a movie one evening?"

Matt grinned "Not backward at coming forward are you?"

"Sorry, I know I come on a bit strong, it's the South African upbringing, I'll try to reign it in a bit."

"Please don't, I like it." He told her.

Without Matt to fool around with Paul had decided to sit in a corner and get quietly drunk, his plan was going rather well until Tessa arrived with three of her friends. He first caught sight of Holly, a demure brunette; Fay a loud and exceptionally funny blond followed Holly across the garden, both girls turned and beckoned to the third friend Tessa had brought, Suzanne.

Rising from his seat and taking the circuitous route around the guests, he stopped by his mother who was talking to Kay; he had managed to put himself directly opposite Suzanne.

She looked sensational, her long, usually straight hair now hung in loose curls around her shoulders. She wore bright red high heeled shoes over a calf length red wrap around dress that displayed her cleavage beautifully and emphasised her tiny waist.

Taking a sip from her glass of wine, she let her eyes wonder around the assembled guests. She spotted Matt talking to a girl she didn't recognise but guessed it was the new girl. Michael was manning the barbeque, Monica was talking to Kay and there he was, standing just behind his mother wearing a black shirt, open at the neck and with the sleeves rolled up, black trousers and the inevitable black trainers, his eyes fixed firmly on hers. She smiled and nodded ever so slightly in greeting then turned her back on him and joined Fay in filling up her glass. He was gone when she turned back; she shrugged and went to introduce herself to the newcomer.

Suzanne enjoyed her conversation with the forthright young woman and even threw in a little light flirting with Matt. Deep in conversation the three of them made their way to the barbeque and that was when she felt his presence behind her, his warm hand pressed against the small of her back, his lips by her ear. She felt his hand slide down to caress her behind and heard the escape of his breath

"You bad girl." He whispered.

She smiled but didn't turn around; he had discovered that she had neglected to put on her underwear. She took one step back and pushed her bottom into his groin, both his hands had come to rest on her hips.

"Pool house?" He asked sliding his hand across her back and stepping to her side.

"Ten minutes." she replied.

He left her side and disappeared into the throng of guests. Suzanne removed herself from the queue of people waiting for food and headed for the nearest bathroom to freshen up before her rendezvous with Paul.

He had closed all but one of the blinds by the time she joined him.

"I could ask Tessa if I can borrow her car for a bit and we could disappear to yours." She suggested "Good idea." He agreed reaching for her "But I honestly don't think I could wait that long before I have you." He attempted to kiss her, she pushed him away.

"I seem to remember you telling me you would do anything I asked of you."

"And I will, just don't make me endure a car ride sitting next to you when you look good enough to eat" he plucked at the tie holding her dress closed, opening the front flap to reveal the inner hidden one;

"Huh, that wasn't as easy as I thought it would be."

"Let me" she undid the hidden tie and held the dress open. Paul stepped back and took his time drinking in the sight of her minus her knickers, her breasts barely concealed beneath a sheer black bra.

"Beautiful." He whispered. She came into his arms then, raising her face to his to receive his kiss. She loved the feel of his hands roaming her body and could feel him becoming aroused as she pressed herself against him. She slid her hands from his neck to the front of his shirt, once it was unbuttoned she pushed it from his shoulders, he dropped one arm and then the other letting it fall to the floor. She pressed her lips to his chest, his skin soft, warm and heavenly smelling, she felt the firm muscle that had replaced the previously slim, athletic build. She ran her hands over his chest and stomach.

"You like?" he asked referring to his now muscled and toned torso.

"Very much." She nodded "You were pretty before but now? Damn boy, you are hot"

He laughed "I do it all for you."

"That's bullshit and you know it" she tutted, he grinned and nodded his agreement

"What do you want me to do?" he asked.

"For starters you can drop your trousers." She told him "Then get on your knees and pay me the attention I deserve."

Doing as she asked, he unbuckled his belt, stepped out of his trousers and underwear, dropped to his knees and grasped her backside in his large capable hands preventing her from backing away from the pleasure his mouth would bring her.

Suzanne's legs began to shake, if it was possible he had become even better at this. Her whole world had dissolved into the feeling of his tongue on her sex and the intense sensations it was bringing her. The strength of her orgasm forced a loud groan to escape from her lips. She was certain she would have fallen to her knees had he not been holding her. He waited for her to stop shaking before coming to his feet and kissing her, his hands never leaving her body.

He shuffled backwards with her in his arms and sunk down onto one of the wooden benches, guiding her legs either side of his, he looked up at her flushed face.

"Fuck me Suzie." He whispered his fingers digging into her hips as she slid her body over his waiting one teasing her tongue into his mouth as she began to rock.

Aware that they would be missed if they were gone too long, Paul grasped Suzanne's hips tighter and eased her into a faster pace. She took her hands from his shoulders and prised his fingers from her flesh.

"Stop it." She hissed "I want to make this last."

"Not this time Suzie, we're at a party, tongues will start wagging if people suddenly realise we're both missing."

"I hate it when you are right." she huffed.

"Turn around, it'll be fast and satisfying that way." He told her watching as she eased herself back onto him helped by his guiding hands, her bottom now pressed into his stomach, her hands on his knees.

"Oh my God." She gasped as she rocked. This way around the feeling was more intense and she couldn't stop herself from accelerating the pace, he had his hands on her bottom, his long fingers sliding into the crevasse, teasingly pushing against the hidden entrance spurred her on. When he grasped her hip with his left hand and wrapped his right arm around her stomach and pulled her back against him she tightened her inner muscles and slammed down onto him feeling him explode. They were both sweating and fighting to control their breathing by now, both wishing they had more time to do this again.

As Paul released his grip on her she removed herself from his lap and slid to the floor in front of him taking his softening penis into her mouth, he jumped as she ran her tongue over the sensitive head but didn't protest as she proceeded to clean him. She licked her lips and bent to kiss him as she came to her feet.

"We have to stop having these clandestine meetings." She told him "I want to take my time and have you worship me properly." She chuckled jumping out of the way as he went to spank her bottom for her last remark and began to get dressed.

"I can probably take a day off this week if you are free." He reached for his boxers.

"I'll make sure I am." She opened her small clutch bag and pulled a pair of sheer black knickers out of it that perfectly matched her bra.

"You did that on purpose." Paul accused looking up from buckling his belt.

"Did what?" She asked, all innocence.

"Forgetting to wear underwear. I should have known. You knew I wouldn't be able to resist."

"Of course I knew. I wasn't going to come tonight until Tessa told me the whole family would be here. You are the only reason I'm here." She admitted.

"We should start dating; this wouldn't be so sordid if you were my girlfriend."

"As much as the idea appeals, you are nowhere near ready to have a relationship where you have to be with only one person. You would hurt me, perhaps not intentionally but it would happen and I'm not prepared to let you do that. What we have right now is fine, we have fun and there are no strings."

"I hate to admit that you are right about me not being ready for a relationship but there are strings Suzie. Wherever I go or whoever I'm with, you are always there in the back of my mind. I never lose sight of the fact that you are the one. I'm going to marry you one day."

Suzanne stepped closer to him and reached up to stroke his face. Unwittingly, he had just voiced the exact way she felt too.

"Little boy, you have a lot to learn." She told him gently "But one day I may just say yes."

He smiled, turned his head and kissed the palm of the hand that caressed his face. "We'd better get back to the party. I'll straighten this place out; grab me a beer would you?"

As it worked out Fay's older brother wanted Paul to give him a quote for renovating and enlarging the pond in his garden. Fay had passed the information on to him along with the keys to her brothers' house as he was currently away on business. As she gave him the keys with one hand, she produced a note out of her pocket with the other.

Unfolding the piece of paper Paul immediately recognised Suzanne's handwriting. The note told him that she was free on Wednesday and would meet him around eleven.

"Suzanne gave you this?" He asked, a frown creasing his brow.

Fay nodded "I know about you two, Suzanne had to confide in someone."

"No offence Fay but I really wish she hadn't."

"Why shouldn't she talk to me about it? I bet you tell Matt."

"Yeah I do but it just means that one more person is lying to Tessa."

"Then tell her."

"Are you insane? She'd go nuts, her best friend and her little brother at it like rabbits would completely flip her out."

"Not if you were Suzanne's boyfriend." Fay pointed out.

Paul shook his head "She won't date me, says I'm not ready for a relationship."

Fay laughed "She does have a point. Don't worry Paul, Suzanne and I will figure out a way to ease Tessa into the idea of you two."

Suzanne found Paul consulting his tape measure and making notes as he kneeled beside the existing pond. Wearing faded blue jeans and a white t- shirt he looked casual but clean, his dark hair stirred in the breeze, he moved around the pond checking his measurements. She saw his frown and stood quietly not wishing to disturb his concentration. He sat on his haunches and pushed his hair back from his face then returned to his note pad, re-calculating his figures.

Watching him Suzanne felt her heart squeeze. She recognised that she was in love with him but refused to put him in a position that would enable him to stomp all over her heart, their time would come, she was sure of it but for now she would make do with their secret meetings.

They spent the entire day together pushing each other to their limits. She watched him sleep until she bored of it and decided the best way to wake him would be to slide her tongue repeatedly over his genitals, it had the desired effect. That day she found out more about him than she had imagined she would ever know, he opened up to her completely telling her all his hopes and dreams as well as admitting to the beatings he had taken from Michael over the years and the story of his short lived stay at boarding school, something Tessa had told her he never talked about, he even told her of his attraction to the teaching assistant.

From Paul's point of view Suzanne was his ideal match. She made him laugh and wasn't afraid to stand up to him. She fulfilled his physical needs and left him exhausted and aching whereas his many other liaisons usually left him wanting more and searching for another lover. He had nothing to hide from her and felt comfortable in her company knowing he could tell her anything in confidence. Because of her he would strive to be a better person. He felt his heart race every time he looked at her and he was being completely honest when he told her that he never lost sight of the fact that she was the girl who had his heart. He fully believed that they would be a couple one day and told her that he knew she would be more than capable of telling him when he was ready to commit to her totally.

Lying on her stomach, her arms folded across his ribs, her chin resting on her hands she looked into his dark brown eyes and saw her own emotions reflected in them so much so that she was almost tempted to throw caution to the wind and actually start to become a couple right now.

"I love you Suzie, I always will." he told her, his fingers entwining in her silky hair.

"I know you do. One day Paul one day."

"I wish I could change, I wish I could promise you that I will only be with you but if I'm going to be honest with myself and you then I have to admit that I'm far too easily distracted by a pretty face to even contemplate a serious relationship. I'm just afraid that by the time I've grown enough to be the man you want me to be, you will have moved on."

"That's a chance we'll both have to take" she paused "Do you know that you are the only one who I allow to call me Suzie?"

"Really? I never even considered that you didn't like it. I won't do it anymore."

"It's fine, I like it when you call me Suzie I just hate it if anyone else tries it, it's something we share, something only you are allowed to do."

"Cool, now I feel special." He grinned "Does it make you jealous when I'm with someone else?"

"Sometimes but as we aren't together I don't really have the right to be jealous. Do you get jealous when I'm with a guy?"

"Insanely but then again, you rarely tell me if you have a boyfriend so I spend most of my time in ignorant bliss."

"I do have a boyfriend." she admitted.

"Is he nice to you Suzie?" Paul asked feeling an instant dislike for the unknown male

"He's very sweet." She nodded "Now ask me what you really want to know."

He chuckled and pulled her closer "Have you got pelvic with him yet and is he as good as me?"

Laughing, Suzanne slapped his chest "No I haven't but I'll let you know how you compare." she snuggled into his side "I start work on Monday as a personal shopper."

"Your dream job, congratulations."

"I get a company car too."

"Awesome, let me know when you want to christen it."

"Is that all you think about?" she tutted.

"It's a little difficult to think about anything else when you are lying naked next to me."

She moved her body to cover his, feeling him harden against her stomach "You want to go again?"

"Well maybe just once more."

Matt had been left to take care of Kay's garden while Paul took a day off to be with Suzanne. Initially disappointed on his arrival as Kay and Hayley were out. His mood improved later in the day as the two women arrived home and Kay made them all something to eat.

Kay had noticed the attraction between her niece and Matt and was a little uneasy with it if only for the fact that Matt was so much younger than Hayley. She decided not to say anything and hoped the attraction would simply fade away. She left Hayley sorting out her new college coursework and Matt in the garden while she went to play bridge.

Returning home a few hours later, Kay noticed her house was very quiet, she called her niece's name and when she didn't receive a reply, she went and checked her bedroom only to find it empty. Next she checked the garden, no sight of Hayley or Matt. She glanced around her grounds, accustomed to finding them perfect under Paul's care, she was astounded that her lawns hadn't been cut and that the ride on lawn mower and other gardening tools were left out. Returning to the house, she picked up the phone.

"I'll get it." Monica called as both Tessa and Paul had moved to answer the phone, the brother and sister heard their mother say "Oh, Hi Kay," before returning to their seats

"You're quiet." Tessa commented.

"Just tired." Paul replied "I'm going to have to look into getting some people to help me out with the amount of customers I have, there aren't enough hours in the day."

"That's good though isn't it?"

"Yeah, I'm just spreading myself a bit thin at the moment and I will need someone to keep an eye on things when I go back to school."

"Why don't you just drop out?" Tessa asked.

"Because I have no qualifications, I need to sit my exams first, and then I'll think about leaving."

Monica came into the room "Paul, Kay would like a word."

Paul got to his feet and went into the hall, perching on his mothers ornate telephone stand "Hi Kay."

"Paul, I think you'd better get over her as soon as you can."

"Is there a problem?" Paul asked.

"You will see when you get here." Kay replied before hanging up.

Paul shuffled his feet into his trainers before joining Monica and Tessa "I have to go over to Kay's; I don't suppose you fancy giving me a lift Mum?"

Monica glanced at her watch, satisfied that it was still relatively early and that she would be home in plenty of time to start Michael's dinner, she grabbed her car keys and took her youngest child to her friend's house.

Kay didn't say a word to him as she preceded him through the house to the garden and gestured to the abandoned tools and uncut lawns. She saw Paul frown and watched him walk down to the grass so that he could get a better look, he returned via the pool.

"Where's Matt?" he asked

"I don't know." Kay replied "This is unacceptable Paul."

"I agree. I'll put the tools away and come back tomorrow to put everything right if that's ok with you, obviously, this week's gardening will be free of charge."

"That's fine just as long as it's you who returns and not your brother."

"Kay, I'm sure Matt just got called away." Monica defended her son.

"It's strange how Hayley is missing too." Kay replied.

"I'm going to kill him." Paul muttered as he walked away to return the tools to the garage his mind running through the next day's jobs he would have to cancel in order to put this right.

Monica glanced at Paul as they began the journey home; his arms were folded across his chest, his face a mask of a deep scowl.

"Paul." she began "Matt was only helping you out."

"Mum, you saw the state of Kay's garden; I would never leave it like that. I now have to cancel a boat load of jobs tomorrow just so that I can go back there and put it right, there are huge gouges in her lawn, God knows what he's been doing but he's just cost me two days money."

"Oh, I didn't realise it was that serious."

"Stop at the park on the way home will you, I have a fairly good idea where he'll be."

"I don't want you making a scene." Monica warned, pulling into the kerb

"I won't." Paul said, his hand on the cars' door handle "I promise. Wait here, I won't be long."

Paul found his brother and Hayley, wrapped in each other in a thick clump of trees, the place both boys used when they were stuck for somewhere to go. Reaching down, Paul grasped the back of Matt's shirt and hauled him to his feet, exposing Hayley's almost naked body.

"Home time." Paul growled at his brother.

"Oh, it's you, I thought it was the Old Bill." Matt shook himself free from Paul's grasp and turned to face his brother "What's up?" he asked on seeing Paul's frown.

"You left Kay's garden unfinished." Paul told him.

"Yeah I know. I'm gonna go back and do it."

"No, you're going to come home so we can talk about this." Paul looked down at Hayley who had made no effort to cover herself, she met Paul's gaze as he surveyed her body "Not a whole lot of class going on there." He said.

"Hey, that's out of order." Matt shoved him "You'd better get dressed." he told Hayley

"Once you are dressed, you can make your own way home" Paul told her "Matt's coming with me."

"Matt, what the hell." Hayley shouted, coming to her feet, re-arranging her clothes "Don't let him speak to me that way."

Matt, in turn, went to shout at his brother, stopping dead at Paul's furious face.

"Shut up Matt." Paul spoke "Hayley, stay away from my brother." he grasped Matt's arm and pulled him with him to Monica's car, opening the back door and guiding him, somewhat forcefully into the seat.

Jumping into the front seat and strapping himself in, Paul half turned to glare at his brother "I trusted you with Kay's garden. I have to go there tomorrow now to put right what you've done, why the hell are there huge bits of her lawn missing?"

"That bloody ride on mower was churning it up, that's why I stopped."

"Ok, that doesn't explain why the rest of the garden wasn't done. I have to cancel tomorrow's jobs now; you've cost me a load of money. Don't think for one minute I'm paying you for today"

"Perhaps if you hadn't skived off today, you would have been there to help me." Matt sniped.

"I wasn't skiving and even if I was, it's my business and I have the right to take a day off." Paul contorted in his seat, dragged his battered note book out of his back pocket and threw it at Matt "I was quoting for a job today as you can see."

Matt glanced at Paul's notes "So this took all day?" he asked "Taking a few measurements for a pond? I suppose it was just coincidence that the job is for Fay's brother."

"Fay put me on to the job" Paul agreed "It could turn into a full garden re-vamp."

"I suppose the fact that you spent the rest of the day banging Suzanne is just coincidence then?" Matt gloated, Paul glared, and Monica slammed on the brakes before pulling the car over to the side of the road.

"Suzanne? As in Tessa's friend?" she asked Paul.

"Yes Mum, Suzann,e" he scowled at Matt "Thanks Matt that was really good of you."

"You shouldn't have left the note lying around."

"You should learn to keep your mouth shut." Paul shot back "You're sacked."

"Does Tessa know?" Monica asked.

"No and I'd prefer it if she didn't." Paul replied, he glanced at his watch "Hadn't we make a move? At this rate, Dad'll be home before his dinner is ready." He deftly changed the subject.

"Bloody hell." Monica muttered on seeing the time "You two are going to have to help me when I get in."

"You can't sack me." Matt finally found his voice "You have far too much work on to do that."

"He does have a point Paul." Monica spoke.

"Ok, I'll keep you on but you won't be allowed anywhere near my high end customers. You can do tomorrows jobs while I sort out Kay's garden, screw this up Matt and I really will sack you."

The following day, Paul went all out on Kay's garden, repairing the damage to her lawns as well as fixing the ride on lawn mower. Kay supplied him with bottles of water as it was a stiflingly hot day.

"I have spoken to Hayley about distracting Matt, she promises that it won't happen again." Kay spoke as she handed over a chilled bottle.

"I know it won't, Matt will be doing the small gardens from now on and I will be the only one who touches your garden." Paul assured her.

"She said that you tracked them down yesterday and that you were quite rude to her."

"Yeah, I was rude; I was also majorly pissed off." Paul shrugged "I know she's your niece but I think it would be better if she stayed well clear of Matt, they don't seem to be very good for each other."

"I agree but if I tell them to stay apart it will just make it more exciting for them to be together so I think I'll let this thing they have fizzle out, I do appreciate your hard work though Paul." She touched his shoulder and smiled before she turned to leave "I have to go out, I've left a salad in the fridge, help yourself."

Paul didn't stop for lunch; he continued to work until his stomach growled. He pulled off his sweat soaked t-shirt and dried himself with a towel before delving into his bag for a fresh shirt. Hayley was standing by him when he straightened up.

"Sorry sweetheart, wrong brother." He snapped.

"It's such a pity you are a twat seeing as you are so pretty." She replied tartly.

"I wouldn't touch you with Matt's, let alone my own." He growled.

"I wouldn't let you touch me, you are repulsive, opinionated and rude." She hissed.

"Meaning I wouldn't blindly follow you into whatever it is you happen to be into like my brother does so therefore I'm not worthy of your attention. Well thank God for that." he turned away from her and headed into the house retrieving the salad from the fridge, he returned to the garden to sit at the sheltered patio table.

"You can't stop us seeing each other." She stood over him.

"Who Matt see's is up to him, don't plan on fixing up any double dates though, you make my skin crawl."

"You just can't handle the fact that Matt is happy with one girl where you jump off one and onto another without a seconds thought for the wreckage you leave behind."

"Let's just get one thing straight, what I do has absolutely nothing to do with you, you stay out of my face and I'll stay out of yours. Don't count on Matt being around anytime soon though, I have the next few weeks full of work for him."

By the time Paul had completed his work, cleaned and tidied away the tools he had used it was getting dark. Kay had returned home and had started to cook for Hayley and herself offering Paul an evening meal and then a lift home when he refused.

"The garden looks wonderful, thank you Paul."

"No problem, I'm going to pop back at the weekend if that's ok just to make sure the repair on the lawn is taking, if it doesn't, I'll re-turf that section for you."

"Ok, let me know how much the turf will cost if you need it."

"Kay, it's free of charge, I'm only putting right what Matt spoiled."

"You are a sweetheart but giving freebies isn't a successful way to run a business."

"It's excellent business sense when it keeps my best customer happy." He smiled "I'll see you Saturday." He let himself out of the side gate and headed towards home, he wasn't even half way there when fatigue hit him and he began to wish that he had taken Kay up on her offer of a lift.

He hopped over the small wall that divided the forecourt of the petrol station from the footpath and was searching his pockets for enough change to buy a drink when he saw her bending over the petrol cap of her car, her tight dark blue jeans clinging to every curve and leaving very little to the imagination. Stopping in his tracks, taking his time to admire the sight before him, he looked into her eyes as she turned, petrol cap in hand;

"Hi Miss" a slow smile spread across his face revealing even white teeth that gleamed in his sun tanned face.

"Hello Paul." Carmen replied, her breath catching at his obvious beauty "What are you doing here?"

"Just on my way home," he sauntered closer. "Don't suppose you fancy giving me a lift?"

"No." She frowned at how bold he was and turned her attention to the petrol pump, squeezing the trigger, ignoring him.

"Oh come on, I've been hard at work all day and it's a long walk home." He wheedled.

"I said no." She replied firmly. She replaced the petrol pump and returned the petrol cap to its rightful place before turning away from him and heading into the shop to pay for her fuel. By the time she returned to her car, Paul was securely strapped into the passenger seat, looking very smug and self assured. "Get out." She hissed.

"Nope." He replied.

"We can't do this."

"It's just a lift, no-one would even raise an eyebrow." He reasoned.

"I'm your teacher, this sort of thing isn't allowed. Get out." She repeated.

"It's Easter holidays; you aren't anyone's teacher in the holidays. You could just take me as far as you are going, I'll walk from there."

"Fine." She conceded "You've got dirt all over my car, you're filthy."

Paul stretched out his hand and placed it on her thigh "You're right, I am filthy," he grinned, winking at her when she glanced over at him and removed his hand from her leg. Paul turned in his seat when the sound of a car horn came from behind them "You'd better get moving, you are creating a queue." He said knowing that now she had no option but to comply.

They drove in silence, Carmen fretting that now he would know where she lived but trying to justify his reasoning that in the school holidays they were in fact just two people not teacher and student, she stole glances at him throughout the trip noting that his lips were twitching, trying to contain his smile berating herself for admiring his perfect profile. She decided to pull into her garage in case the neighbours were home and saw her with him in his more than obvious youth. She was out of the car before he could turn to her, waiting for him to get out.

"You can leave through the side door." She told him, deliberately keeping her voice cool and her eyes cast away from his.

Not wishing to push his luck and therefore push her away, Paul was more than happy with the steps he had taken today and was about to voice his thanks when she bent to collect her mail from the doorstep stretching the seam of her jeans tighter across her full behind before stepping into the kitchen not realising that Paul had thrown caution to the wind and was behind her as she turned to close the door.

"Paul. Go home."

"Nice house." He roamed the kitchen.

"You need to leave." She said, hands on hips.

"Actually, I need a shower, it's this way I take it?" He asked rhetorically as he moved out of the room and up the stairs, coming to what was obviously her bedroom at the top of them, pleased to find she had an en suite and stripped with lightning speed.

Carmen was stunned into immobility until she heard the shower start up making her sprint up the stairs and into her bedroom, wrenching open the door to the en suite she screamed at him to get out of her house, her words dying on her lips as he turned to face her, water cascading over him, he opened the shower door, he made no effort to cover himself.

"Why don't you join me?"

"This is bad, very bad." She muttered as she backed out of the room, closed the door and sunk to the floor by the bed, her head in her hands, trying in vain to block the image she had just seen from her brain which is where Paul found her when he stepped out of the shower, a towel draped around his hips, his body glistening with droplets of water as he hadn't bothered to get dry. He regarded her in her hunched position and briefly wondered if he should take this next step quickly deciding that it was now or never.

He stooped and grasped her hands, bringing them to his lips as he guided her to her feet then taking both her hands in one of his; he pressed them to his chest as he closed in to kiss her, stilling the protests that spilled from her lips. Releasing her hands, he used his own to let her hair down from the constraints of the band currently holding it then set about removing her clothes, her thin blouse was no contest for his deft fingers, her jeans putting up a minimal protest as both hands slid inside them, over her bottom and shoved, dropping them at her feet.

"Stop." She whispered, her hands still resting on his chest and although she continually protested that this was wrong, she made no effort to push him away but he found the lack of her caresses was a little discouraging.

"Ssh." His lips against hers as he began to push her backwards, her calves against the bed before he reached down to her behind, spreading his hands for maximum coverage as he lifted her and positioned her legs around his hips and in the same movement, stepped forward and lay her on the bed before freeing his hands, one flicked away his towel, the other found her breast, swiftly followed by his mouth as he took complete possession of her bringing forth an unrestrained moan of longing as he ploughed into her.

She went from rigid with guilt to clawing at him as he filled her without hesitation; she closed her eyes hoping she wouldn't feel so depraved if she couldn't see him but the feel of his young flesh under her hands was preventing her from fooling herself. She could only marvel at his confidence and obvious skill as subconsciously she began to match him move for move, she had been with men twice his age and not one of them had been bold enough to just take her. She recognised that at just fifteen, Paul Jensen was every inch a man.

Paul was lost, he knew without doubt that he would do anything for this woman and although he had promised Suzanne his heart, he admitted to himself that a tiny pocket of it had been taken over by Carmen. He loved her restraint and her protests; they only served to make him want her more. He had dreamed of this moment and perfected his skills on the many girls who had passed though his bed. He knew they wouldn't last, the age gap between them and her chosen career would, he was certain, come between them at some point but for now, he was going to milk whatever it was that they had until the well ran dry.

It was quick and brutal and immensely satisfying. He continued to kiss her deeply as he softened not wishing to hear further protests when she had clearly enjoyed the ride, his grazed skin a visual testament to that. Eventually he removed his body from hers, turning away to save her blushes and retrieve his clothes.

Carmen was dressed by the time he returned from the bathroom now also fully clothed, she pushed him away when he tried to hug her, her eyes blazing.

"Leave." she ordered.

"Ok." He agreed "Don't worry, no one will know about this but us," he hesitated, waiting for her reply and when she failed to respond, he headed downstairs and let himself out of the house. He felt like he was walking on air during the rest of his journey home.

"Dinner will be ten minutes Paul." Monica told him as he entered the kitchen "You have time to shower and change."

Paul made a show of getting clean clothes and going into the bathroom, he had no intention of showering again that day not when he smelled of her and could still feel her wrapped around him, he took note of the raised welts across his ribs where her nails had caught him and smiled at his reflection. He had scored big time and he knew it, there would be no more teenage girls for him now. Intuition told him that for all Carmen's protests, he had her hooked and she would allow him into her again in the very near future.

Chapter Seven

The encounter with Carmen was enough to keep Paul smiling throughout the rest of the holidays and he was only just beginning to get pangs of withdrawal a few days before the start of the new term.

Carmen, on the other hand had spent the remainder of the holiday in turmoil. She was convinced that people were looking at her sideways when she went out; she felt their knowing eyes were boring into her and while she hadn't encouraged him, she couldn't equate her conscience with the fact that she hadn't done enough to deter him either. Raised a strict Catholic, she tended to let some of the rules fall by the way side, sex with a minor however wasn't a rule she had been prepared to break and since her encounter with Paul, she had spent a fair amount of time in confession. She was dreading the start of the new term.

Monday morning found Paul raring to go and Matt dragging his heals much to his brothers' frustration, they got to school in record time and were soon immersed in school life and their many friends.

Carmen was summoned to the head teachers' office on entering the school. With her heart in her throat, certain that someone had seen her with Paul and she was about to get her marching orders, she knocked on the cherry wood door and took a seat in front of the desk. When she emerged from her meeting, she was filled with trepidation after being told that the science teacher would be off sick for an indeterminate amount of time and she was to take over the science lessons, her hours and salary had been increased accordingly. She was now officially the teacher of the boy who had possessed her totally.

By the third lesson of the day Carmen was in full swing and enjoying her new role, she had relaxed slightly as she hadn't caught even a glimpse of either Jensen boy but was more than a little concerned that both boys would be present in her classroom immediately after lunch. She toyed with the idea of rearranging the seating plan but dismissed it almost immediately as she didn't want to give him the satisfaction of knowing he had rattled her.

Paul sauntered into the classroom, his arm around a petite brunette, his school tie all but completely undone, his shirt sleeves rolled up and the buttons open half way down revealing the broad expanse of his tanned chest, the girls hand resting there as they talked by his desk, he didn't look in her direction although he was more than aware that she was watching his charade and complied when she told him to take his seat and correct his uniform.

The lesson was torture for both of them, Carmen battled with her guilt, stealing glances at him as he worked occasionally catching his eye but she was pleased that he seemed to be behaving himself for the moment. Paul's eyes had almost popped out of his head when he saw her; God this woman knew how to dress to accommodate her curves. Her blouse strained across her full breasts, he could picture her dark rose coloured nipples pushing at the lace of her bra underneath the material, he was amazed that she could walk in that skirt and the way it clung to her thighs and hips, she unknowingly revealed the thigh high split in the back of the garment when she turned to write on the board making the hand holding his pen still in mid sentence as he cleared his throat and battled his growing arousal under the desk.

Just as she was beginning to think that he had gotten over his crush and would cooperate in class, he beckoned her over and asked for help, handing her a sheet of paper which told her in no uncertain terms what he would like to do to her. She read the note, blushed then ripped it in two;

"Wrong." She frowned at him and returned to her desk, ignoring him for the rest of the lesson.

Paul tried to get her attention throughout the remainder of the lesson, failing at every turn, he also failed to get her alone during the day, every time he passed her in the hallway, she either had another teacher with her or was talking to a student, the only time she looked in his direction was when he kissed one of his many female admirers whilst waiting to enter a classroom, looking up to see her staring and knowing he still had her attention. He was stupendously frustrated by the end of the school day but as he had work to go to, he couldn't linger after school to talk to her.

On entering the science room the following day, looking forward to a double lesson, Paul and the majority of the rest of the class stopped and surveyed the re-arranged desks. Having decided that Paul obviously wouldn't behave himself in his prime position at the front of the classroom, Carmen had asked the Principle if she could have single desks for this room and keep just the one freestanding work bench, front and centre of the room, she had remained at the school late the previous evening re-arranging the room and making sure there was enough work space for experiments on the built in work stations around the edge.

She called out each student's name in alphabetical order, pointing to the desk she now wished them to occupy resulting in Paul being placed in the far right hand corner of the room, his desk one side of the store room door with Matt's on the other side. Once each student had found his or her seat, she explained the experiment she had set up on what had once been Matt and Paul's work bench at the front of the room, asking her students to gather around the bench, keeping Paul firmly on the opposite side to her. With the experiment complete, she asked them to return to their desks and write up the theory for it after which would follow a test to be taken in exam like conditions.

During the second part of the double lesson, Carmen handed out test papers and answers sheets to her students and set them a time for the test to be completed. Once the class had settled into taking the test, she finished some marking she hadn't got done the previous night before setting off around the class, peering over her students shoulders to apprise their work. Reaching the back of the classroom, she slipped into the storage cupboard to retrieve some whiteboard markers and was stopped dead on her way out when Paul's hand clamped around her left calf and pulled her closer to him with surprising strength, lifting that leg slightly and placing it on his lap, pressing against the solid length there.

Swapping his grip from his right hand to his left, holding her leg in place, he let his right hand drift to the hem of her skirt, a different one from yesterday but with an equally easily accessible split in the back of it. He stroked the back of her knee, his fingers gliding over her nylon covered leg and sliding upwards without hesitation. His fingers found the lace top of her hold up stockings and played alternatively with the material and the soft flesh of her inner thigh. She made to move away, making him clamp his left hand harder around her left leg as his right hand speeded upwards to the heat radiating from between her legs, his fingers swiftly brushing aside the material covering her and gliding along the silky hairs he encountered before parting the lips and delving inside. He smiled as he felt how wet she was and the tremble in her thigh, she might try to deny how much she wanted him but he wasn't fooled for an instant and neither was her body that had betrayed her. Pushing another finger inside her, he began a slow in and out motion while rotating his wrist bringing forth more moisture.

Carmen couldn't believe the front of this boy or that she was just standing there letting him finger her, she wanted to pull away before anyone noticed but it felt so good, his fingers inside her felt so good that she simply couldn't bring herself to move. She was jolted back to reality when another student raised her hand, needing help and she wrenched her limbs away from his prying hands, straightening her skirt as she went to assist, finally able to return to her desk, she looked to the rear of the classroom, wholly unsurprised to find him looking at her but blushing furiously when he raised his hand and slid his fingers into his mouth, sucking every last drop of her from them.

Wiping his damp fingers on his trouser leg to dry them, Paul bent his head to his work, glancing sideways at his brother who had witnessed the entire charade. Matt was grinning broadly and shaking his head, his admiration for his brother escalating tenfold by the younger twins' unflappable boldness and ability to take advantage of any situation.

The students jumped to their feet as the bell that marked the end of the lesson and the end of the day sounded, Carmen calling out instructions for homework as they packed their bags. Matt stopped by Paul's desk as he packed his books away.

"You're a dog." Matt grinned at him.

"Nah." Paul shook his head "I am a God." He laughed as he stood making sure he was the last one to leave the room.

Carmen dropped into her chair, vastly relieved that he hadn't found an excuse to stay behind; she really had to find a way to discourage him she told herself. She wanted nothing more than to go home and take a long hot bath to try and scrub away the sensations his prying fingers had caused, hot tears of shame pricking her eyes as she recalled how much she had enjoyed it, she reached for a tissue and was dabbing away the tears when the door to the classroom opened.

As he packed his bag at the end of the lesson, Paul considered the possibility of remaining behind after class and taking things further, eventually deciding that it was a little too risky right at that moment and he left the room with his brother without a backward glance. Reaching the school gates, he told Matt that he wasn't done yet and he'd be home later.

"What do I tell Mum?" Matt asked to make sure the brothers' had their stories straight

"I dunno, er, tell her I went straight to a job or something," he stepped closer to his brother, lowering his voice so that only Matt would hear "Tell her anything other than I'm fucking the science teacher." He grinned.

"Are you though? I mean, have you actually been there?" Matt asked, grabbing Paul's arm to prevent him from leaving.

"Yeah, once. Matt, don't go shouting this from the rooftops ok?"

"You know I can keep a secret." Matt stepped back.

"Uhuh, oh yeah, like the me and Suzanne secret?" Paul accused.

"Hey, you pissed me off and insulted my girlfriend." Matt defended.

"Even so, it was a cheap shot and you know it." Paul replied "You'd better have my back on this one."

"I do, trust me, catch you later." Matt turned out of the school while Paul sprinted over to the main building and did a quick sweep of the corridors, glancing into classrooms as he made his way back to the science room.

She was where he had left her, sitting at her desk but now she was dabbing at her eyes.

"You can't be here." she said in a voice barely above a whisper as he pulled the roller blind down over the glass door and swiftly made his way across the room, dropping his bag when he was halfway to her. Paul grabbed her hands, pulled her out of her seat, turned her and pushed her back onto her desk on top of the test papers. Positioning himself between her legs, he roughly wrenched her skirt up over her thighs before releasing the belt holding his trousers and letting them drop.

"No." she protested in her sternest voice.

"You can stop with the protests." he told her as he stepped closer, one hand going to her hip while the other moved the material of her underwear aside "You know you want this, you just have to admit it to yourself" a half a step closer still and he was inside her, once again,

119

she made no attempt to stop him or push him away, she closed her eyes and hung her head in shame at her inability to stop her legs from parting further, her eyes opening when he paused, seeing in front of her evidence of her arousal on the firm flesh that had stopped half in and half out of her.

Paul was so lost in the moment that it took him precious seconds to realise the noise he had heard wasn't coming from either of them. He was relishing how damp she was and the delightful wet noise that filled the room at each and every thrust and that was when he heard it, laughter and the clang of a metal bucket, the cleaners had arrived.

"Fuck." He hissed, unceremoniously pulling out of her and carefully easing his still hard cock back into his trousers, he reached for her skirt and pulled it back down over her hips, smoothing it down her thighs "Meet me in the park, by the top car park, I'll be there for the next hour" he said, she recognised it wasn't a question but a demand.

"No, I won't, this stops now." she answered, finally finding her resolve.

"It's up to you." he shrugged "You either meet me in the park or I'll come to your house, which would you prefer?" he picked up his bag and looked at her questioningly.

"Fine, I'll come to the park." she agreed knowing she couldn't allow him near her house.

She parked her car in the top car park as instructed; apart from one other car the place was deserted. Stumbling from the vehicle, she took the most obvious, well beaten route from the gravel surface of the car park, cursing her shaking legs, blaming it on her stiletto heels which were wholly unsuitable for this type of terrain, her tight skirt wasn't helping matters either and she found herself hitching it up to allow a more purposeful stride.

As she walked, avoiding pot holes and the delightful parcels left by inconsiderate dog owners, she went over in her head what she was going to tell this persistent boy, she would have to be firm and take no objection from him, this ended today, after this meeting she would not allow herself to be in this position again. She jumped when he stepped out of a clump of trees just a few feet in front of her, a cigarette clamped between his lips, he smiled at her around it as he unbuttoned his shirt and pulled it out of his trousers, exposing his body to her gaze. Carmen could swear that he knew exactly how good he looked, he had testament to that fact every day at school with hoards of girls salivating over him, all of which he took in his stride with an extremely dirty laugh and easy smile. She looked away, annoyed that despite the firm warnings she had given herself she still felt the heat rise between her legs, her nipples hardened as he removed his shirt and threw it into the clump of trees he had so recently stepped out of.

Paul's smile widened when he saw her look away from his naked torso, he saw the slight hesitation in her step and also the way her nipples pushed at the material of her blouse, in that split second he wanted to roll them between his lips but that would have to wait for another day. He gestured to her the way through the trees, finally reaching the spot that served as a smoking den and love nest for him and his brother, the large trunk of the fallen tree had proved useful in its death more than once.

"Paul, you have to listen to me." She rounded on him when she found her way blocked by the tree trunk "This is wrong and dangerous, I shouldn't have let it get this far. I'm flattered that you are attracted to me, I really am but I am at least ten years your senior and your teacher, this will have serious consequences for me and I'm concerned that it will also harm you psychologically."

Paul had listened to what she had to say but her words hadn't stopped him from divesting himself of the rest of his clothing, he took a pull on his cigarette before reaching forward and stubbing it out on the dead tree, blowing out the smoke before looking her in the eye "I realise this is a bit dodgy for you but if no one finds out, there isn't a problem." He shrugged, one hand idly stroking his erection.

"I am your teacher." She repeated "And you are only fifteen years old, you aren't even legal."

"It's just a number, I feel legal." He grinned, he reached for her hand and wrapped it around his hot, rock hard flesh.

She whipped her hand away, glaring at him but inside she was shivering with desire "If you don't stop this, I will report you for harassment and have you expelled."

"You don't believe a single word you just said, you tell yourself that you do and try to convince yourself that you are doing the right thing but all the while there are tiny tell tale signs that you know you are fooling yourself and I know it too. You don't resist me, you are dripping wet every time I touch you and you want nothing more right now than for me to bend you over that tree and fuck you like your life depended on it. So if you have the courage of your conviction, go ahead, walk away, report me, get me expelled, it's not like it'll be the first time, you'll be doing us both a favour because that way, you won't have the teacher card to play which, in case you haven't noticed, doesn't bother me in the slightest."

"Stop it." Firmer this time, she pushed against his chest as he moved closer; regretting her decision to touch him, the feel of his firm skin beneath her fingers wasn't helping her cause.

"You don't mean that." He had lowered his voice and continued to move closer, his hand cupping her face, his tongue in her mouth before she could speak again. She was breathless when he broke the kiss, swiftly turning her around, pulling her behind into his erection as he ground his hips into her bottom, he stepped forward, pushing her before him, over balancing her deliberately so that she reached out for the tree trunk, once he had her bent at the waist it was easy, he lifted her skirt, moved her panties aside and slid two fingers inside her with ease, leaning back to watch as they cavorted in her slick hole, noticing the dampness extended to her thighs, knowing he was the cause of it. Easing his fingers out of her, he held her lips open, letting the air hit them and cool them slightly before thrusting his hips forward, her wetness allowing him full penetration in a single stroke, he grasped her hips as he withdrew and powered into her making her moan again and again as his thighs collided with hers. Close to orgasm, he altered his stance and still deep inside her, folded his body over hers, one hand sliding into the front of her knickers, manipulating the stiff rose bud of flesh he found there as he picked up the pace again "Come for me." He breathed in her ear, knowing the last thing she needed was encouragement. He clamped his other hand over her mouth as she began to moan louder with every thrust and tweak, her cunt squeezing the last of his orgasm from him as she came, holding him fast inside her.

Turning her to face him, Paul caught a glimpse of her inner turmoil in the expression on her face; he pulled her closer, kissing her tenderly before smoothing her skirt down then moving away to dress.

Carmen's legs gave way and she sat heavily on the tree trunk, her body telling her that what she had just experienced was fantastic her mind screaming at her to get out of there, to get out of London and flee back to everything she knew in Gloucester, she jumped back into the present when he closed in on her again.

"Don't look so sad." He spoke quietly, pressing kisses to her cheeks, neck and lips.

"You've ruined everything." She whispered closing her eyes against the desire his touch was causing to course through her veins "Paul, please, I can't keep doing this with you."

"Yes, you can." He disagreed.

"Please just listen to me." She forcefully pushed him away "If anyone finds out about this, I will lose my job and I could possibly go to prison."

"What? Why? It's not like you led me on."

"You are fifteen and I am in a position of influence, it doesn't matter which one of us started this, in the eyes of the law I am the responsible adult and you are a child, at the very least they'll say I've molested you, I could even be done for rape. Now do you see why this can't happen again?"

"I'll make it very clear that I did the pestering and made you give in," He shoved his hands into his pockets but he kept his distance.

"It doesn't work like that," she shook her head "I will lose everything."

"So what now?" he asked.

"You find a nice girl your own age and forget this ever happened." She told him.

"Girls my age are boring and I won't be able to forget the way you feel, I don't want to."

"You can't keep cornering me like you do, I won't be influenced by you anymore." She told him sternly "I'm not some love struck teenager that's going to spread her legs every time you smile in my direction."

"And yet you do." He was sideways on to her, glancing back at her over his shoulder while he kicked at the undergrowth with his trainer. "You aren't just a quick fuck for me, there's more to it than that, I can get sex anytime I want it, it's different with you, more intense, better than anything I've ever had."

"It only feels like that to you because you know it's wrong. I'm going now, if I have to move you out of my class, I will so if you want me to remain as your teacher, I suggest you start to tow the line."

He realised that she had finally found the courage to stand up to him and the consequences for her were far more serious than they were for him, he couldn't bear the thought of her leaving the school or banishing him from her lessons, at least seeing her would keep the fantasy alive even if he couldn't touch her, he recognised it was time to back down.

"I'm sorry," he turned to face her "I didn't know how much trouble you could get in. I won't ask you to do this again and I'll behave in class."

"Thank you." She stood, pleased that her legs seemed to have found their strength, his dejected expression squeezed at her heart but she wouldn't allow him to have any kind of hold over her anymore. She made her way out of the trees and to her car.

Chapter Eight

Paul made every effort to turn himself into the epitome of the perfect student, he worked hard and was polite and made sure to hand in his homework on time but for all this, his attitude outside of school had suffered, he had had a few arguments with Matt and Tessa resulting in violent clashes with his father and a very large black eye which Carmen eyed suspiciously in class. He threw himself into his gardening business and was even lucky enough to be in the right place at the right time in the local hardware store where another local gardener was loudly complaining that some kid was taking all his business and he was thinking of letting some men go. Paul stepped forward and introduced himself, recognising the need to maximise the potential of his own business, he offered a generous partnership to the older man and within a few days and with a substantial loan from his grandparents, Paul was the proud owner of two companies as well as five full time staff and vans thus leaving him free to concentrate on the larger gardens of his prestige clients.

After the meeting in the park with Paul, Carmen had rushed home and settled into a steaming hot bath washing every last vestige of his scent from her, she had put the clothes she was wearing in a bin bag and threw them away. As she soaked, she analysed the way he made her feel, the things he made her feel and even through her guilt, she knew there was something special about this boy. When the water cooled, she wrapped herself in her huge purple bath robe, curled up on the sofa with a bar of chocolate and a chic flick, picked up the phone and called Helen, her closest friend, holding the receiver away from her ear when she shrieked down the line as Carmen revealed the age of the boy who had her world in turmoil.

When Paul passed her at school, he would politely acknowledge her but wouldn't look her in the eye, instead turning his attention to the nearest available female to distract him but she was constantly in his thoughts and she was a regular feature in his dreams.

"Morning Miss." He mumbled as she walked by, his eyes to the floor, hands in pockets

"Good morning Paul, Matt" She greeted both brothers as she passed through the door to her classroom.

"What's going on with you and her?" Matt asked, they were swapping books over at their lockers.

"She ended it." Paul replied "Said it was too risky."

"Well, you can see her point of view." Matt reasoned.

"Yeah, doesn't mean I have to agree with it."

"Ah, so that's why you've been a miserable git at home." Matt grinned "Come on Paul, it's not like you can't get some any time you want."

Paul slammed his locker shut and glared at his brother. "That's hardly the point though is it? How would you feel if Hayley suddenly cut you off and wouldn't have anything to do with you?"

"Gutted." Matt admitted.

"Bingo." Paul replied and steeled himself to sit through double science. A warm hand slipped into his as he neared the classroom and he looked down to see the adorable red head he'd had a few encounters with, he smiled.

"Hey Paul, what you up to at lunch?" She asked as they entered the classroom, stopping by her assigned seat.

"Nothing." He replied.

"Wanna hang?" She beamed.

"Yeah, ok, meet you out front?" He asked and received a nod in response. He prised his hand from hers and went to his seat, slouching comfortably in the corner as Miss Scott began the lesson.

Carmen headed to the staff room after her lesson, she was handed a cup of coffee and grabbed her sandwich from the fridge, eating it quickly as she had playground duty that lunchtime, a hated chore but one made bearable by the maths teacher who joined her as they strolled around the tarmac grounds, pausing now and then to exchange a few words with students or to kick a stray ball back to its owner.

"Hey Miss." Paul smiled as he walked by on his way to the main playground, jumping down the steps and into the arms of Melanie, a nubile blond with a reputation for being easy.

Carmen and maths teacher Julia watched as he dropped his bag and enveloped the girl in a hug, inclining his head as their mouths met and Carmen could swear she saw his tongue slide into the girls open mouth.

"Shouldn't we stop that?" she asked Julia.

"We could try, but in my experience, he'll only do it again just to wind us up, he knows we can't touch him, all we can do is shout at him which, I guarantee will just make him smile at us, he's far too cocksure of himself that one." Julia replied.

"Hmm" Carmen agreed "That isn't the girl he said he'd meet during my class." She commented.

"Is he still getting himself dates during lessons?"

"Oh no, this was just before the lesson started, do you know, it's because of him that I had to re-arrange my seating plan, it was a nightmare trying to stop him from turning around and talking to the girls."

"Tell me about it, does your seating plan work?"

"Not really. I've put him and his brother at the back of the class where I have to admit, they do behave but now I have the girls turning around to talk to them, I give up."

"I have the pair of them surrounded by boys in my class, it seems to be the only way I can get them to work, I've moved them away from each other too, they work better that way. Don't be fooled by Matt Jensen, he may not be as obvious as his brother but he's every bit as much of a ladies' man as Paul is."

"I'll keep an eye on him. Uh oh." she finished as the red head from her science class appeared, the girl grabbed Paul by the arm and dragged him away from the blond, slapping her soundly across the face before turning to Paul, scowling at him before wrapping her arms around his neck.

"Dear God, when will these girls realise that he's the rat in all this and not the other girl?" Julia asked "This, we will have to stop."

The blond, having recovered from her slap, proceeded to lay into the red head with vigour; hair pulling and nail scratching ensued amidst lots of screaming. Paul stepped back and let them continue, he circled away as he saw the teachers coming towards them, wanting no part of the blame for this.

He still found himself outside the principal's office though not for himself. Matt had been caught smoking behind the equipment shed and was waiting his turn to see the head of the school.

"Mum's been called." Paul told his brother as he stood in front of him "Makes a change you being here instead of me." He grinned.

"Yeah, first time for everything." Matt smiled in return "Look, take these for me, if I haven't got them on me, they can't prove they caught me." Matt handed Paul his cigarettes and lighter. Paul quickly stuffed them into his pocket.

"I'd better go before Mum gets here." He told his brother then stopped as the two girls he'd been with at lunch were marched down the corridor accompanied by Carmen and Julia

"Bollocks," he groaned "They've blocked my exit route."

"Matthew, come in please," the head called from his office door "Paul, why are you here?"

"Sorry Sir, I was just keeping Matt company." He shuffled uncomfortably under the man's gaze.

"You can go now." The Principle stood aside to let Matt into his office "Ladies, take a seat, I'll be with you shortly. Miss Scott, Miss Meacher, you can return to your playground duty."

Julia Meacher gestured to Paul to move on down the corridor before resuming her conversation with Carmen not noticing that her colleague was a little distracted.

"I'm having my lawn re turfed at the weekend." Julia gabbled, this was information Paul already knew as two of his workforce had been hired for the job "It'll be so nice to have the garden done in time for summer." She continued.

"My garden's a mess." Carmen admitted, she was watching the teenager saunter ahead of them, noticing for the first time how his white school shirt strained across his broad shoulders "I really ought to do something about it but I hate gardening and hiring someone can prove to be expensive."

"The guys I have aren't bad, granted they aren't the cheapest but they have an excellent reputation and they guarantee their work, I've had them do a few repairs around the house too."

Paul had heard enough, he side stepped into the boys' toilets, a plan of how to get back into his favourite teachers affections forming in his head.

The rest of the week proved uneventful and somewhat boring as Matt had been put on a two week suspension despite Monica and the Principle being unable to find his cigarettes, he'd reeked of smoke and that was enough to suspend him. Monica had also grounded Matt indefinitely and had even refused to let him accompany Paul on jobs leaving the younger boy to work alone and pass a very quiet weekend.

Paul daydreamed his way through Monday morning assembly, silently lamenting that school was terribly boring without his brother even though he was surrounded by friends, no one got him quite like Matt did and also, the two girls who had been fighting over him had been suspended leaving him little to look forward to at lunch time. He was jolted back to the present when the Principle announced in front of the whole school that he was to make his way directly to the office after assembly.

"What did you do?" Jake asked.

"Nothing" Paul frowned; he shrugged at his friend and headed to the principal's office "Mum? What are you doing here?"

"I was hoping you would tell me that." Monica replied.

"I haven't done anything," he told her "I definitely haven't been in any trouble."

"Do you have any work that's overdue?"

"No, I'm up to date with everything."

"Mrs Jensen, Paul, come in, take a seat." Principle Williams called them into his office; he waited for mother and son to be comfortably seated before he began to explain about the cat fight that had happened the previous week.

"I don't understand what this has to do with Paul." Monica said at the end of the explanation.

"Both girls have said that they were fighting over Paul."

"Yes, yes, I understand that but as Paul wasn't actually involved, I fail to see why we are here."

"Mrs Jensen, I would just like to say that I am impressed with the way Paul has applied himself to his studies, however, he is very mature for his years and is causing somewhat of a distraction among the female students. I'm not sure if this distraction is intentional or not but I am not able to let it continue particularly this close to exam time. I have discussed this rather unique situation with the school governors and we agree that it would be best for all concerned if Paul is released on study leave."

"You're suspending him?"

"No, not at all. Paul is not in any sort of trouble and he is more than prepared for his exams, I just feel it would be advantageous for him to be out of the school environment, away from distractions."

"Sir, I'd rather remain in school and the distractions you are referring to have been suspended so I don't see a problem." Paul spoke

"I'm sorry Paul, the decision has been made. You can remain in school today, I have arranged for your teachers to put together study packs for you. You only need to come in when you have an exam, you won't be required to wear uniform for that."

"I can't believe I'm being punished because a couple of girls can't keep their hormones in check."

"Be quiet." Monica said sharply to her son, instantly stilling his tongue. "Although I am inclined to agree with my son, I do see your point and as he is up to date with his studies, I see no reason why he shouldn't remain at home."

"Please don't view this as a punishment." the principle smiled.

"Oh come on. Only the trouble makers get put on study leave. I admit that in the past I probably deserved it but not now, this is totally out of order." Paul folded his arms across his chest.

"That's quite enough from you." Monica turned to her son "Go back to your lessons while I iron out a few final details here." She told him.

Paul quite enjoyed not having to get up for school; it was even better as Matt was still home and therefore also not getting up early and disturbing him. Monica was enjoying having both boys at home as well and while Matt was on strict punishment when his father was home, the rules where relaxed when Michael was at the office and the boys would spend some of their time kicking a ball around the garden or playing video games until she insisted that they get some school work done.

Paul stretched and looked up from his book "Bored" he groaned, drawing out the word for effect.

"I'm going shopping, you could come." Monica told him.

"Er no! Take Matt, he's the one being punished."

"Thanks bro, remind her why don't you." Matt griped, throwing an apple at Paul

Reaching out and catching the apple, Paul closed his books and stood "I'm going to the park for a bit, I won't be late back." He told his mother.

Paul knew exactly where he was going but he headed in the direction of the park as he knew Monica would be watching him leave from the living room window, he skirted around the edge of the park then turned in the direction of town and the house where he would spend a few hours each day. He was covered in dirt when he returned home, carefully coming in the back of the house and catching Matt's eye "Where's Mum?" he asked.

"Out" Matt answered "What have you been doing, you're filthy."

"I've been working on Carmen's garden."

"Carmen?"

"Miss Scott, moron. I need to get changed."

"Didn't she end it?"

"Yeah it's over but I overheard her talking about her garden and I did cause her a bit of hassle, it's just my way of saying sorry."

This behaviour became the norm for Paul. He would wait until the usual urbanites would be at work and Monica was occupied with one of her many coffee mornings before leaving the house and working on Carmen's garden. He carried out small tasks at first, a little bit of weeding and edging, nothing obvious that would make her think someone had been at her house. He considered leaving her a note on the day he cut her lawn, just in case it freaked her out but decided that he was probably the last person she wanted to hear from.

Within two weeks he had her garden looking perfect and had started to repair little bits and pieces on her house, sanding down and painting the window frames at the rear of the garage. This particular day, he lost track of the time, he had begun pointing the brickwork below her kitchen window when the window opened, startling him and making her scream at what she thought was an intruder.

"What are you doing here?" She screeched, wrenching open the back door to confront him

"I'm just doing a few jobs for you."

"You are the one who has done all this to my garden?"

"Yes."

"Why?"

"I wanted to make up for what I did and for putting you in an impossible position." He explained "I'm sorry if I frightened you."

She regarded the boy in front of her; he hadn't made any move to come closer, if anything he had backed away "You have done a very good job."

He shrugged "It's what I do, this is my job."

"What do I owe you?" She asked, she had moved further into the garden, admiring his work then she noticed the freshly painted window frames and the pointing he had started.

"Nothing. I don't want you to pay me. I'm doing it to apologise to you. I'd appreciate it if you let me finish what I've started.."

"I don't think that's a good idea." She told him.

"Look, I don't have an ulterior motive, I just want to help."

"No ulterior motive huh?" she questioned.

"Ok, I like you, a lot, those feelings aren't going to vanish overnight but more than anything I want to show you that I'm a nice guy, I can be responsible for my actions and I enjoy being kept busy." He gestured to her brickwork "And there is a lot here to keep me busy."

Carmen sat heavily on her garden bench "You are very sweet." She swallowed back a tear.

"Please don't cry, I didn't mean to upset you."

"You haven't. I'm just not used to people being genuinely nice."

"Look, I'll finish this bit of pointing then I'll go. I won't come back if you don't want me to."

"I shouldn't want you to, maybe I want you here for the wrong reasons, I don't know, but it would be good to have the house looking nice. Thank you Paul for everything you've done."

"So, I can come back?" he asked.

"Yes, you won't have to sneak around anymore." She stood "Would you like a drink?"

"No thanks." He turned back to his work "I won't be much longer on this and then I'll get out of your hair."

"What did you mean when you said this is your job?" She asked.

"I have my own gardening and Handyman Company. A couple of the guys that work for me did Miss Meacher's lawn."

"Oh, I didn't know."

"It started with me just doing a couple of gardens for my Mum's friends and kind of escalated, I went into partnership with another company and now I own the majority of that company, thanks to my Grandparents and business is good."

"You are quite the entrepreneur." she smiled.

"Nah, I'm just lucky," he returned the smile "Don't let me stop you from whatever you have to do. I'll let myself out."

Carmen began to look forward to going home, knowing he would be there. On several occasions, after a heavy overnight rainfall, he would present her with flowers he had cut from her garden that the rain had battered down. She convinced herself that there was nothing wrong in letting him do odd jobs for her and her garden looked amazing. They got into the habit of sitting and talking when she returned from school, Paul would have the tools packed away by the time she changed into casual clothes and they spent the summer evenings sitting on the patio talking about anything from the latest event on the news to nature and Paul's hope's for his future and as she got to know him, little by little, she began to realise what a sensible and mature young man he was and she enjoyed his company immensely.

The more time he spent with Carmen, the more time he wanted to spend with her. Being in her company was bittersweet, while he happily chatted to her and maintained her house and garden, he ached to touch her, knowing if he did, it would freak her out and probably bring to an end what they had so for now he was happy to sit back and get to know her, let her realise there was more to him than meets the eye.

"You'll have to teach me the basics of keeping the garden looking good." She told him one evening.

"It's pretty simple really," he replied. "But if you want to learn, I'll be glad to show you."

"I have a half day tomorrow. Do you think you might be able to spare me some time?" She asked, she had seen him arranging jobs in his diary and completing job cards for his staff and knew he was a very busy boy, she hated to think that by being here he was losing money.

"Of course I can be here tomorrow, that's the beauty of having people work for you." He smiled.

"I wish you'd let me pay you."

"Don't start that again. I don't want payment from you." His standard answer and one that always, without fail, caused her brow to crease.

And so it began the following afternoon, the gentle dance of seduction as he guided her through planting and weeding working on their hands and knees, side by side. He listened when she began to talk about her family, of her father who had died in a tragic accident at work when she was five to her mother and brother who barely spoke to each other and who she rarely saw. He learned that she had a quirky and somewhat sassy sense of humour and that she was, at all times, mildly flirtatious but also that she was quick to put him in his place if he overstepped the mark.

Carmen would often watch him as he worked, he was thorough and very particular that everything was just so and he always, without fail, tidied up any mess he had made. She found the days when he didn't come to her house very long and lonely and knew, without a shadow of a doubt that she was falling for him, as his physical attractiveness had initially drawn her in, his personality had sealed the deal and try as she might to avoid her feelings, she knew deep down that she wanted to spend more time with him in a more intimate setting. She relished the scorching summer days that followed his exams as he would arrive at her house in shorts and a baggy t-shirt, the latter garment would soon be discarded when he began to work and she would find herself positively drooling at his sweat slick body that slowly turned an even golden brown in the sun.

Chapter Nine

As the Jensen family prepared for their annual pilgrimage to Spain, Paul made sure he had so much work on that he couldn't possibly be spared. Presenting Monica with his diary one Sunday afternoon, he explained that he needed to stay at home and with the diary in front of her, she couldn't deny that her youngest child had made a success of his business and was indeed, very busy. She agreed to let him stay at home, telling him that he would need to check in with Michael's parents and Kay at least once a day and under no circumstances was he allowed to have a party in the house. Promising reverently to obey the rules, Paul was smiling smugly to himself when Matt finally entered their room and prepared for bed.

"Are you really that busy?" he asked.

"Certainly am." Paul confirmed.

"You know Kay's going to be watching you like a hawk right?"

"I know, but I'll be working most of the day so all I have to do is drop by her place on the way home, show my face and then I'm good to go."

"When you go to see her, make sure you keep your hands off Hayley." Matt warned.

"Ergh." Paul shuddered "I wouldn't touch her if she was the last woman on earth," he assured. "Besides, I have bigger fish to fry."

"Oh yeah?" Matt sat on his brothers bed. "Who?"

"Carmen. I've been doing a little work for her, strictly off the books, we've become quite good friends as odd as that sounds. She still denies any interest in me but I find it funny how she appears out of nowhere when I take my shirt off, she pretends to sunbathe but I can feel her watching me, she's so ripe right now that a few coy smiles and carefully placed compliments and she'll be putty in my hands." He gloated.

"But she ended it because of the whole teacher, student thing."

"True, but I've left school now, she isn't my teacher anymore. A point which I intend to force home leaving her with little doubt what I want."

"Let me get this straight, you've spent your own time and money doing her garden just so that you can get in her good books?"

"It's not her books I want to get into but yeah, you've pretty much got the jist"

"Well, you're persistent, I'll give you that" Matt climbed into his own bed "This holiday is going to suck balls without you"

"I'm sure you'll find something to keep you amused." Paul winked at him as he turned off the light.

Carmen was hanging washing on the line when Paul arrived after saying his goodbyes to his family. Dressed in a pretty yellow blouse that tied under her breasts and tight white shorts, the sight of her had him hiding the first signs of his arousal.

"Hi," she smiled "What's that?" she pointed to him, waist level.

"Shit." He thought, willing his groin to behave before realising she was pointing to the sprinkler he had picked up on the way over "Oh, it's a lawn sprinkler," he replied, relief flooding through him "You won't have to spend ages watering the grass anymore"

"Thank you." She turned back to her washing. "There's a fresh pot of tea in the kitchen if you fancy a cup" she called over her shoulder.

Declining her offer, he set to work, keeping his gaze fixed firmly on the plants, stopping only to eat the sandwich she provided and drink the ice cold glass of cola before setting back to work.

"You don't usually come on a Saturday," she was beside him, he had been so engrossed in planting that he hadn't heard her approach and jumped at the sound of her voice "Sorry, I didn't mean to startle you." She touched his shoulder.

"My family has gone on holiday; I have plenty of free time."

"Why didn't you go?" she asked as she crouched beside him.

"Work. I like to keep an eye on things." He sat back on his haunches not realising she was so close, his arm knocked her shoulder, overbalancing her, she squealed as she began to topple. He reached out and grabbed her arm, swiftly coming to his feet, dragging her with him, her hands flailed and came to rest on his bare chest, by now he had hold of both of her arms, they were face to face and he couldn't help himself, he lowered his head, his lips brushing hers.

"Don't," She breathed "I thought we'd moved past this?" She couldn't bring herself to move away, silently begging him to kiss her again.

"Crap." He thought as he searched her eyes for signs of anger. "Do I back off or just go for it?" He asked himself, his eyes travelled to her lips, slightly parted, begging to be kissed, they travelled back up to her eyes, he saw some confusion but also a glimmer of desire and that was enough to spur him on. He closed the gap between their lips, taking advantage of the fact that hers were parted to slip his tongue into her mouth, the jolt that ran through him when she responded was magnificent, he pulled her closer, never wanting to let her go.

"No. Stop." She pushed him away. "We've been through this." She told him, hands on hips.

"You don't get it do you?" He asked, he kept the distance between them "This isn't some silly school boy crush I have on you. I'm in love with you, I've tried to ignore how I feel but I can't."

"Can't or won't?" She asked.

"Won't," he admitted "I want to be with you and you can't keep denying that you feel anything for me, if you didn't, you would have sent me packing long ago, you like having me around." he accused.

"Yes, I do." She was flabbergasted that she had spoken those words out loud, now she had to explain herself "I do like having you around and yes, I am attracted to you but I'm still your teacher and I still can't do this."

"I'm not at school anymore, I'm just some guy."

"Until you get your certificates in September, I'm your teacher." She protested but she didn't remove her hand from his.

"Then teach me," he challenged "Teach me everything you like doing and how to do it" a quick tug and she was in his arms again.

"Not out here," she breathed against his lips "Inside." She ordered, all reasoning behind her now, she dragged him into the kitchen "take your shorts off." She ordered, not wishing to let him dominate her as he had done previously.

Watching as he wasted no time in slipping out of his trainers and pulling his shorts down, she sat back on the table and began a slow strip tease "You want me to teach you little boy?" she asked, he nodded, unable to speak "I want to watch you pleasure yourself," she said and saw him hesitate "The only way this is going to work is if you do what you are told." She sat forward, grasped the back of his neck and pulled him into a kiss before pushing him back and purring "Now grab hold of your dick and stroke it until I tell you to stop," she watched him, his right hand slowly stroking his hard flesh as she untied and unbuttoned her blouse, his eyes watching every move, her hands flicking open the catch of her bra and letting it fall followed by her fingers teasing her nipples until they were hard, bending her head, stretching her tongue to flick at the hardened nub. His left hand touched the soft skin of her breast "No touching." She said, softly slapping his hand away.

She hopped down from the table, pressing her naked breasts to his chest while one hand covered his and squeezed it tighter against his organ the other unbuttoned her shorts and she wriggled against him as she shimmied out of them before sitting back on the table and suggestively parting her legs, letting her hands trail to her secret place, bringing forth an unstemmed flow of desire, he groaned as she began to play with herself, all the while watching his face, seeing the change from mere arousal through to passion then lust, treading the fine line between teasing and torture as she screamed her way through her first orgasm.

Carmen beckoned him closer, positioning him between her legs, the head of his cock just resting on her lips "Keep stroking yourself, don't fuck me just yet, just slip the head inside a few times." She told him, returning her fingers to her clit bringing herself off again as his hand flew along the length of his shaft while just the tip of him rocked inside her. As her third orgasm built to a crescendo, she shouted at him to fuck her, he didn't need telling twice, with a huge thrust of his hips he was inside her, bucking hard, growling with each breath, fighting for control, finally admitting that he had willingly handed it to her as he covered her and pumped harder.

Lacing her fingers into his hair, she pulled his head up as he rested on her shoulder, swiftly, she kissed him;

"Go and get cleaned up and we'll try this again." She told him.

"Upstairs?" He asked, she nodded, shoving him away from her and towards the door.

Standing in the shower, Paul's head was reeling with what had just happened, he'd expected a little more protestation, anger even, not the complete turnaround that had just happened, never in a million years had he imagined the firecracker that had given him orders. Thinking about that too, he wasn't sure he liked being dominated, up until now he had been the dominant party with everyone he had managed to sleep with, he smiled, perhaps once or twice he had let Suzanne take over but that had been more by mutual consent than anything to do with a power struggle. He sighed as he washed the soap from his body, for now, he would play along and let her have her way, knowing that if she pushed him too far he had the physical strength to stop her and assert his authority.

She was waiting for him when he stepped out of the bathroom, determination fixed on her face as she told him to lose the towel seconds before her mouth was on him again taking control as she pushed him back on the bed and covered him swiftly, riding him hard, leaving him drained.

Snuggling into his side, she revelled in the feel of his large warm hand resting on her hip, who'd have thought he could take direction so well? Thinking about it made her want more and she let her hand trail down his body, figuring that since she was going to hell anyway, she may as well go in style.

"Carmen." He smiled into the dimly lit room as his hand grasped hers. "Not again."

"Yes, again." She kissed his chest.

"I should make a move." He sat up "I need to check in with my Aunt before she checks in with me."

"You'll be back tomorrow." She told him, not asking the question.

"I'll be back tomorrow" He confirmed. He spent the remainder of the evening with Kay and Hayley, eating his evening meal with them before Kay dropped him home.

"Will you be ok here on your own?" Kay asked as she pulled up outside the house

"I'll be fine. I'm so tired, I'm just going to go to bed" he told her.

Carmen was waiting for him when he let himself in via the back garden the following day, she had lunch laid out on the garden table and told him to sit with her and have something to eat.

"We have to talk." She said as he tucked into lunch.

"Came to your senses overnight did you?" He asked.

She snorted "I wish," and shook her head "There needs to be some ground rules to our sordid relationship," she started "Firstly, no one can know about us."

"Matt knows." Paul stopped her "He saw what I did to you in class so it's a no brainer that he knows."

"Fine, just make sure he's the only one who does know. We can never been seen together, we won't be able to go out anywhere, I can hardly take you into a pub for a nice sociable drink now can I?"

"I can get served in pubs." He mused.

"That's beside the point Paul, what we are doing is wrong and will need to remain behind closed doors. I'm a teacher, you are a minor."

"The fact that it's wrong just makes it more exciting. I have no problem keeping it within these four walls" he smiled then and watched the tension leave her. "Now, is there anything you want me to do in the garden today or do you just want me to do you?"

By the time Paul's family returned from Spain, his relationship with Carmen was in full swing. He quickly learned that she preferred to jump on him when he had been working and was sweaty and dirty. She quickly learned that he preferred her in dresses or skirts to trousers or shorts and that it was harder to turn him on when he was occupied. Carmen was pleased with the way he listened to her and followed her direction as she taught him new things but once or twice she had given him a sharp order and been on the end of his whiplash like tongue as he protested, dressed and left, on those occasions, he would take days to calm down before returning to her and trying again.

During one particularly long and sticky afternoon, Carmen snapped at him as he penetrated her, telling him in no uncertain terms that the angle he had his hips at was not what she'd told him to do, she saw the flash of anger in his eyes as he complied but it was soon forgotten as she began to climax, reaching out and digging her nails firmly into the flesh that covered his ribs.

Paul gasped in pain and decided that enough was enough. Slipping half way out of her and supporting his weight on his hands while he shifted position, he pinned her thighs beneath him with his knees before grasping her hands and pinning them over her head with his.

Stretched out on top of her, knowing his weight would eventually hurt her, he leaned closer to her as she glared at him. "No." He growled.

"Get off me." She tried to struggle, for the first time realising that he was heavier, bigger and stronger than her.

"No," he repeated "Do not scratch me again, I've told you before, I don't like it, I don't like pain,"

"Ok." She agreed.

"While I have your attention," he shifted one of his knees, making himself more comfortable but causing her to gasp as his weight pinched her skin "You aren't to boss me around anymore, I don't like that either."

"You asked me to teach you." She accused.

"Yes," he agreed "Teach me, not tell me, there's a difference. You seem set on commanding my every move, that's not how this works and it stops now."

"Fine, you stay at the level you are now."

"You aren't in a position to argue," he countered "I want to learn Carmen, I don't like to be told like I'm a kid, if I'm doing it wrong, let me know, there have to be more subtle ways than snapping at me."

"Ok, I'm sorry. Now, could you please get off me, your knees are hurting me."

He eased his knees from her thighs and released her hands but instead of backing off, he grasped the back of her knees and spread her legs wide, raising her hips to meet his, using the strength of his arms to raise and lower her hips for his pleasure.

She watched him as he manipulated her body to satisfy his needs, there was no hint of malice in his actions and she loved the way his biceps and chest muscles flexed and relaxed when he moved her onto him.

Matt's return home also signified the homecoming of most of their friends and party season ensued before the return to school and sixth form for Matt and college or work for their friends. Even though Paul and Matt's girlfriend Hayley didn't exactly see eye to eye, she always made sure to invite him to parties and he had to admit that she had some excellent contacts and that summer the Jensen twins attended some extremely hedonistic parties.

Carmen was secretly pleased with the way her relationship with Paul was going, she liked to watch his comprehension as the things she would do to him would bring pleasure but it seemed the more she pleased him, the more he wanted and he was becoming confrontational and demanding, something she would have to curb. When Matt returned from Spain, Paul and Carmen began arguing when he would announce that he wouldn't see her for most of the weekend as he would be out with his brother at parties or hanging out with friends in their gardens and swimming pools. Paul would turn up at her house on Sunday's, tired, hung over and evasive about what had happened at the parties he had attended.

"Did you have a good time?" she asked looking over at him.

Paul, stretched out on a sun bed beside her, dark shades covering his eyes, smiled lazily "I think so," he replied "I don't remember a lot of it."

"What's the point of going to all of these parties if you don't remember them?" She asked.

"It's a laugh and a good chance to catch up with friends," he waved a dismissive hand at her "I'm tired." He announced.

"So who else is at these parties?"

"Oh, you know, the usual guys, some of the girls from school, Matt and his skank girlfriend."

"I'll bet the girls from school are pleased to see you." She pressed.

"Dunno," he sighed "I don't take a lot of notice." He knew where this was heading.

"I think you should ease off on the partying for a bit, all you seem to do is get drunk with those girls then spend Sunday recovering here."

"I don't get drunk with girls, I get drunk with my friends, and it's what partying is all about. What's up with you? Jealous?"

"You forget that I've seen you around the girls you are partying with, I've seen you around school, your tongue was down the throat of a different girl every time I saw you, you only need to smile at a girl to have her falling at your feet."

"Hold on," Paul sat up and removed his shades, squinting against his headache and the bright sun light. "Do you seriously think I go to these parties just to get laid? I don't need to be with any of those girls anymore, I have you, I want to be with you but equally, I like to kick back and relax with my friends, come September most of them will be going to college and I won't see them again until Christmas so how about you just chill over me going to parties and make the most of the time I'm here?"

"I know you, you can't help but flirt, you like to spread yourself around, I don't believe it when you say you aren't sleeping with these girls. What exactly is there to stop you?"

"There isn't anything to stop me." He agreed "Apart from the fact that I've realised sex with them is a brief in and out, over and done, whereas with you it's mind blowing, why would I want to ruin the chance of being with you by having a five minute bang with one of them?"

"Everything that comes out of your mouth is bullshit," she hissed "You criticize me when I try to teach you new things...." she started.

"That's because you've stopped teaching and started giving me orders," he cut her off and jumped to his feet "I get enough of being told what to do from my old man; I don't need it when I come here as well. I think the age gap is beginning to show and perhaps we shouldn't see so much of each other." He grabbed his shirt and pulled it over his head. "You need to learn to trust me." Was his parting shot.

Paul returned five days later only to announce that he would be attending yet another party that Saturday night and he would, if she preferred, spend the night at her house rather than going home to prove that he wasn't sleeping around. He offered no apology for storming out and not contacting her earlier.

Carmen was still angry with him and refused to answer any of his questions but she had missed him and made no move to ask him to leave, she moved around him as she carried out her house work only protesting when he grabbed her and pulled her into his arms, holding her fast against him, her protests being silenced by his persistent mouth and hands as he lifted her and laid her on the living room floor, she responded by digging her nails into his flesh, ignoring his protests but smiling every time he complained, she abruptly told him to shut up, she was making the point that she was in control of this relationship and marking his body in case he decided to cheat on her therefore making the other party well aware that he wasn't entirely single.

He stayed with her until the early hours of the morning only to receive a stern reprimand from Monica on his return home, he just managed to talk himself out of a weekend grounding by turning on the charm and when that failed, begging his mother not to tell Michael of his late arrival home and pleading her to let him attend the party the following night at the same time as informing her that he and Matt would be staying out Saturday night.

Carmen was surprised when she heard Paul's knock on her door shortly after one in the morning the following day she had thought he would have been home much later than that. Opening the door, she was dismayed to find him leaning on her porch, supporting the weight of his brother.

"What is he doing here?" She asked as Paul hauled an inebriated Matt into the house.

"He'll have to stay here if that's ok, he can't go home without me and he's far too drunk to stay at the party alone." he replied, stifling a hic cup.

"You're drunk." She stated.

"Oh yeah." He grinned.

"Gonna be sick." Matt mumbled.

"Quick, get him in the kitchen." Carmen moved out of the way in time for Paul to shuffle his brother into the kitchen. Matt didn't make it to the sink.

"Ah, gross." Paul dropped Matt in the closest chair and backed away.

"Help me clean this up." Carmen shot at Paul.

"Can't. Puke makes me want to add to it." He covered his mouth with his hand, standing as far away from the mess as possible without actually leaving the kitchen.

Carmen scowled at him but grabbed a bucket and sponge and cleaning up the mess. She had to stop several times as Matt staggered to the sink and continued to vomit. Looking to Paul for support, she realised that he had disappeared. She found him passed out across her bed still fully clothed.

Returning to the kitchen, she found Matt once again hanging over the sink, his stomach now empty, he was dry heaving in-between apologies not only for his sickness but also for his presence.

"It's ok Matt." She told him as she made herself a cup of tea and handed him a glass of water. "Once you are sure you've stopped puking, I'll show you to the spare room."

"Thanks." Matt sipped his water "Paul thinks the world of you although I doubt he'll ever tell you that."

"Does he really? Did he tell you that?"

"Not in so many words but on the odd occasion he utters your name at home he can't help smiling and his whole demeanour changes when he talks about you."

"I didn't realise he liked me that much." She smiled.

Matt nodded "Even if he didn't talk about you, the fact that he spends so much time here speaks for itself, he usually just gets what he wants then leaves and forgets about the girl he's been with and he rarely goes back for seconds." He finished.

It was a little while later that Matt assured her he was no longer going to vomit and she escorted him to her spare bedroom before closing the door on her own. Paul, now flat on his back, stirred when she walked her fingers up his torso over his shirt and placed a kiss on his slightly parted lips, her fingers easing the buttons open on his dark blue shirt.

Paul woke when he felt Carmen's cool hands stroking their way down his body, his head was beginning to ache already which dismayed him as he hadn't actually had that much to drink. He sat up and wrenched the shirt from his shoulders, throwing a sheepish smile at the woman sitting beside him.

"Sorry I bolted, I can't stand to see someone throw up." He mumbled.

"I gathered that much when I found you passed out across the bed." She ruefully replied

"I need some water, my head is pounding and my mouth feels like Ghandi's flip flop." He climbed off the bed and headed for the bathroom, she had a glass of water and a pain killer waiting for him when he returned. "You are so good to me." He smiled as he slipped under the covers.

"I know I am." She told him "Just you remember that the next time you decide to throw a strop."

Summer sped by and Carmen watched her young lover's skin darken in the sun, she watched him grow broader and taller and far more confident and mature and their relationship took on an easy, comfortable air although she often worried that he would outgrow her even though he had so far not shown any signs of it and appeared to be happy with the way things had progressed.

As September approached, Carmen readied herself for her return to school and also began making plans for Paul's fast approaching sixteenth birthday. She announced that she had been invited to a friend's wedding the weekend before she was due to return to work and once again found herself explaining to Paul why he couldn't come with her and wishing he was older. Paul walked out of her house while she was packing to leave, telling her that he wasn't angry that she was going but equally, he didn't want to watch her leave; he kissed her passionately and left.

Chapter Ten

Carmen returned home in the early evening of the following Sunday to find Paul in her living room watching television. His face lit up when he saw her and he rushed across the room to wrap her in a hug, easing her down onto the sofa and attempting to wriggle his hands under her clothes.

"I'm too tired." She protested. "And I could murder a cuppa." She sighed as she relaxed back against the soft fabric. Paul left her for a short while, returning with tea and crumpets on a tray. "I take it you missed me?" she asked, amused by his attention.

"Of course", he stroked her arm.

"You're making me suspicious, what have you done that you feel you need to atone for?"

"I have nothing to feel guilty about." He told her. "But I did do something for you." He stood and reached for her hand. "Come with me." He said as he began to lead her up the stairs

"Paul," she protested "I've already told you I'm too tired."

"Trust me." He replied and reaching the top of the stairs, he turned towards the closed bathroom door. "You've been so kind to me and patient when I decide to sulk so I thought I'd do something for you for a change." He pushed open the door to reveal a gleaming white, brand spanking new bathroom suite.

Carmen stood on the threshold, speechless, admiring her beautiful bathroom; everything had been replaced even down to the flooring and the wall tiles. Her bathroom had always been a bone of contention for her. She had loved the house on her very first viewing; the only thing that had made her hesitate in putting in an offer initially had been the hideous avocado coloured bathroom, however, the large kitchen and pretty garden had swayed her and she had purchased the house despite the bathroom.

Paul's smile broadened as he watched her take in her newly re-vamped bathroom. He had tried several times to fix the leaks which occurred with alarming regularity only to discover that for all his handyman skills, he most definitely wasn't a plumber. Carmen's weekend away had given him the perfect opportunity to solve the problem once and for all and when he had told her that he didn't want to watch her leave, in reality he was making plans in his head and re-allocating gardening jobs in order to free up some of his staff for the bathroom re-fit.

It had proved to be a manic weekend with three hulking great men crammed into the bathroom leaving Paul to make sure they had a never ending supply of sandwiches and tea. The bath he had purchased was larger than the existing one and able to hold more water therefore requiring the bathroom floor to be strengthened to accommodate the extra weight. The re-fit had been completed a mere forty minutes before Carmen had returned home.

"The paint is still wet" Paul told her as she took a further step into the room "That tub can hold at least three people with ease, we'll have to give it a try when you aren't so tired." He smiled.

"Paul, this must have cost a fortune," she turned to face him "It's beautiful and what I've always wanted but it'll take me forever to pay you back."

"It's a gift, I don't want you to pay me back." he folded his arms across his chest.

"Don't go getting all defensive." She warned "I'm overwhelmed that you've done this for me, at least let me give you something towards it."

"No, honestly Carmen, I can afford it, I just wanted to do something nice for you. Up until now I'm the one who's done all the taking in this relationship; I thought it was about time I gave something back."

"You haven't done all the taking, you've fixed up my house and garden, I didn't even have to ask, you've done more for me than you could ever imagine." She reached up to kiss him "Will the floor withstand the weight of the bath when it's full of water?"

"Of course," he replied, his arms fastening behind her back "Everything has been done properly. Do you want to try it out?"

"I think it would be a terrible shame not too."

Carmen returned to work that Monday, happy and content and eager to meet her new students knowing full well that Paul would be waiting for her when she returned home that evening.

Paul had been spending so much time at Carmen's house that Monica had begun to question his whereabouts each time he returned home.

"Nice of you to show your face." She commented as her youngest child breezed into the kitchen and kissed her cheek.

"I've been working." his standard reply.

"Twenty four hours a day?" she questioned.

"Er, no. I do have a social life Mum and it's not like I don't let you know if I'll be home or not."

"Agreed, you are very good at keeping in touch but where do you stay? Most of your friends have gone away to college and even you don't have in inexhaustible supply of them" she stopped stirring the gravy for a moment to look at her son, amazed by how much he had grown over the summer and at how breathtakingly handsome he was.

"I have a number of places I can stay, usually one of the guys who works for me will put me up if we have an early start." He hedged.

"And the rest of the time?"

By the time Monica got around to asking this last question, Paul had usually managed to subtly back himself out of the kitchen, today he was stopped by Tessa on a rare day off of work, the result of a migraine earlier in the day.

"Don't be so blinkered Mum," she edged past her dirt covered brother "He has a girlfriend, I'll bet anything that he spends most of his nights with her."

"Paul? Is this true?"

Paul pushed his hair out of his face and glared at his sister "Yeah, I have a girlfriend." He admitted.

"Is she from school?" Monica asked.

"Kinda, she's a little older than me."

"Oh, do I know her?" Tessa asked.

"I don't know, we don't talk about school." He was becoming very uncomfortable with conversation.

"Don't her parents get a little tired of you staying there?" Monica this time.

"She doesn't live with her parents," he replied, consoling himself that it wasn't an outright lie "Mum, I gotta get cleaned up and make a move, do I have any clean clothes?"

"Of course you have clean clothes" Monica frowned "I take it you aren't staying for dinner?"

"Not tonight." He called over his shoulder as he bolted for the stairs.

"You'd never have let me stay out the way he does at his age." Tessa accused her mother

"I know darling but at his age, you were still at school, not running your own business, he pays rent now and therefore I feel he has every right to come and go as he pleases, he's far more mature at fifteen that you were."

"God," Tessa sighed "He's always going to be your favourite isn't he?"

"I don't have a favourite Tessa. You all have qualities that I like and some that I don't but you are all my children and I love you all equally."

"And yet Paul gets away with everything."

"Not where your father is concerned he doesn't, you and Matthew get an easy ride there, he needs to have at least one parent on his side." She tried to explain.

"His beef with Dad is entirely his own doing, you shouldn't baby him the way you do." Tessa protested.

"I'm sorry, didn't I run around after you this morning when you couldn't stop being sick and had the headache from hell?"

Tessa nodded, suddenly feeling guilty "You did, sorry Mum."

Within weeks of school resuming, they had once again settled into a steady routine. Paul remained at home on Monday and Tuesday evenings in order to appease his mother even though he became uncomfortable when the conversation inevitably turned to his love life but it was good to re-connect with Matt and even though the two days away from his lover dragged, he enjoyed spending time with his family.

With Tessa out with Suzanne for the evening and their parents joining friends for dinner, Matt and Paul were left to their own devices resulting in Matt cajoling his brother into helping him with batting practice for his forthcoming cricket match. Paul became adept at ducking the cork and leather bound missile that Matt fired back from his haphazard attempts at bowling.

As he straightened up, Paul heard the thwack of the ball connecting with Matt's willow bat, the projectile heading straight for his face. He dropped to the floor as it hurtled over his head, so close that it ruffled his hair, the next thing he heard was a smash and he turned from his crouched position in time to see the glass of the huge patio doors shatter into a million tiny pieces as the ball shot through the double glazed panels and on into the dining room and Monica's collection of Wedgewood tea sets, the resulting crashes turning both boys to stone, neither could move, both filled with fear of the inevitable repercussions.

Slowly, Paul came to his feet and joined by his brother and they stood and surveyed the damage from the garden.

"Now you've done it." Paul told his brother.

"Me?" Matt's voice rose in shock "You threw it." He accused.

"You hit it." Paul retorted.

"We are totally in the shit." Matt said.

Paul nodded in agreement "I think I'm going to take the coward's way out and disappear to Carmen's."

"You can't leave me to deal with this on my own." Matt protested.

"Oh I think I can."

"Come on Paul, it won't be so bad if we own up to this together."

"It won't be so bad for you, you mean. Dad will turn the whole thing around so that it's my fault when I am only partly to blame."

"I won't let him, I'll tell him that it was my idea in the first place." Matt nudged him.

"Alright Matt, stop shitting yourself, I'll stay," Paul stepped over the shattered glass "Give me a hand to tidy this up."

The boys waited nervously for their parents to return, both knowing that Michael's reaction was pretty much guaranteed but they worried about Monica's reaction to the destruction of her collection of tea sets, many of them priceless.

"This is going to be one hell of an insurance claim." Paul muttered as they heard the sound of Michael's Mercedes pull into the drive way.

Matt stood and made his way from the kitchen to the front door, greeting his parents and explaining what had happened. As expected, Michael exploded halfway through Matt's attempts at apologising. Monica stood in silence as she surveyed the remaining pieces of her china that Paul had managed to salvage from the mess on the floor.

"I want both of you in my study. NOW." Michael demanded, preceding the two boys up the stairs.

"I'm so sorry Mum." Paul hesitated, he wasn't in any rush to join his brother and father.

"I'm sure it was an accident." She replied, she looked into her son's eyes and saw the slightest hint of fear there.

"It was a total accident."

"Your father will understand if you keep your cool and explain it clearly." she told him "It's best not to keep him waiting"

Closing the study door behind him, Paul stood beside his brother as Michael proceeded to tear strips off both of them.

"What the hell were you thinking?" he shouted.

"I needed the practice Dad." Matt explained. "I asked Paul to bowl for me and he did even though he didn't really want to, we made a mistake, it was an accident. In hindsight, perhaps we should have gone to the batting cage." He shrugged.

"What do you have to say for yourself?" Michael turned his attention to Paul.

"Matt pretty much covered it." Paul replied not wishing to be drawn into the conversation.

"I cannot believe you could be so careless." Michael exploded "What the hell is wrong with you that you can't catch a ball?" he directed at Paul.

"It was coming at me so fast, the only thing that would have stopped it was my face." Paul lost his cool, his voice rising to the same level as his fathers.

"Rather that than my windows." Michael sniped back.

"Nice." Paul retorted, "Told you it would be my fault." He said to Matt.

"Dad," Matt stepped between Paul and Michael. "I hit the ball so hard there was no way he could have caught it, he'd have broken his hand if he had, this isn't Paul's fault."

"I do not understand why you feel the need to defend him Matthew." Michael bellowed.

"We fucked up Dad, we didn't deliberately set out to break the window." Paul shouted resulting in Michael removing his belt.

"I'm told I can't leave visible marks on you boys, doesn't mean you won't be punished, I'll leave it up you to decide who goes first" he turned toward his desk to await his first victim.

Matt and Paul faced each other both of them had expected this. Paul shot his brother a wry smile before prising open the button of his jeans.

"Sorry." Matt murmured.

"It's ok," Paul grasped his brothers' shoulder and squeezed "I pity the fielders of the other cricket team." He finished as he stepped up to Michael's desk and dropped his jeans to the floor.

The following evening, the twins were hustled into Michael's car having been told in no uncertain terms that they couldn't be trusted alone in the house and so they would both attend Matt's parent/teacher meetings.

"I don't even go to school any more." Paul complained as he adjusted his seating position, favouring his left cheek as the right side of his behind had taken the brunt of Michael's beating.

Monica turned in her seat to look at him. "Do you really think your attitude is the best course of action?" She asked "Given recent events, I think it may be prudent for you to keep your mouth shut."

"Why does it seem like the whole thing is my fault?" Paul hissed back at her.

"Matthew got the exact same punishment you did." Monica replied.

"Really? Funny that because my arse cheeks seem to be far more painful than his." Paul scowled.

"I just have more muscle on my bum than you." Matt nudged him "Shut up dude or we'll get more."

Arriving at the school, Paul suggested that it might be a good idea for him to stay in the car;

"If I were to allow that, what are the chances that you would have disappeared by the time I return?" Michael asked, holding open the back door of the car and glaring at his son.

Paul shrugged and unfolded himself from the back seat ."The chances would be pretty high." He admitted.

"That's what I thought." Michael slammed the door and locked the car "You stay in my line of sight at all times, do you understand?"

"Yes Dad." Paul mumbled.

Paul managed to keep himself in Michael's peripheral vision throughout the evening and gave his father no course for further repercussions. He became uncomfortable as Matt led their parents towards the science labs but knew if he asked to wait outside the room that it was likely to arouse more suspicion than if he accompanied them into the room and did his best surly teenager act.

Entering the room, he felt his temperature rise and his groin tighten at the sight of her. She looked good enough to eat in that sweater, it was deep red and Cashmere, he knew that because he had bought it for her, he didn't remember the fit being quite as snug though, she had coupled it with black jeans that clung to her shapely legs and bottom and had him mentally kicking himself for staring. He hadn't seen or spoken to her since Sunday and he was hungry for her company.

Carmen looked up from her pile of student files and smiled;

"Mr and Mrs Jensen, so nice to meet you, please take a seat. Matthew, sit there." She gestured to the chair in the centre of the two adults "Oh, hello Paul, I haven't seen you here for a while." she at last acknowledged his presence.

"Hi Miss." Paul answered making brief eye contact with her, memories of the way he pursued her and teased her in this very room flooding back. Shoving his hands into his pockets, he moved over to the work benches by the window, keeping himself in Michael's sight at the same time as he turned his back on those present and pretended to look out onto the school grounds.

There was quite a lot of discussion over Matt's work, from what he could gather from the snippets of conversation he could hear, Carmen was telling his parents that Matt's work had suffered since Paul had left school and he had dropped several points in his grade average which surprised him as Matt had always been the one who was far more interested in science but thinking about it, they had bounced ideas off each other, their differing personalities covering every angle of the problem presented to them.

"Paul was a very good student." Carmen was saying "He always had a healthy input into class discussions."

"He always has liked the sound of his own voice." Michael sniped.

"Oh, I think you may have misunderstood me Mr Jensen. Paul's opinions were usually spot on and between him and Matthew, they got their peers far more interested in the lesson than I ever seemed able to and while Matthew still holds the attention of the class, it isn't quite the same without Paul's input. Both boys are excellent students and presented their ideas in an extremely mature manner, I am so pleased to have been able to teach them." She beamed as she closed Matt's student file. "Do you have anyone else to see?" she asked, deftly changing the subject..

"Just my English teacher to go." Matt confirmed.

"I'd better let you get over to her then. Do you mind if I borrow Paul to help me put the room back to normal? I'll escort him to the English block when it's done." She saw Michael hesitate and Matt grin as he rose from his chair.

"Well, Paul's only here as he is grounded as punishment for breaking a window and some very valuable china," Michael started "I'd rather keep him with me to make sure he behaves."

"I see. If it's of any comfort, I have never known Paul to misbehave here, I'm sure he won't give me any trouble." Carmen countered.

"Michael, we will only be down the hall a little way and Miss Scott did say she'd bring him to us, let him help her with the desks." Monica cajoled.

"Very well," Michael conceded "Paul, make sure you behave."

"I will," he replied as he came to stand next to his lover "I always do." he shot a smirk at his father.

Michael huffed but opened the door for his wife saying as he did so "What an exceptionally lovely looking lady." His comment causing Paul to scowl after him.

Carmen made sure the door was shut on the Jensen family "You're grounded?" she asked.

"Yeah and sore, my backside looks like it has stripes." He stepped closer "God I've missed you." He reached for her then surprised when she allowed him to kiss her.

"I've missed you." She answered easing herself from his grasp "I take it I won't be seeing you this week?"

"Not unless I can persuade Mum to let me off the hook. At the moment Dad is going to pick me up from my last job and take me home every night for the foreseeable future."

"That's a pity. The bath tub is far too big for one person." She shot him a sly smile.

"I'm very tempted to bend you over the desk and have my wicked way with you right here and now."

"I'm very tempted to let you but we both know it's too risky." She answered "Come on, help me with these desks." She moved away. "If you have any local jobs, I could always pop out at lunchtime to see you." She casually dropped the temptation into his consciousness.

Paul put the end of the desk down that he had been manoeuvring and reached into the back pocket of his jeans to retrieve his battered but up to date work diary and quickly flicked to that week's work. "I'm not close by until Friday but I could slip away at lunch time. Do you want to meet me in the park, same place as last time?"

With the time and date agreed and the science room once again looking presentable, Carmen walked Paul to the English block. To the outside observer, it looked and sounded as though they were deep in conversation, discussing the things that Carmen wanted done to her garden with Paul suggesting alternatives to the usual winter planting regime, only Matt knew better as he watched his brother, he saw the way Paul's hand softly traced down her back as he held the door open and allowed her through ahead of him.

"I'd be interested in you giving me a quote." Carmen said within earshot of his parents.

Paul dug a business card out of his pocket "Take my card." He told her "Give me a call or let Matt know when you are available and I'll pop over."

Chapter Eleven

Matt stopped by her desk before taking his seat on Thursday that week, handing her a note from Paul. The note told her that he couldn't make their arranged Friday meeting and as Michael was still escorting him home from work, he didn't know when he would see her again. As the end of the lesson approached, she told Matt to remain behind after class, asking him to pass a message to his brother that she would be home Saturday afternoon if he was free to come and give her a quote.

"Make sure you tell him in front of your parents." She told him.

Early Saturday afternoon, Carmen opened her front door to a beaming Paul, his face turned away from Michael who was standing just behind him.

"Hi Miss Scott." He grinned "I'm a bit dirty, shall I let myself in through the side gate?" he asked.

Carmen let her eyes travel down the length of his mud caked clothes "That would be the best idea." She replied.

"Paul, I'm going to run a few errands, how long do you think you'll be?" Michael stepped back as Paul brushed past him.

"Oh, it should take about half an hour. Are you sure you can trust me enough to leave me? Don't you want to wait in the car like you usually do?" Paul smirked; he had succeeded in making his father look like a fool.

"As Miss Scott is one of your former teachers, I am sure she is more than adept at keeping you in line boy. I will be back in thirty minutes." Michael replied.

By the time Carmen had closed the door and gone through to the back of the house, Paul had stripped off his top and had started on his jeans.

"I know it's been a while." Carmen smiled "But don't you think you are being a little forward?"

"Huh?" he looked up from unlacing his work boots "Oh, no, I'm not stripping ready for action honest," he laughed "I haven't worked this morning, I only put these clothes on to piss Dad off, they have left mud and dust all over his white leather seats, I didn't want to bring the dirt into the house."

"I was only kidding, get naked and get in here." Her answer which had Paul nearly falling over himself in haste.

Sweating and breathless, Paul glanced at his watch as he snuggled closer to the curvaceous woman at his side and softly stroked her flushed cheek.

"You do know I'm with you for more than just the mind blowing sex, don't you?" He asked.

"That's a nice sentiment but it's a little hard to believe in the circumstances." she replied.

He propped himself up on one elbow, looking down at her. "I'm serious, maybe this is the wrong time to be saying this but with my watch dog due to return in the next few minutes, if I don't say this now, I don't know when I'll get another chance. Sex with you is out of this world, there's no denying that and in all honesty, I was beginning to question my motives about being with you but this enforced separation has made me realise how much I enjoy spending time with you, how good you make me feel. You treat me like an adult for the most part; you listen to me and discuss things with me as well as take care of me. I like the way you do things, silly things like turning the bed down before we get into it and the way you turn your teddy bear to face the wall when we get busy just cracks me up. I love you Carmen, I'm in love with you and I like who I am when I'm with you, being apart and not even able to speak to you is killing me, I can't concentrate, I'm making stupid mistakes, I can't eat or sleep, all I do is think about you and when I might be able to see you again," he looked up as he heard a car horn. "Shit, Dad is here. I have to go."

Carmen reached for him and pulled him into a kiss "I love you." She whispered. "Try to get some time away from your parents if you can, we need to talk about this."

"Ok," he slid from the bed and pulled on his shorts "I'll try to ring you." He told her shortly before jogging down the stairs and throwing on his dirty clothes, he hated leaving her and was quiet on the journey home, pretending to make notes on his quotes pad.

"Don't think you've got a free afternoon." Michael told him, reaching for the Hoover, "You can get all that muck out of my car before you come in for lunch."

Carmen returned to school as usual on Monday morning, she hadn't heard from Paul and found herself thinking about him constantly, his admittance of his feelings for her had touched a nerve and everything she had repressed until then came washing over her, she knew she felt every bit as strongly about him as he did her and that her actions from here on in had the potential of shaping his young life whether that was good or bad she was yet to decide.

A cold wind had got up as she walked to her car a few nights later and she pulled her jacket closed only to find that it would no longer fasten over her chest. Knowing that the contentment her young lover bought her had caused her to put on a few pounds, the shock that this particular jacket, bought large to accommodate a jumper, wouldn't do up over her blouse had her frowning and contemplating the snide remarks she had encountered in the staff room over her expanding chest. Sitting in the drivers' seat, she paused before starting the engine and looked down at her chest, unbuttoning her blouse slightly she saw them spilling out of her bra and noticed for the first time the blue veins crisscrossing the smooth skin. Almost as if a light bulb had switched on in her head, she scrabbled in her bag for her diary, counting back the days since her last cycle, closing the book slowly and dropping it back into her bag when she realised how long it had been.

PRODIGAL SON

It was over a week later when Paul appeared on her doorstep, finally released from his parents grounding punishment. During the week, Carmen had made several calls to her best friend Helen to discuss her predicament. Helen advised her to seek an abortion, spelling out in no uncertain terms what this would do to her career and calling into question her morals for continuing her affair with a teenage boy. Helen went on to explain that being a single parent was horrible, her husband had left one evening on the pretence of going to buy cigarettes and never returned leaving her and her almost three year old son Luke on their own with Helen struggling to earn enough money to keep their house let alone feed her fast growing son.

"Dad's away for a few days." Paul explained as he helped her prepare dinner "And Mum's a push over. I can stay if you want me to."

"Ok." She replied.

"Are you alright? You've hardly said a word since I've been here." He stroked her arm.

Carmen looked into those beautiful dark brown eyes filled with concern and confusion "I'm fine, I had a tough day at school that's all." She smiled "I'd love you to stay."

She woke in the early hours of the morning, unable to sleep or lead him on anymore; she shook him awake, turning on the bedside light, making him squint.

"What's wrong?" he asked, his voice thick with sleep.

"Paul, I can't do this anymore," she started "We have to end this."

"What?" He sat up "What's brought this on?"

"My career is taking off and we are playing a very dangerous game, I can't afford to be caught with you and it's only a matter of time before one of us slips up. I'm so sorry, I feel like I've led you on. We're finished, you should go home."

"I don't understand," he turned around, crouching on his knees "What have I done that's upset you so much?"

167

"You haven't done anything; you are such a sweet boy. I have just come to my senses." She stroked his sleep messed hair away from his face

"I still don't get it," he brushed her hand away "You cook me dinner and tell me you'd love me to stay then you milk me dry when we come to bed only to have an epiphany during the night that makes you want to end everything?"

"It sounds strange but that's about it, I know you feel angry and hurt but you're young, you will find someone your own age that can make you happy."

"You make me happy, I don't want anyone else. Do you really think I would have kept coming over if I wasn't happy or if I didn't want to be with you?" He was standing now and unbelievably angry, his anger fuelled by the pain in his chest as her words cut him "If I wasn't happy, I'd fuck you and leave and wouldn't give you or your feelings a second thought."

"I know and I'm sorry Paul but I have made my decision, I can't be with you anymore."

"Don't I get a say in this?" He asked, Carmen shook her head "Please don't do this." He begged.

"I'm not going to change my mind, I never wanted to hurt you Paul but you do have to leave."

It was getting light by the time he got home. He tried his key to no avail as Monica had deadlocked door, she hadn't expected him home that night. The side gate was also locked and with the heavily laden trellis on top of it, climbing over was out of the question. Hurt and still angry, Paul surveyed the front garden for small stones to throw against his mothers' window in an effort to wake her knowing as he searched that there were no stones, he had made sure of that. Sighing, he lent against Monica's car, his hand groping for the handle, hoping that she had forgotten to lock it; he would spend the rest of the night in the car.

"Bollocks." He spat as the door refused to budge; he turned to look at the vehicle, an idea forming. Placing both hands on the side of the vehicle, he lent his weight onto his arms and pushed repeatedly causing the car to rock and the alarm to sound. Monica's light came on within seconds of hearing the obnoxious noise.

Muttering about the bloody faulty car alarm, Monica grabbed the spare set of keys she kept in the bedroom and threw open her curtains, aiming the keys at the car, she jumped when she saw a man by the car, not instantly recognising her son until he looked up and waved. She switched off the alarm then hurried down the stairs to let him in, realising she had locked him out.

"I didn't think you were coming home tonight." She said, re-locking the door behind him

"I hadn't planned on it," he replied "Sorry I woke you."

"Are you alright?" Monica caught his arm before he reached the stairs; he looked haggard and older than his fifteen years.

"I'd rather not talk about it Mum."

"You wouldn't be home if everything was fine." She countered.

"Mum, please," he frowned but made no attempt to pull out of her grasp. "My girlfriend dumped me." He stated.

"What did you do?"

"Nothing as far as I can work out, she went on about not being ready for a relationship, I don't know, I stopped listening after a while," he shrugged "I have work in the morning Mum, I should get some sleep."

Carmen collapsed on the bed after he had gone, she felt dreadful over having hurt him and her heart was breaking knowing she wouldn't see him again but she couldn't saddle a fifteen year old boy with a baby, she just couldn't, it was better for everyone this way she told herself. Picking up the phone, she left a message on the school answering machine stating that she wouldn't be at work the following day. She used that day to call old contacts in Gloucester and before the weekend dawned two days later, she had secured a job in a newly opened private school.

Paul threw himself into work and would return home exhausted and filthy. His mind was reeling and he couldn't shake the feeling of abandonment caused by Carmen's rejection of him. He would strip down to his boxers in the utility room before going upstairs to shower then taking advantage of his weary body, he would grab a couple of hours sleep before his insomnia woke him and he would spend the rest of the night alternating between paperwork and wondering what Carmen was doing.

Monica watched her son carefully, she had taken note of his withdrawal from his social and family life in general, and he said very little to anyone and when questioned, would usually reply with a one word answer before leaving the room. She worried that he barely ate enough to sustain his large frame and she often heard him get up in the night, he rarely returned to bed once he was awake. She was sorting the washing in the utility room the following Saturday morning, a mere week before her beloved twins turned sixteen when she inadvertently overheard the conversation between her two boys.

Paul passed his brother the cereal and milk then joined him at the breakfast bar, pressing a tea towel full of ice to his right eye having been exceptionally rude to Michael moments earlier, he now bore the beginnings of a black eye. He had considered retaliating against the blow and the thought had clearly been written on his face as Michael had told him in a menacing snarl;

"Think twice boy."

He hated himself for backing down, knowing he only did so as not to cause further friction in the house.

"Is Carmen alright?" Matt asked around a mouthful of cereal.

"As far as I know." Paul replied.

"How come she hasn't been to school?"

Paul put the ice down. "She hasn't?"

"Nah, how come you don't know?" Matt questioned.

"She dumped me." He picked up the ice again.

"That makes sense now," Matt mused out loud "I wondered why you were spending so much time at home.

"How many days has she been off?" Despite telling himself he wouldn't ask, he just couldn't help it.

"Since last Thursday. When did she dump you?"

"Last Thursday," he answered "Have you been given any reason why she's not there?"

"Nope but there's a rumour flying around that she's leaving, someone said she's moving to Gloucester."

Paul's heart dropped, she was going home, he couldn't let her go without seeing her one last time "I gotta go." He mumbled and bolted for the door.

Carmen looked up from wrapping glasses in newspaper when she heard footsteps on her patio, seeing Paul, red faced, chest heaving from his sprint over here made her catch her breath. Initially surprised when he hadn't made any contact with her, she was only just becoming accustomed to life without him when he appeared. He reached for the door handle, finding it locked; he looked up at her and spread his hands, a silent plea to be let in.

"You shouldn't be here." She told him, opening the door and gesturing for him to come in.

"It's true, you're leaving." He stated looking around at the many packing cases.

"Yes. How did you find out?"

"Matt heard rumours at school about you moving to Gloucester. Did you forget that I know that's home for you?" He spun to face her "Why are you doing this?"

"I'm giving you your life back, you should be grateful."

"You've ripped my world apart, I can't sleep, I don't care about anything, I'm empty from losing you, all my feelings are directed towards trying to get you back. You weren't even going to say goodbye."

"I thought a clean break was the best thing for both of us." She walked away to answer the phone before he could reply.

He sat at the kitchen table, ripping small pieces off the piled newspapers there and rolling them into balls, flicking them into one of the empty boxes. Carmen, a mere three feet away from him, watched as she spoke to her friend, keeping her voice low, knowing he could still hear her, hoping he wouldn't understand the conversation.

"It's kind of hard to talk right now." She spoke into the phone.

"Is he there?" Helen asked.

"Yes."

"I thought you finished with him?"

"I did, this is the first time he's been here since then."

"I see, I hope you aren't considering getting back with him."

"I don't know Helen, it's so hard. You can't help who you fall for."

"You can when he's fifteen years old. Come on Carmen, get your head straight, finish packing and get up here then we can see about getting rid of that baby."

"Actually, I have made that decision, I'm going to go through with it, I've taken on board everything you said about how hard it is but I'll manage somehow, I know I will."

"Christ," Helen sighed "Are you absolutely sure you're pregnant? It's not just some wishful thinking, phantom thing?"

"I'm sure."

"You've done tests?"

"Yes. Four to be exact."

"Have you seen a doctor?"

"Not yet, they are 99% accurate though."

With that last comment, the penny dropped for Paul. Her growing breasts, the way her tops were now far too tight, the thickening of her waist that he had noticed at their last meeting. He jumped to his feet and pulled out the kitchen bin, finding it empty, he glanced up at Carmen and saw the stricken look on her face as she realised she had said far too much then he headed for the dustbins, up ending them and kicking through the rubbish by the time she reached him.

"Stop this," she screamed at him, then "No," as he bent to retrieve what he was looking for

"You're pregnant?" He stated, holding out the positive test. "You should have told me."

"I finished with you so that you didn't have to know." She replied quietly, defeated.

"Whoa, this is huge," he sat suddenly on the wall surrounding the patio "I don't understand why you wouldn't tell me."

"Come inside, I'll make some tea."

With the hot drink slowly going cold in front of them, they tentatively began to talk;

"So, what do you want to do?" He asked "About the baby, I mean."

"I've decided to keep it." She answered "I have a job to go to in Gloucester, I'm going to stay with Helen until this place sells then I'll get a house close to work and take it from there."

"Do I figure in any of this?"

"I didn't want to put you in this position which is why I ended it. In reality, I think I just didn't want to see you run away."

Paul huffed at her last remark. "Don't get me wrong, every nerve ending is screaming at me to bolt but what kind of person would that make me? I was serious when I said that I'm in love with you, I can't help that. I can support you; you won't have to work once the baby is born."

"With the sale of the house, I'll have enough to keep me going for a while even with buying another house, you don't have to worry about any of this, I won't tie you down to fatherhood or child support."

"I want to be part of this baby's life and yours, moving to Gloucester is perfect, I can come with you, we can be a family."

"You are fifteen; you can't possibly take responsibility for me and a baby."

"I earn more than enough to support you, in fact, I earn more than you do and I have a fair bit saved and I'm only fifteen for another week. By the time you move, I'll be legal and nothing can touch us."

"You can't come with me, it simply won't work."

"I want to be with you, how many times do I have to say it before you will believe me? Come on Carmen, you know me; if I was going to run I'd have done it the moment I realised what you were talking about. I'm not going anywhere; I'm in this for the long haul. If you really don't want anything to do with me then fine, I'll deal with that eventually but at least let me be a part of my kid's life."

They talked late into the night, Paul's arguments finally winning her over. They decided that she would move and he would stay here, he vowed to visit her regularly and promised to support her in every way he could.

"Telling my parents is going to be epic." He commented as he closed his eyes.

"Do you think that's a good idea?" She asked as she snuggled into his side.

"Nothing is a good idea where my parents are concerned but I will have to tell them at some point." He reasoned.

"I suppose. I must say, you have taken this remarkably well"

Paul laughed dryly and turned towards her "I'm shitting myself Carmen, I mean, ok, I can and will support you but at the end of the day, I'm still a kid and I have no idea if I can do this."

"Which is why I wanted to make a clean break."

"Have you even considered abortion?" he asked.

"I thought about it. Is that what you would prefer?"

"I don't think so," he mused "I wasn't suggesting it either, I just wondered if it was ever an option."

"Paul, you don't have to do this, I can manage on my own."

"I know you can but we did this together so we'll deal with it together. I wish you'd reconsider moving though."

"My friends are in Gloucester, that's where I'm going to get the most support. I need to go home."

"Yeah, I understand that, I just wish you wouldn't."

He was alone in the bed when he woke later in the day, he reached out to the crumpled sheets where she had been, finding them cold, she had obviously been up for some time and then panic began to set in as he remembered the packing cases all over the house and his sleep addled mind crashed upon the idea that she had left while he was sleeping. Jumping out of the bed and dragging on his jeans he called her name as he reached the bedroom door, relieved to hear her answering call from the bathroom.

"I thought you'd gone." he perched on the edge of the bath

"No. I couldn't sleep." She stroked his hand, she loved him like this, dressed only in jeans, his toned and tanned torso was very easy on the eye "There's fresh tea in the pot if you want some" she handed him her mug encouraging him to make her one too. He returned a few moments later with two steaming mugs of tea, balancing one on the edge of the tub; "Are you getting in?" she asked.

"Actually, could I use your phone; I have a few things I need to re-arrange?"

Matt, meanwhile, completely oblivious to his brothers' anguish, finished his cereal and went to put some bread in the toaster as Monica came out of the utility room.

"Do you fancy pancakes instead of toast?" she asked.

"Maple syrup?" Matt grinned as she nodded. Reaching into cupboards, he handed her the ingredients she would need before re-taking his seat at the breakfast bar.

Monica piled pancakes high onto a serving plate and put them in front of her son, giving him a fork and a smaller plate along with the maple syrup before taking her seat opposite him, watching as he eased vast amounts of the cooked batter into his mouth.

"So. Paul's girlfriend? How much do you know about her?" Monica asked.

Matt looked up from his plate into his Mothers' eyes and swallowed almost half of the food in his mouth, thinking "Crap," as he frantically tried to come up with a cover story for his brother while he finished chewing. "Er, not much."

"Come on Matthew, you need to give me a little more than that."

"Honestly Mum, I don't really know that much about her."

"Let's start with the basics shall we?" Monica asked "What is her name?"

"Carmen." Matt replied. He gathered his plate and put it into the dishwasher "Mum, I don't have time for this now, I'm meeting Hayley at the gym."

"SIT DOWN." Monica rarely raised her voice but her family jumped to do her bidding when she did, it only took seconds for Matt to return to his seat "Spit it out Matthew, what aren't you telling me?"

"Nothing!" Matt's voice rose with the lie.

"Paul usually brings his girlfriends home, why haven't I met this one?"

"She has her own place, it makes sense that they would go there rather than here."

"Exactly how much older than him is she?" Monica frowned.

"I don't know, a few years maybe." Not totally a lie as he really didn't know.

"Matthew," Monica warned "I know something isn't quite right with what's going on with Paul and this girl so you may as well tell me."

"Look, all I know is that she's older than him, she has a job and her own place ok?"

"What else?"

"He loves her." Matt shrugged.

"That much I did know." Monica sighed "Are they sexually active?"

"This is Paul we're talking about, what do you think?" Matt shot back.

"Have you met her?"

"Yeah, a couple of times," he answered but he was thinking "So have you."

"Describe her."

"Brunette, curvy, a little taller than you although it's hard to say, she always wears stupidly high heels, she seems to care for him a lot."

"Do you know where he met her?"

The words "At school" were out of his mouth before he had even formed the thought.

"I don't see how she can afford to have her own place if she's just left school" Monica mused.

"I think it's been a while since she left school but she is there pretty much every day." Matt sniggered.

Then Monica realised "She works at the school?"

Matt remained silent trying to think of all the ways he could make this up to his brother as although he hadn't actually blurted out the fact that Carmen was a teacher, he had provided the information that led Monica to the correct conclusion.

"Oh my God, she's a teacher?" Monica gasped, waiting for her son to deny it, his silence speaking volumes "Tell me I'm wrong" she almost pleaded.

"I'm sorry Mum; I've already said too much, you should talk to Paul about this."

"Oh I will, don't you worry about that." Her expression hardened "How could you keep this from me?"

"He's my brother, he keeps my secrets, I keep his." Matt shrugged "Can I go?"

Chapter Twelve

During that next week, Paul was rarely home, he flitted in and out between jobs and the rest of the time he spent with Carmen, helping her pack and taking full advantage of the fact that she was beginning to feel guilty for leaving him. He spent the early part of his sixteenth birthday with her, leaving only to return home to ready himself for a meal out with his family.

The Jensen family were in full preening mode when he arrived home to the sound of hairdryers and the shower running, he found Matt in their bedroom, buttoning a whiter than white shirt.

"Paul, I am so sorry."

Matt's words stopped him dead "What did you do?" Paul's reply.

"Mum, kind of cornered me and started asking questions about you and Carmen." Matt hesitated "I didn't say too much but she twigged big time, basically, I dropped you in the shit."

"She knows Carmen's a teacher?"

"Uhuh" Matt nodded "I'm sorry." He repeated.

"Tonight is going to be fun," Paul replied as he began removing his clothes "I don't understand why she hasn't said anything to me, I've been here a few times this week."

"I think she's waiting for the right moment. You know Mum, she'll tackle you when you least expect it and when Dad's not around, she is going to go nuts though."

"She has no reason too, I'm sixteen, totally legal, there's nothing she can do now."

"Yeah, I wouldn't bet on it" Matt commented.

"Carmen's leaving in the morning; at least she won't be around to take any of the flack. I'm going back there later so I need you to cover for me."

"It's the least I can do. Hayley and I are going to catch a late film after the meal; just pretend you are tagging along."

The meal was torture. Matt had obviously clued Hayley into his conversation with Monica over Paul's current romantic entanglement and she made leading comments all evening.

Sitting opposite his Mother, Paul found himself on the end of more than a few stern looks but those he could take it was the ones filled with disappointment that squeezed his heart. He was on the verge of blurting out that, yes, he was dating one of his former teachers and that, yes, he was madly in love with her when Monica pushed two gift wrapped boxes across the table, one for each of her sons.

Ripping open the paper revealed a mobile telephone for each of them, quelling any further thoughts of proclaiming his love for the woman carrying his baby. The teenagers left the restaurant shortly after desert was served and after walking a short way, Paul veered off in the opposite direction from his twin.

"How was it?" Carmen asked wrapping her arms around his neck as he joined her on the sofa.

"Horrible," he huffed his lips playing with hers "I think I may be in need of your undivided attention," he smiled and pulled her closer "How about you undress me and do lots of unspeakable things to the impressionable teenager currently in your care." He chuckled.

"You just made me sound like a dirty old woman." She rolled her eyes.

"I wouldn't be with you if you weren't." He answered.

The removal vans arrived promptly at ten the following morning and Paul set about helping the hired hands load the larger items of furniture into the vehicle.

"What am I doing?" He asked as he jumped down from the back of the van "I'm only speeding things up by helping them." He explained to Carmen vainly trying to wrap his arms around her.

Almost three hours later and the final van was closed up, the workers climbing aboard to start their journey as Carmen and Paul headed back into the empty house, their voices echoing.

"I should make a move." Carmen told him allowing him to hold her.

"Let me come with you." He whispered, his lips pressed to her temple.

"Don't keep asking that, you know the answer," she reached up and wrapped her arms around his neck, pressing her body into his as he kissed her "Just give me a little while to get settled then come and see me, we'll talk again then, perhaps by that time I will have missed you so much that I won't want you to leave."

"Alternatively, by that time, Helen will have poisoned you against me and you will never want to see me again."

"Never going to happen. You are a very special young man, you are going to achieve many things in your life, I knew it the moment I set eyes on you and I now know it to be true having spent some time with you."

"I won't let you down Carmen, I'll always be here for you." He allowed his hand to glide over her stomach "For both of you," he corrected himself."Take care of my baby" he told her, letting her ease out of his grasp "Call me when you get there, let me know you are safe."

Knowing he would more than likely have to face Monica's wrath, he still chose to return home after watching Carman's car disappear from sight. He felt empty and incredibly sad, he knew he would see her again but the distance she was putting between them seemed like an impossible chasm to cross at that particular moment in time. He heaved a sigh of relief on reaching home when he saw that Michael's car was nowhere in sight and on entering the house, realised that he was alone. Pouring himself a cold drink, he went out into the garden and rescued the lawn mower from the mangled bits of push bike that Matt was working on and set about tidying the garden.

Tessa was the first to return home, spotting her brother in the garden, she asked if he wanted anything to eat or drink before she made a start on dinner and when he had told her that he would wait for the evening meal, she returned to the kitchen.

Monica was next to arrive. Matt and girlfriend Hayley in tow having bought them with her from Kay's house where she had spent most of the day. With her blond son and the girl disappearing upstairs and her daughter busy in the kitchen, she joined her youngest son in the garden taking note of the perfectly cut grass as well as the bits of her lawn mower strewn within easy reaching distance of the boy sitting cross legged on the grass.

"Thank you for cutting the grass." Her opening mantra.

"That's ok," Paul looked up and smiled at his mother "I broke the lawn mower," he gestured to the parts surrounding him "I should be able to fix it though." He finished turning his attention back to the part in his hands.

Monica, glass of wine in hand, sat at the patio table and watched him work "Are you out tonight?" She asked knowing she would have to start the conversation somewhere.

"I don't think so," came the reply, he didn't stop what he was doing, he didn't look up but he felt his stomach begin to squirm, knowing the conversation would soon turn to his affair with his teacher.

"Paul..." Monica started, she stopped when she saw him rest his hands on his legs and look over at her.

"I know, you know Mum." He cut her off and turned back to fixing the lawn mower.

"What were you thinking?" Monica, now kneeling the other side of the broken machine, reached out and stopped his hands from working.

"She's hot," he shrugged "She treats me like an adult, listens to my ideas and she believes in me."

"I believe in you."

"Yeah, it's different Mum, I fell for her the moment she walked into the class room, I couldn't help it."

"She should have known better."

"So should I, I knew what I was doing was wrong on so many levels and she repeatedly pushed me away but that just made me want her more. I was the one who pursued her; I made it impossible for her to refuse me. I backed her so far into a corner that the only place she had to go was into my arms." He explained.

"Does she teach Matthew?"

"She did until Friday. She's moved back to Gloucester, I won't be seeing her for a while."

"How much older than you is she?"

"Trust me, you don't want to know. I love her Mum, I want to be with her, I'm considering getting a place closer to where she is and starting a branch of the business there."

"Give it some thought before you do anything." Monica advised.

"I will. I thought you would tear me a new one."

"I want to but that's a sure fire way to lose you and you have always been able to talk to me, I don't want that to end. Promise me you'll keep me in the loop, I will try to support you in whatever you do, you surely know that?"

"I do, thanks Mum. I'd better get this fixed before Dad gets home." He changed the subject and went back to work.

Paul spent the evening watching films with his mother and sister, trying everything he could to avoid his bedroom what with it currently being occupied by his brother with his girlfriend being most intricately wrapped around each other the last time he had checked. His mobile phone rung as midnight approached, making him jump out of his chair and bolt for the kitchen.

183

Monica said goodnight to her daughter then turned down the volume on the television so that she could listen to her son, now she knew why he had been jumpy all evening. He sounded far more animated in those few moments than he had been throughout the entire evening.

Returning to the living room, he gave her a sideways glance, flopping into the armchair he said "That was Carmen."

"I gathered." Monica replied "It's a little late to be calling" she sniffed disapprovingly.

"I asked her to let me know she had arrived safely." He countered "Mum, is this going to cause problems between us?"

"I don't know, I'm trying to understand what a young boy would see in an older woman but I'm failing to grasp it at the moment."

"Then let me spell it out for you," Paul sat forward, irked by Monica's attitude "She's physically very attractive with curves in all the right places, she's caring and funny and her age gives her the experience that girls my own age lack, even if I didn't have feelings for her, the sex alone would keep me with her."

Monica gasped "I cannot believe you would be so shallow or that you would speak to me in that manner."

"You wanted to know," Paul shrugged "Perhaps I shouldn't have been so blunt, but you did want to know."

Over the following weeks, his contact with Carmen became hap hazard at best and when they did speak, she seemed closed off to him and their conversations were brief. It became increasingly clear to Paul that she was being ever more influenced by Helen about their relationship and he wasn't in the least surprised when Carmen once again called a halt to it in their most recent conversation and while he regretted some of the things that came out of his mouth, he still wasn't ready to give her up.

His behaviour deteriorated along with his attitude and while he was fine working on his own, when he had someone with him, he was quick to snap and often found himself apologising. At home, things were tense, Monica avoided the subject of Carmen altogether not wishing to hear any more of her sons' admissions of his physical draw to the woman in question, things hit a further downward spiral when Paul snapped at Michael over dinner and then proceeded to dodge every blow the older man aimed at him, infuriating him further and causing him to storm from the house. Monica realised around this time that her youngest child was out to irritate his father by any possible means and promptly moved him to his grandparents to avoid further confrontations.

Although Jackson and Paula didn't understand their Grandson's attraction to a much older woman, they did listen when he explained the situation of her living with her best friend who was slowly but surely poisoning her against him and that he needed to borrow some money short term to invest in a property for her, he carefully omitted the fact that she was carrying his baby.

Using Paul's absence from the house, Monica systematically went through all of his belongings, gleaning as much information on the woman as possible, finding photographs and notes that had been passed between them, then she approached the school armed with her full name, even more furious that she had sat across a desk from this woman discussing not only Matthew but Paul, she mentally kicked herself when she recalled that it was her who had allowed Paul to remain behind on the supposition of helping the woman straighten the classroom.

Horrified and shocked at her allegations, the school launched an immediate investigation and took full responsibility for Carmen's actions as well as contacting the school she was due to start at the following week.

Leaving the school, Monica went straight to her parents' house and confronted her son with the facts about the relationship that she had found in his room. Infuriated beyond belief that his mother had violated his privacy, Paul, for the first time in his life, raised his voice and directed all the frustration and hurt he was feeling about his situation at her.

"What gives you the right to go through my things?" he shouted.

"You live in my house." She responded.

"I pay rent to live there." He barked back absolutely seething. It was at this point that Monica's brother John stepped in. Placing a hand on Paul's shoulder, he guided the shaking, angry teenager from the room.

"Ok, I understand why you are angry but do you really want to be talking to your mother like that?" He asked, his voice calm.

Paul closed his eyes and hung his head at his Uncle's words, hating himself for shouting at Monica, taking a deep breath and making a huge effort to compose himself he replied "No, I shouldn't be speaking to her that way."

"Good. Let's go back into the fray then, you keep calm, I want to talk to my sister before you open your mouth again ok?"

"OK, thanks John."

"Hey, I'm on your side kid, don't ever forget that," he answered and led the way back into the living room "Monica, what on earth made you decide it was a good idea to search Paul's things?" he asked his sister.

"I wanted to know more than he was telling me." She defended herself "He still lives under my roof and at sixteen he isn't considered an adult yet, I'm only trying to protect him"

"But he doesn't need protecting Mon, take a good hard look at the boy, he mature beyond his years, responsible and sensible. We all have our vices and I believe Paul has just found his."

"Older women?" Monica questioned, tutting when John nodded "I think I would prefer it if he smoked." she folded her arms across her chest.

"I do smoke." Paul this time "I drink too" in for a penny in for a pound. "Mum, I'm sorry I shouted at you it won't happen again but you were wrong to go through my stuff."

"Thank you for the apology." She paused "You smoke?"

"Yep."

"Do you think you can stop?"

"I can try," he shrugged "We're getting off point here. Mum, you need to accept that I'm dating someone older than me, your disapproval isn't going to change that."

"Perhaps it isn't but have you given any thought as to why she keeps pushing you away and ending the relationship?"

"I don't have too; it's her vindictive friend who's making up her mind for her."

"Or perhaps she has finally realised that entering into a physical relationship with a fifteen year old boy, one who was her student no less, is completely immoral as well as illegal?"

"I'm sixteen, no longer at school, there's nothing illegal about it."

"You seem to be forgetting that I have seen evidence that suggests your relationship started while you were fifteen and still her student. I have spoken to the school and made them aware of this fact, they are taking the appropriate steps to ensure she never works with children again." Monica raised her chin in defiance.

"Oh Monica." John shook his head.

"No, you have to tell them you were wrong, you'll ruin her career, she loves teaching and this will destroy her." Paul ran his fingers through his hair "Mum please, don't push this, call the school."

"I can't, wheels have already been set in motion, I am expecting that she will be arrested any time now and the police will want to talk to you."

"I have to talk to her." he made to leave the room.

"You will do no such thing." Monica's voice took on the tone that brooked no arguments causing Paul to look up from his mobile phone.

"She needs to know it wasn't me who did this." He protested.

"I hope she thinks it was you," she replied "Oh, I have cancelled the contract on your phone and instructed your Grandparents to forbid your use of theirs; you will have no further contact with that woman."

"You can't stop me from seeing her." It was his turn to fold his arms over his chest.

"I don't have to, once she's arrested, she won't want to see you again."

"I beg to differ," Paul replied "You have seriously underestimated me." He told her before he bolted not only from the room but out of the house.

"Paul." Monica called after him, using her best stern voice.

"Let him go Monica," John said, stopping her from following her son "Whether you approve of his actions or not, you won't be able to stop him, he was right when he said that you underestimate him."

"You don't understand John, you aren't a parent." Exasperated, she knew her brother was right.

"No, I'm not and I don't understand your point of view but I totally get where he's coming from. Do you think you could let me deal with this?"

"What are you going to say to him that's any different to the things I've said?"

"For starters, I'm not going to forbid him to see her and I'm going to allow him to talk to her. If this is just a crush which is what I suspect you think it is, he'll get over it and move on. If in fact, he's in love which I think he is, these next few months are going to be hell for him and for us. He needs support Mon not conflict."

"He knows I'll support him."

"You have a very funny way of showing it."

Paul only had to go as far as the corner of the street to reach the nearest phone box. Filling the instrument with all his spare change, he dialled Helen's number and waited an eternity for an answer. Helen went berserk when she heard his voice, screaming at him and confirming his worst fears that Carmen had been arrested and was currently being held at the police station. He tried several times to cut into her tirade but finally gave up and let her rant only getting to speak and profess his innocence once she had exhausted herself. He calmly explained what had happened between his mother and himself and relayed his Grandparents phone number to her before hanging up and returning to the sanctuary of their house.

Letting himself in though the back door, he closed it silently and lent against it, breathing in the heavenly smell of his Grandmothers kitchen before steeling himself to face his mother again. Prising his body from the door, he raided the biscuit tin and then the fridge for Apple juice and once fully stocked, made his way through to the living room, stopping in the doorway, mouth full of biscuits, he briefly considered doing a runner when he set eyes upon the two uniformed officers talking to his Mother before Jackson saw him and beckoned him into the room, telling him in Spanish that the officers would like to talk to him and that he should be as honest as possible shortly before John cut in with the helpful fact that if he refused to say anything, they couldn't press charges on Carmen from anything he passed on, all they had to go on were the notes and photos he had kept.

Sitting opposite the officers, he listened as they spoke while munching on his biscuits, growing more resentful with each word that came out of the officers' mouths.

"You don't have to talk to me like I'm a child you know," he finally replied "Sugar coating things isn't going to change them."

"Very well, would you like to tell us what happened?"

"No. I have nothing to say on the matter." He sat back in his chair, took a large gulp of Apple juice and regarded the officers and his mother. "You can ask as many questions as you like, you won't get any information out of me."

"So you will neither confirm nor deny that you were molested?" The second officer asked

"Do I look like I've been molested?" He sat forward, the officer was young and pretty, her tunic hanging open in the warm house. "You'd look fantastic with your hair down," he told her.

"Paul!" Monica breathed, shocked at her sons' words.

"I feel you are being inappropriate." The female officer commented.

"I'm just stating a fact and I'll bet it's nothing your male colleagues haven't been thinking, I'll bet you would rock a short skirt too, you appear to have endless legs."

"Young man, stop this now, you are bordering on harassment." The male officer spoke.

Paul smiled as he got to his feet "There's the basis of your case," he said as he leant close to the male officer, "You have nothing on Carmen, you have nothing on me and you won't get anything from me except that I wasn't in any way forced to do anything I didn't want to do, I dictated the way things were, none of this is an act, it's just me and the way I am, I'm so good at this that no judge or jury would rule any different so you have no case and you may as well get in touch with the Gloucester Constabulary and tell them to let her go." He left the room in astonished silence and climbed the stairs to his room.

As her parents showed the officers to the door, Monica slipped by them, dodged John's attempt to stop her and shot up the stairs to her sons' room, throwing open the door and making him sit up from his prone position on the bed.

"Pack your things, you are coming home." She told him, furious that he had embarrassed her in front of the Police officers.

"I'd rather stay here." Paul stood "Even you have to admit that things are easier at home when I'm not there."

"I can't keep such a close eye on you here, you need to come home." She replied as she pulled his bag from the wardrobe and began throwing clothes into it.

"Monica, he's better off here for the time being." John said as he watched from the door "Nice work with the officers by the way". He addressed Paul now.

"Encouraging him is not helping," she rounded on her brother "He is my son; he will do as I say."

"Sorry Mum, not this time." Paul spoke up "I'm staying here, there are some things I need to sort out and I'm working on a job just around the corner so it's more convenient for me to stay here right now."

"What exactly, do you need to sort out?" she asked, hands on hips.

"I have to get some money together to get Carmen out of Helen's house, she can't move until her house sells, Grandpa is lending me some money to buy her house so that she can move." He explained.

"You are buying her house?"

"Well, technically, John is, I'm too young. We're going to do a little more work on it then sell it on."

"Unbelievable. Am I the only one who can see how wrong this whole situation is? Is there anything else I should know?"

"I can't tell you everything" Paul replied, he couldn't look at her now, knowing the last piece of the puzzle would hurt her beyond belief, "I want too but now's not the right time."

"You can tell me anything." Monica spoke gently.

"Judging from your reaction to my relationship, I honestly don't think I can. You need to get the police to back off and drop the case then maybe I will tell you everything."

"How dare you give me an ultimatum." She flared.

"You aren't exactly giving me a lot of choice."

"You are behaving like a child."

"Give it a rest Mum. I'm doing what I think is right. Whether you like it or not is a mute point right now. I love her, I would move heaven and earth for her if I could, you attempting to make things difficult isn't going to change anything, it's just going to make me move away sooner than I had planned."

"You aren't going anywhere," she fumed "Until you are eighteen you are still my responsibility, you've had a free rein up until now Paul but I expect you to start towing the line. You can start by apologising to those Police officers on their next visit."

"Huh," Paul smiled ruefully "Not going to happen. I only did what I did to prove a point, without my help they have nothing, that officer was a very nice piece of ass though." He chuckled.

Thwack – Monica's hand connected with his face with surprising force, making his head snap back as he took a step away from her, "I expected more from you. I raised you to respect women."

"And yet you married someone who treats you like a slave," he shot back, rubbing his cheek and keeping his distance "I think you should leave before we both say something we'll regret." He frowned, the blow from her hand wounding him deeper than any words ever could.

"He's right Mon. You need to go home and take stock of things." John finally spoke again "Come back when you've both had a chance to calm down." He stepped aside as his sister left the room and followed her down the stairs, wrapping an arm around her shoulder before she stepped out into the street "Monica, you need to handle this more carefully, keep going the way you are and you'll lose him."

"It feels like I already have," she leant on him "He's my baby John; we've always been so close."

"You have to let him grow up, he's already very much his own man, he still needs you but he's having trouble admitting it, he'll come around. Whatever it is he isn't telling you right now is obviously something he's struggling with himself and he will need to get it straight in his own head before he can let you in on it. You know he'll come to you eventually."

"I hope he does," she kissed his cheek "Look out for him, I'll leave it a few days then I'll have another chat with him."

Paul was unpacking his bag when John returned to his room;

"Ok, spill." The older man spoke.

Pushing a drawer closed, Paul put shorts, a t-shirt, trainers and a towel into the bag "I didn't tell her, what makes you think I will tell you?" he asked.

"Well, it's just me and you here, you know I won't tell anyone anything you don't want me too."

"Thanks John but I do need to keep some things to myself. Eventually I guess I'll have to say something but right now, I'm happy keeping it to myself." He hefted the bag onto his shoulder.

"Where are you going?"

"To the gym, want to join me?"

"You mean you want to be seen with this old codger?"

"Yeah, besides, you keep yourself in good shape, let's see which one of us has more stamina." Paul grinned. A swift phone call to Matt while waiting for his Uncle assured Paul that his brother would also be at the gym to prevent any further pertinent questions.

After a friendly warm up session on the treadmills and a more aggressive speed competition on the rowing machines, the boys left their uncle to the static weights while they hit the free weights, Paul spotting for Matt, amazed at the size of his twin's massive shoulders as he hefted the bowing bar above him repeatedly.

"If this bar drops, I don't think I'll be able to hold it." Paul admitted as Matt lowered the bar to his chest. Although he worked out regularly, he was nowhere near as large as Matt; his lengthy, naturally athletic build prevented him from becoming too bulky resulting in his body being sleek and toned with perfect muscle definition. Matt's short, stocky form took well to weights and his already large chest and shoulder muscles took no time at all in filling out, along with his rock solid thighs and halo of blond curls, Matt truly was a sight to behold.

"You should up the weight and lower the reps." Matt grunted with effort as with one final heave, he allowed Paul to guide the bar back into its stand.

"I swear this thing has just heaved a sigh of relief," he muttered as he began to remove weights for his standard twenty four reps. "I like the way I look," he said to Matt "Besides, I'd look odd if I got any bigger."

"I wouldn't look as big if I had some of your height." Matt grumbled.

"Bullshit." Paul laughed "You're lifting over twice as much as I can, maybe you should lower the weight and increase the reps." He jibed as he lay back on the bench and waited for Matt to lower the bar to him.

"Yeah, maybe," he mused, watching his brother "Watch your breathing." He warned, Paul was prone to going at the weights hell for leather and not concentrating on his breathing. which often left him out of breath. "How're things at Grans?" he asked.

"Ok, Mum called the Police in, she got a bit narked when I came on to the female officer and then wouldn't give them any information."

"She's told Tessa and I not to make any plans for tomorrow as they are coming to talk to us."

"Tessa doesn't know anything." Paul replied pushing the bar above him and counting "Seven," he was already beginning to feel breathless and concentrated harder on his brother as he dictated the pace of his breathing.

"I do though."

"You can't say anything Matt." Paul warned "Mum's already had Carmen arrested once and all Helen does is scream at me down the phone, I haven't been able to talk to her for nearly two weeks all because people have interfered."

"Don't worry about it; I have your back on this. If it wasn't for me opening my big mouth, Mum wouldn't have twigged in the first place, they won't get anything out of me."

"Thanks Matt, I owe you." Paul finished his reps and replaced the bar in its stand.

"We're cool and even." Matt slapped his sweating brother on the back then wiped his damp hand down Paul's t-shirt "Gross," bending to get a drink from the water fountain, Matt straightened up when Paul tapped his shoulder.

"Take a look at John," he grinned, gesturing to the other side of the gym where their uncle was in full Casanova mode, assisting a pretty young thing on the weights "At least I know where I get it from." he laughed.

"Yeah," Matt agreed "Jesus, look at him go," he sniggered "There's life in the old dog yet, come on," he nudged Paul "Let's go and ruin his style."

They sauntered over to their relative, wiping sweat from their arms and faces "Hey, Uncle John, we're going to hit the sauna, are you coming?" Paul smiled at his Uncle and the young girl next to him.

John looked up from the most welcome sight of the nubile young woman and pulled a face at his sniggering nephews "Hello boys," he said in the most derogatory tone possible "I'm just helping out Mandy here, I'll be with you shortly."

"Hi Mandy," Matt smiled "I'm Matt, this is Paul, we're twins."

Mandy stood, she barely reached Matt's chest and with him being the shorter of the three men, this made the girl positively tiny. "You don't look like twins," the standard reply.

"We're paternal twins, not identical." Paul replied casting a glance at his uncle "If you look close enough, you can see the similarities," also a standard reply but one that had worked on many occasions.

Mandy stepped closer as they knew she would "You are both lovely looking boys," she said as she scrutinized them "But I'm afraid I prefer something a little more mature." She stepped back beside John who was now smiling broadly.

"Fail," he laughed "I honestly will be with you in a moment boys," he turned his back on them and continued his previously interrupted conversation with Mandy.

"Wow, we just got turned down." Matt said as they walked away.

"I know, it kinda hurts." Paul answered.

"Maybe John really is that good." Matt pondered.

"Yeah or maybe the twins' thing is getting old."

Chapter Thirteen

Over the following two days, the two police officers paid several visits to Paul coming away empty handed each and every time. With the winter fast approaching, gardening work was at a minimum and Paul had his men working on house maintenance but with the weather now dictating his work schedule, he was becoming increasingly frustrated at being held back by the rain and while he had plenty of indoor work to occupy his work force, his own job close to his Grandparents house was going painfully slowly as it was all outside work.

Although Friday morning dawned grey and cold, the weather forecast didn't predict any rain making it possible for him to work. He left the house early, telling his Grandmother he would work until the light faded and not to bother with lunch. Working quickly and carefully, he was interrupted once by the offices again trying their luck; he gave them a cursory glance before returning to work, not even bothering to throw his now customary sarcastic greeting at them. He packed up his work tools early and caught the bus into town where he purchased two mobile phones, one for Carmen, the other for himself, on the way out of town he passed a jewellers, glancing in the window, a silver Celtic knot ring caught his eye, he stepped off the street and into the old fashioned shop, not hesitating or wanting to look at anything else, he purchased the ring knowing without a doubt that Carmen would love it.

Returning home to his Grandparents house, he showered and changed before joining both Grandparents and John for their evening meal of Paella, the discussion around the table conducted in Spanish and only covering that days current events had Paul relaxed and feeling very much at home it was only when Paula dropped into the conversation that as it was his parents wedding anniversary at the weekend, a small get together consisting of his family and

Michael's parents was planned for Saturday evening. He enquired if it was strictly necessary for him to attend, the stern look he received from Jackson told him that yes, his attendance would most definitely be required. After dinner was over, he disappeared into his room, making a number of phone calls, one in particular to a mini cab in order to get his gifts to Carmen even though it would cost him hundreds.

Monica was shocked by Matt's refusal to give the police any information on Paul's relationship with Carmen. Apologising profusely to them for her son's lack of co-operation as she guided them to the front door. The officers informed her that they hadn't had any luck with Paul either and with her permission they would like to take him to the police station and question him further as they often encountered a change of attitude when teenagers were confronted with a station environment. Monica readily agreed.

Matt was waiting for her in the kitchen when she had finished with the police officers and launched into a well practised speech of how out of order he felt she was in pursuing this situation and for trying to put words in his mouth during his interview. The realisation dawned that Paul and Matt had spoken before the police arrived hit her like a freight train, it was more than obvious to her that Paul had asked his brother to stay silent and that Matthew was doing as his brother asked, the pair of them as thick as thieves. She turned her anger at her youngest child onto the one standing in front of her and a full scale argument ensued complete with slamming doors and stomping up the staircase.

Carmen opened the package given to her by the taxi driver shortly before eleven o'clock that evening under the sceptical gaze of her friend. She knew the reason for the phone, Paul had explained to Helen that his mother had stopped his contract and his original phone was as good as useless, the reason behind the ring was less clear but she loved it and prised it from its decorative box, sliding it onto the middle finger of her right hand. The letter Paul had enclosed with the gifts had her in tears, for all the trouble his mother had caused, he apologised, the rest of the letter was filled with his feelings for her and his plans for their future and all of the things he had so far kept locked inside.

She waited until she was sure Helen was asleep before she removed the mobile phone from its box and turned it on. Her heart was pounding as she dialled his number, knowing it was late but needing to talk to him, to hear his voice, she jumped as the phone on the other end of the line began to ring, the sound seeming unbearably loud in the otherwise silent house.

Paul turned over in his sleep and pulled the covers up over his shoulders, the ringing phone had disturbed him and he wished someone would answer it. Suddenly he jumped on realising the sound wasn't the house phone, it was his new mobile and only one person had the number.

"Carmen?" He asked feeling stupid as it had to be her then comforting himself with the knowledge that she didn't know he had purchased the phone for the sole intention of talking to her. He struggled with the covers and managed to sit up as he listened to her speak, his hopes swelling with every word from her mouth. They talked for hours, finally getting to say all the things they had yearned too until eventually, Carmen told him that the battery on her phone was just about to die, he promised to call her the following day, smiling and happy as he snuggled beneath the covers again.

When he finally crawled out of bed the following morning and sauntered down to the kitchen, it was to find Monica sitting with her parents waiting for him to surface. He greeted all three adults and then proceeded to make some breakfast while Paula provided him with a steaming cup of tea.

"Once you have eaten, you need to get dressed, you are coming to the police station with me." Monica told him.

"Has something happened?" he asked.

"Everything is fine, you're presence has been requested."

"This again? What's the point Mum? I'm not going to tell them anything." The bright, sunny mood he had woken up with evaporated with her words.

"You will do as you are told, it's only a matter of time before you realise that what happened was wrong and then you will want some recompense."

A silent car journey later and Paul and Monica were shown through to an interview room where they were left to wait. Monica passed the time rummaging through her sizable handbag while Paul looked around the dismal grey room, drumming his fingers on the melamine table in front of him as he observed the chips in the paint and scrapes along the walls giving the room a general unkempt air. He sat forward, elbows on the table as two officers entered the room and introduced themselves.

Sitting opposite the boy, the female officer could clearly see what her colleague who had previously interviewed him was talking about; he was a work of art to look at with dark brown, almost black fashionably scruffy hair, olive skin and large almond shaped, inscrutable brown eyes rimmed with thick black lashes above impressive cheek bones, a straight nose and full lips. The green t-shirt strained over broad shoulders, the sleeves clung to the muscled upper arms and the fibres stretching under the expanse of chest with each breath. His lower arms were tanned and tapered down to large, work roughened hands with long, elegant fingers. She couldn't see his legs but deduced that they were long as she pulled her chair closer to the table as his feet were resting on the floor, crossed at the ankle almost on her side of the table. She made eye contact with him as she finished her evaluation and was surprised to see that he was appraising her with equal interest, he didn't look away when her eyes met his but the lazy grin that twitched the side of his lips and the twinkle in his eye was unmistakeable and she knew without a doubt that this boy would stick to his guns, making this little episode nothing more than a waste of everyone's time, he exuded confidence and arrogance in equal measure, he knew without a doubt that if he didn't give anything away, they didn't have a case.

Try as they might, they couldn't get him to own up to having an underage relationship with his teacher, the situation not helped in the slightest by the prompting from his mother. Eventually, Paul smiled, crossed his arms over his chest and leant back in his chair, his bulk making it creek in protest.

"I'm pretty sure I am correct by thinking that you have nothing to go on, you can't bring charges against me in any way shape or form therefore, if I were to get up and walk out of that door, there is absolutely nothing you can do to stop me?" He questioned, the most he had said all morning.

"That's right." The male officer confirmed.

"Fine." He stood, putting his weight on his fingertips as he leant closer to the officers "I'm sure the taxpayers would appreciate you wasting their money on this fruitless venture especially as you have failed on no more than five separate occasions to get me to talk. Did you really think I would be intimidated by this situation?" He turned to Monica "Are you coming? I'm done here."

"No you are not." Monica scowled.

"Look Mum, if you want to stay in this.." he paused, looking around the room "Ahem, delightful room, that's up to you, I'd quite like a lift home but I'll happily catch the bus if you feel you need to stick the knife in further." He held the door open for her and before passing through himself, turned back to the officers and shot them a dazzling smile.

"Bloody full of himself that one." The male officer commented, shuffling his notes

"Yeah but you have to hand it to him, he handled himself very well, mark my words, he'll be a force to be reckoned with when he's older."

Paul went straight to his room when Monica dropped him off at his Grandparents house, he had left her no room or cause for conversation on the way home and Monica knew that if she didn't let this situation lie she would lose her son. She resolved to tell him at the weekend that she was prepared to drop the charges and that she would very much like it if he were to return home.

He helped his Grandparents over the weekend to prepare for the meal they had planned for his parents, setting up the long dining table, extending it and adding the additional leaves so that the guests would be seated with plenty of elbow room. He attempted to help Paula in the kitchen but only managed to get in the way; he ran laughing from the kitchen, his Grandmother brandishing a large wooden spoon at his retreating back.

After a stint at the gym and a quick shower on returning home, he settled down on his bed and flicked on the television, finding nothing of interest to watch, he reached for his phone and dialled Carmen's number, smiling broadly when she answered. His smile was short lived however as he explained the police station fiasco, kicking himself for mentioning it as Carmen flipped out, screaming down the phone at him, telling him in no uncertain terms what she thought of his mother.

Although he wasn't exactly seeing eye to eye with Monica at that precise moment in time, Paul felt his hackles rise at Carmen's insults of the woman who had given him life and he let his temper have full rein, keeping his voice low, he told her succinctly how he felt, not giving her room to defend herself and when he had finished, promptly hung up and turned off his phone, breathing heavily. He lay back on his bed, his hands in his hair as he replayed what he had said in his mind "Shit," he whispered, knowing he now had an awful lot of apologising to do to both women.

It was with a heavy heart that he set out on his shopping trip to find an anniversary gift for his parents, well, for Monica; he had already given Tessa some money to buy a bottle of vintage brandy for Michael, what he wanted for Monica would take hours of sorting through pawn brokers and second hand shops, he exhausted every avenue but was pleased with his finds, he was weary and grimy on returning to his Grandparents house, wrapping the gifts before allowing himself a long soak in a hot bath.

With his skin tingling pleasantly from the hot water and wrapped in a towel, he sat on the edge of his bed and, steeling himself, called Carmen. He relaxed when the first thing she did was apologise for shouting at him the previous evening and he offered his apology in return only to become irritated when she berated him for turning off his phone, his mood turning sour when she once again began to point out Monica's failings as a mother.

"Aren't you going to say anything?" She asked upon realising that the protestations on the other end of the line had stopped.

"I don't think I have anything to say." He sighed "I don't want to argue Carmen but you must know Mum was only trying to protect me."

"And in doing so, she ruined my career; I have been suspended from my job pending an investigation. The police are in regular attendance here and at the school and now the local press have got hold of it, she's made me look like a paedophile."

"I'm sure it wasn't her intention, I'm sorry for all the trouble I've caused."

"So you should be, I told you this was a bad idea from the start," she snapped "You'd better be prepared to start supporting me as it's looking highly likely that I'm going to lose my job."

"That's fine, you know I will support you," his reply "I want to see you."

She replied after a short silence "I'd like to see you too."

"I'll see if I can get someone to drive me up."

It was her turn to sigh, the fact that he was too young even to drive bringing home how young he was "You are such a child" she whispered, she had meant it kindly but Paul took a firm grasp of the wrong end of the stick and gave it a thorough shake

"I was man enough for you." He spat.

"Paul, you took that the wrong way, I wasn't having a dig."

"How was I supposed to take that comment?" He growled, he raked his fingers through his hair, jumped up from his bed and began pacing his room, "I'm going to go before I say something I shouldn't."

"Fine, you do that, you made your feelings more than clear last night, I hadn't realised you were such a Mummy's boy."

"Ah, you know what Carmen, out of the two of us; it's you who needs to grow up, not me. Call me when you are in a better state of mind." Tiring of pacing, he sat once again on his bed, his head in his hands, admitting that the situation he was in was a little too much for him to deal with on his own, he needed help.

Only a few short hours later, his family arrived for the opulent meal provided by his Grandparents. Studiously ignoring his father, Paul managed to get Monica to one side;

"Happy anniversary Mum." He said, presenting her with a sizable box "It's from me and Matt." He finished; he would have to tell his brother later what they had bought their Mother.

"It's heavy," she took the box from him, placing it on the kitchen table, she began to break through the wrapping, opening the box to reveal vast amount of packaging material, delving into the polystyrene quavers, her fingers connected with smooth cold china. Freeing the first of many cups and saucers from the box, she gasped as she recognised the pattern "Paul, where did you find these?"

"I've been searching since we broke them," he explained as he removed further items from the box "They're the same pattern and batch number as the pieces of the tea set you already have so they should match perfectly."

"Thank you," she reached for him then, hugging him fiercely "You shouldn't have."

"I'll keep looking until you have a complete set again." He told her.

"Matthew doesn't know anything about this does he?" she asked, willing him not to lie to her.

"No." He answered "I meant to tell him but I forgot, don't say anything to him."

"I won't." She smiled, he had spoken the truth.

"Mum, can we talk?" he asked, shuffling his feet.

"Of course."

Paul opened his mouth to speak but before he could make a sound, Jackson called her name asking her to join them in the living room.

"Can you keep it until later?" She asked, he was deflated as he nodded at her and followed her out of the kitchen.

"You ok?" Matt asked as he flopped onto the sofa next to Paul.

"Yeah," Paul grinned at his brother "We have started replacing Mum's china by the way, we got her some bits as an anniversary present."

"Cool, you are the best brother a guy could have," Matt heaved a sigh of relief "So what you been up too?"

"Work mainly. I got a new mobile; I'll give you the number before you leave."

"So you aren't coming home anytime soon?"

"I don't know," he shrugged "I love it here but it's not the same as being at home, I miss my bed and the sound of you farting the night away."

Matt laughed "I aim to please."

Monica surveyed her family gathered around the table. Her parents at one end and Michael's at the other, her brother, seated opposite her had resisted the urge to bring his current conquest with him and was therefore seated next to Paul who had Matthew on his right followed by Michael holding court with Charles and Penelope. Tessa sat next to her with Kay completing the party on Tessa's other side.

As always with one of her parents' parties, the food was opulent and the wine flowed freely along with the conversation and laughter. She appraised each of her children as they held their own in the conversations around the table, Tessa, mature and sure of her opinion but prepared to listen to an alternative point of view, considering it before she put forward her reply.

Matthew, smiling, taking comments lightly and bringing his sense of humour to the forefront of his replies, his face was red and Monica realised that he was slightly drunk; she leant forward and got his attention before softly telling him to lay off the wine and eat a little more.

And then there was Paul, her troublesome son who she loved to distraction, he was quiet today which was unusual when near his Spanish family as the knowledge that his father couldn't understand a single word he said usually buoyed him up and made him a lively contributor to conversations, but not today. He used the fork in his left hand to push the food around his plate but not once did he lift it to his mouth, his right hand was wrapped around his wine glass, his eyes lowered as he watched the food move from one side of his plate to the other.

He drained his wine glass and reached for the bottle, upending it over his glass and sitting back in his seat, he murmured a reply to some comment John made, the jist of which she didn't quite catch but whatever it was brought a frown to her sons' brow. She wished she had made the time to talk to him when he had asked her for he was obviously on the verge of what his sixteen years would consider a great revelation and she knew from experience that his brooding silence was never a good thing.

"Paul? Perhaps you would like to come home tonight?" She asked, her hand touching his as he reached for another bottle of wine

"I think you should know the whole story before you make that offer." Unsurprisingly, he had answered in Spanish.

The discussion at the other end of the table had become loud and heated in the exchange between Charles and Michael. As usual, they were talking about the direction Charles had seen his company heading in before Michael had taken over the former now berating his son for his slow action and lack of forward planning, he proceeded to tell his son in no uncertain terms to pull his finger out and put the plans into fruition and that perhaps he would someday actually be man enough to run the company without his added assistance, Charles was, after all, supposed to be in retirement.

More than a little drunk and with his manhood in question, Michael raised his voice above that of his fathers' and let rip with a steaming diatribe of what made a man, which according to Michael's philosophy included running one's own successful business, make enough money to support oneself and sire a child.

To each point his father had made, Paul had replied, again in Spanish, "Done that, doing that and huh, hatrick"

Monica had shot Paul a warning look as he answered each of Michael's comments in turn, nearly choking on the food in her mouth at the last word.

"What did you say?" she asked, speaking English.

Knowing he had allowed the alcohol to loosen his tongue and he had said too much, Paul backtracked "Nothing, I was just amusing myself."

"You said hatrick when your father mentioned children." Monica hissed but by now the conversation had died down, she had everyone's attention.

"It was nothing, I was messing about." Paul replied to Monica in Spanish, painfully aware that all eyes were on them.

"What are you talking about?" Michael's voice broke the silence in the room.

Monica cleared her throat, tearing her eyes from her son, she addresses her husband, "We were just discussing the points you made Michael, would you mind repeating them?"

"I was merely saying my dear that in order to be considered a man, one should have a successful business."

"Done that" Paul answered, in English this time.

John hastily lent towards his nephew telling him that he needed to find another answer to the third part of Michael's statement to which Paul had shrugged and easily switching back to Spanish said "What's the point, it's out there now." while Michael continued; "One should also make enough profit from said business to support oneself."

"Doing that" Paul reached for the wine, filled his glass and downed it quickly.

"And of course, the ultimate proof of manhood, sire a child" Michael sat back, pleased with himself.

"As I said before." Paul stood and looked at Monica "Hatrick."

"What do you mean Hatrick?" Michael asked confused "Sit down boy, you are making a fool out of yourself."

"Well Dad." Paul started, he stumbled slightly as he pushed his chair away, the wine rushing to his head, "I run my own successful business, I do make enough money to support myself and I have, with the help of my older, school teacher girlfriend, sired a child so I guess that makes me a man doesn't it?" He asked the silent room, taking a further stumbling step away from the table, he turned to face them, "Ladies, I apologise if I have spoiled your afternoon," he was slurring his words now "But fuck this, I'm going to bed."

"He's going to regret those wine filled balls very soon." John sighed.

"You've done WHAT?" Michael shouted also on his feet and making quick strides towards his son, there was a commotion on the other side of the table as Monica extricated herself from her seat and was encouraging Paula to move out of her way. Michael had Paul pinned against the wall by his throat by the time she reached them.

"Michael, he's drunk, he doesn't know what he's saying." She protested.

Ignoring his wife, Michael addressed Paul "Not only have you brought shame upon this family from your endless fist fights, you have in the past been expelled from school and now you take up with a teacher and get her pregnant, how much more do we have to take from you boy? You have been trouble from the day you were born, I saw it, it amazes me that no one else has and that they repeatedly defend you but this is the last straw, you are no son of mine."

"That's fine." Paul slurred "But according to your little speech back there, I am a fully fledged man, I am successful and people do genuinely like me so perhaps you," he poked Michael in the chest "should show me a little more fucking respect." His reactions slowed by alcohol, Paul didn't actually see the fist that knocked him out cold.

Michael felt something snap inside his head, the fact that his very first blow knocked Paul out cold only served to fuel his rage, by the time John, Matt, Charles and Jackson managed to pull him away from the beating he continued to give his unconscious son, he was sweating profusely and panting from the effort of it.

"Who the hell does he think he is to speak to me like that?" He howled as he was dragged out of the room.

"He's a child Michael and he needs our help, you only make matters worse," Monica screamed at him "Don't you ever touch him again."

A few hours later, Paul opened his eyes and very quickly closed them again; the pain in his head was similar to a jack hammer, intense white noise accompanied by throbbing;

"Ow." he murmured, his fingers pressing into his eyes, trying in vain to still the pulsing light that flashed behind them.

"I take it your hang over is in full swing?" John asked from his perch on the side of the bed.

"Uhuh," Paul replied "pain killers would be really helpful right about now."

"Dude, you are my hero." Matt's voice now "You fronted up to Dad big time, his head almost exploded when you told him to show you some respect."

"I did what?" Paul sat up, clutching his head and groaning at the intense pain in his head the movement had caused, as the duvet fell away, he saw the bruises that were starting to form on his body "Why the hell did you let me say that?" he asked his brother.

"There was no stopping you, you were on a roll." Matt told him "Mum's in shock at your revelation."

"Will you stop talking in riddles?" Paul snapped "Just tell me what happened, I don't remember anything after talking to you yesterday afternoon." And by the time John and Matt had filled him in on the afternoons event, Paul felt nauseous, sitting with his head in his hands, he groaned "I have seriously fucked up," he threw his legs over the side of the bed, wincing as he felt the bruises across his ribs accommodate themselves to the movement, standing in front of the mirror, he surveyed the damage and was surprised that it was remarkably less than he had received before and his face only had a few marks across his left cheek bone and a slight split in his lip

"Where's Mum?" He asked, taking the shirt that Matt held out to him.

"Downstairs." Matt replied.

"And Dad?"

"He went home with Tessa."

"I have to talk to Mum." Paul told the men in his room.

"I'm not sure that's advisable right now," John spoke "She's reeling, she knew you had something else to tell her but she never guessed that it would be a potential grandchild."

"There's nothing potential about it," Paul's shoulders sagged, "It's going to happen." Sighing then, he reached for the door handle "If I'm the man I proclaim to be, I have to tackle this head on." He told them.

Monica looked drained when he approached her, for the first time he noticed the strands of grey in her hair and her usual graceful stance had disappeared.

"Mum?" He said softly "Do you feel up to talking?" He asked, painfully aware of his Grandparents watching them.

"Let's go into the garden," she left her chair and led him outside, down the garden to the pergola where she sat heavily in the wooden chair.

"I'm so sorry." Paul blurted sitting beside her.

She didn't answer or look at him for a very long time, lost in her own thoughts, the sound of him striking a match and lighting a cigarette bringing her back from the turmoil of her mind.

"You should have told me sooner." She said quietly

"I know. I wanted to. I just didn't know how to go about it."

"Blurting it out in a drunken stupor seemed like the best idea did it?"

"I don't even remember doing it," he admitted "Mum. I need your help."

"Yes you do." She looked at him then and saw that the strain of keeping this secret had taken its toll on him "You are too young to be a parent."

"I know but it's going to happen, there's nothing I can do about it and I don't want to be one of those guys who doesn't take responsibility for his actions."

"What were you thinking when you went with her?"

"Like I told you before, she was hot and she made it a challenge, clearly I wasn't thinking with my head." He admitted the hint of a smile on her lips wasn't lost on him.

"You told me you loved her."

"I do," he pushed his fingers into his hair, a gesture she loved and she felt her heart begin to melt "It's difficult being apart from her and we have been arguing a lot," he took a deep pull on his cigarette, blew out the smoke then stubbed it out "I have to talk to her face to face at some point."

"So do I." Monica told him, holding up her hand to quiet his protests "Paul, if you want my help, I will have to talk to her, especially if you are set on being a father to this child, we will need to arrange visits, maintenance etc etc."

"I intend moving up there after its born."

"Absolutely not! I forbid it and you are not to argue with me on this. Believe it or not Paul, I do know what's best for you and if you are prepared to listen and work with me on this, I will help you as much as is humanly possible. First things first, you pack your things, you are coming home."

"Do you think that's a good idea as I have clearly visible bruises?" He asked,

"I want you home. Your father and I will discuss it when you are there but I warn you Paul, if you do anything to provoke him, you will receive a far harsher punishment than any you have had so far."

"I don't want him to have anything to do with this." Paul put his foot down.

"He knows of course but I will ask him to leave it to me to sort out." She confirmed. "You should have come to me sooner."

"I know, I wanted so badly to tell you when I realised I had actual feelings for her but it's so difficult to tell your parent that you are banging your school teacher, are madly in love with her oh, and have possibly got her pregnant." He sighed "Where do we go from here?" He asked.

"From now on, you need to tell me everything and it needs to be the complete truth. I'm so angry with you right now, you know you can trust me but you chose to keep it to yourself, I am very disappointed in you."

"I'm sorry, I promise, I will tell you everything from now on. I love you Mum."

"You break my heart, do you know that?" She responded unable to stop the tears gathering on her lashes "I love you so much and yet around every corner there is some problem or other waiting for you, you used to come to me."

"I'm growing up," he reached for her hand "I know I can't make this right Mum but I can make it better for you and Carmen, I just need time."

"You are going to be a good father to this child whether you want to or not." She told him. "You do know there's no future in this relationship of yours?"

"Don't say that, it feels right when I am with her, it's everyone else's reaction to it that makes it seem sordid and dirty."

"It is sordid and dirty, there are no two ways about it. Paul, you will have to behave yourself when you come home, you will have to obey the rules that will be set out for you."

Paul sighed "I know," he looked down at his hands "I'd better go and pack."

She watched him walk away, his head bowed but his back was straight, his shoulders squared. She admired him for facing his responsibilities; she just wished that trouble and problems weren't his permanent companions. He was such a loving soul, kind and thoughtful, his anniversary gift bore testament to his thoughtfulness. She shook her head, she had firmly put herself between her son and her husband, a place she didn't want to be but the son needed protection from the father and from his own quick temper which would flare at the slightest provocation from Michael.

Chapter Fourteen

The atmosphere in the Jensen house could be cut with a knife. Tessa had up until now, denied all knowledge of her fathers' treatment of her brothers' and Michael's attack on Paul had chilled her to the bone. Admitting that although Paul had provoked the reaction, the fact that Michael had continue to beat him once he was unconscious made her feel sick every time she thought about it. She had never seen her father quite so angry and focussed and Paul had been defenceless, her sympathy and understanding were now on the side of her brother.

While Paul unpacked his bags and reacquainted himself with his siblings, Monica and Michael discussed what they should do with their wayward son and built their own bridges towards forgiveness and understanding.

Sitting opposite each other on their beds, Matt and Paul listened to the raised voices coming from the study. Paul jumped when their bedroom door opened, relaxing at the sight of his sister. Tessa sat on the bed next to Matt, leaning her back against his muscled bicep as she lit three cigarettes, passing her brothers' one each.

"You've really done it this time." She said, glancing sideways at Paul.

"Yeah I know. I'm sorry guys, I realise that you are going to get some of the backlash." He replied.

"What are you going to do?" She asked.

"I think that's being decided for me." He inclined his head towards the voices of his parents.

"I can't believe you will go along with everything they decide." She scoffed.

"I probably won't in the long run, there's only so much time they can dedicate to watching me and as far as they are aware, I work all day and that gives me plenty of opportunity to make my own plans."

"You aren't even going to try are you?" Tessa accused.

"Of course I am, if I'm going to get Mum's help, I have to but they have to realise that just because they say something, doesn't make it so. I have things I need to discuss with Carmen and there's the purchase of a house which is going to happen whether they like it or not. What it all boils down to is I got my girlfriend knocked up, in reality, it wouldn't matter if she were my age or not, they would still have reacted the same and so would I , I'm going to take care of Carmen and the baby, they can't prevent that no matter how much they try."

"I have to admire you for taking reasonability." She conceded.

"I can't just walk away from this Tessa, you know me well enough to know that."

"I think you're stupid" Matt blurted.

"Thanks Matt," the sarcasm was thick in Paul's voice

"Face it Paul, you've ruined your life, you are sixteen and you're thinking about raising a kid, seriously stupid. If I was you, I'd insist she got rid of it, cut all ties with her and get a life."

"You aren't me. We discussed our options, adoption isn't one of them and neither of us could come up with any real reason to get rid of it and I haven't ruined my life. I'll admit that this is a setback in the grand scheme of things but my life is in no way ruined and I will make sure that my child has a good life too just you wait and see."

The house phone stopped their conversation as Tessa bolted into the hall, returning and telling Paul the call was for him. The resulting conversation couldn't have come at a better time for him; he was smiling and already forming plans in his head when he hung up from speaking to the local council. He had completely forgotten submitting the quote for re-designing areas of the local park over the winter in preparation for it re-opening in the spring; it was a massive undertaking and one that would keep his work force busy over the winter months and make him an awful lot of money along the way.

PRODIGAL SON

Upon his summons to the study, Paul studiously kept his gaze from meeting Michael's for fear of what might be misconstrued in his own eyes. He sat and listened to the rules laid out to him with which he was expected to comply without protest or complaint.

Having owned up to the purchase of another phone, this was the first thing that was taken from him although he was told he would be allowed to speak to Carmen but only in the presence of one or both parents. He would not be permitted to socialise for the foreseeable future either after work or at weekends, he was expected to fill this time helping around the house and learning aspects of Michael's business, further restrictions were placed on the amount of time he would be permitted to watch television or listen to or practise music. They recognised that he was now a young man and did concede to one outing a month for him in which he would be allowed to see his friends but there would be a strict curfew to be adhered too.

Michael and Monica had decided that he should no longer pay rent, that money would be put into a high interest savings account and he was expected to honour his commitment to the child by adding to the account each month, the account would be held in Michael's name, the money would be returned to Paul for him to pass onto his child upon reaching the age of twenty one provided Paul hadn't sired any further children outside of marriage. If however, more children were born, the money would be split equally between them.

Paul felt he had little option but to agree to the terms, he did however, ask to put on hold joining Michael even part time at Jensen's, all Michael's protests were put on hold when Paul explained about the prestigious job he had won for the local council, pointing out that the park was within walking distance from home and therefore they would easily be able to check up on him. He also asked to be allowed to go to the gym three times a week under the guise of working out, he had made a lot of friends at the gym and the time spent there would kill two birds with one stone. After a brief discussion, he was given permission for this but informed that he should go straight from work on the agreed nights and under no circumstances was he allowed to be out after seven o'clock.

Within a few weeks, Paul found that playing by the rules made life at home surprisingly pleasant, not that he had much time to dwell on it, the work in the park was extensive and exhausting and, given the current horrendous weather conditions, extremely messy. Monica refused to let him in the house wearing his work clothes, insisting that he strip down to his boxer shorts and put his soiled clothes into the washing machine before being allowed upstairs to shower. Shivering from the icy air in the unheated utility room, he adhered to this rule every night before making a mad dash for a steaming hot shower.

Monica was especially impressed with his behaviour. Not once had he complained or sulked at the restrictions placed upon him, in fact, he seemed to be positively thriving under the circumstances, making her wonder why she hadn't been stricter with him earlier.

She allowed him to hold his meetings with his staff at the house, letting them use the kitchen and making sure they had a healthy supply of sandwiches, impressed with the way her son conducted himself with these much older and far more experienced men. She watched their faces as he talked and saw not one hint or resentment that this mere boy was running this business and taking home more than each man present.

As the meetings became a regular occurrence, she learned the names of Paul's workers, she heard them talking and discussing ideas when Paul had left the room to take a call or to fetch some plans and with a start realised that these men held enormous respect for her son and the more she listened the more she understood why. Paul listened to his men, often implementing their ideas alongside his own and freely admitting when one of them suggested something, that he had no clue where to start with that and would they teach him. She realised Paul had the potential to be an extremely successful business man and made it her personal goal to make sure she helped him every step of the way.

"He's a good kid Mrs Jensen; maybe you could lighten up on him a little." Phil, Paul's foreman commented as he left the house one evening after handing in that week's time sheets.

Secretly, Monica was inclined to agree but succinctly informed the man that rules were rules and Paul had done his fair share of breaking them in the past for which he was now paying the price.

A week previously, Phil had listened to Paul's explanation of his drunken stumble down the stairs, the reason for the bruises on his face and his stiffness in moving, the bruising over his ribs jabbing him each and every time he stretched.

"Come on lad," Phil cajoled as he and the rest of the men warmed their hands on their plastic cups of tea on a break from digging "It's well known that your old man is harsh with his discipline, you don't have to cover it up, we know he's knocked seven types of shit out of you."

Paul looked into the murky brown liquid squirming over the serrations in his cup, for some unfathomable reason, he felt ashamed, he couldn't admit that Michael had done this to him, not meeting Phil's eyes he simply replied "We'd better get this finished" neither denying or confirming their suspicions.

He was allowed a phone call to Carmen once a week, during which both Monica and Michael were present making conversation between them strained and stilted, only once did Carmen crack, asking quietly when she would see him.

"I don't know, they have me locked up tighter than a nun's arsehole so it's anyone's guess when I will be allowed out into the big wide world again." His comment earning him a scowl from Monica, Michael was unable to suppress his smile.

"I want you." Carmen whispered.

"Oh God." Paul groaned, closing his eyes. "I have to go."

The news of Carmen's affair with a student hit the Gloucester papers like an atomic bomb once she was officially sacked from her job. There had been rumours of course, but it was only when the school confirmed her dismissal and the reason behind it that she began to be hounded by the local press. It wasn't long before the news went national and from there it took very little time to connect Carmen to Paul thanks to one or two of his previous girlfriends.

"Mum!" Paul shouted as he let himself into the utility room and began to strip "There's press everywhere." He finished as she opened the door into the house.

"Haven't you seen the paper?" She asked, Paul shook his head.

Clothed only in his shorts, he stood by the breakfast bar and began to read the article, "Shit, how did this get out?" He asked then groaned as he read the names of the girls who had eagerly parted with information. "Has Dad seen this?"

"I would expect so judging from the phone call I had from him" she replied, and there it was, that flash of fear in her son's eyes "He's furious but it will be alright, you should stay out of his way for a few days." she placated.

"A few days? Mum, Carmen's' not due for another few months, this isn't going away any time soon." He answered, his mind was reeling, he suddenly felt trapped and wanted to run "He's going to kill me this time" he had spoken quietly, more to himself than her.

"No he's not, he won't touch you." She reached out, smoothing down his windblown hair "I promise you that," she closed the paper and threw it in the bin "Go and get cleaned up, I'll bring your dinner up to you, stay in your room this evening."

Paul flinched when two hours later, the front door slammed and Michael bellowed his name from the bottom of the stairs. Now he didn't know what to do for the better, stay in his room as directed by

Monica or go to his father. He was saved from his indecision when Monica quickly stuck her head around his bedroom door and told him to stay put, the row between husband and wife that ensued was of epic proportions the like of such would never again be repeated within the walls of the Jensen house.

When Matt returned home, he found his brother a quivering wreck on the edge of his bed. Having read the newspapers, he knew what the argument was about. Sitting by his brother, he nudged him with his shoulder;

"It's going to be alright." He told him.

"I don't know Matt. Have you ever heard Mum shout at Dad like that?" Paul asked.

"Nope, didn't know the old girl had it in her." Matt admitted.

"What if he lashes out at her? It'll be my fault."

"He won't. Dad's not that evil." He assured.

"Can I borrow your phone?" Paul asked, he couldn't stand it anymore.

Matt knew better than to ask what Paul was going to do, he didn't want any part of it, the less he knew, the better off he would be "I won't say you can borrow it," he said "But I'm going to hop in the shower, if you should happen to find it amongst my stuff while I'm in the bathroom then I'd know nothing about it." He grinned as he left the room.

Paul made three calls, the first to Phil with a brief explanation of his plans and asking the older man if he could carry on with the job in his absence, adding that he would send time sheets and job cards in the next few days. The next was to Carmen, telling her he was on his way and would explain when he got there, the third and possibly most important call was to his Uncle John, pleading for a ride to Gloucester. When John heard the raised voices carrying to him down the phone line, he agreed to get his nephew as far away from the house as possible, hastily dressed and kissed the breathless girl in his bed goodbye before setting out into the cold winters' night.

Half way into the journey, they stopped for fuel and food. John observed his nephew over the melamine table between them. The boy had been visibly trembling when he jumped into the car and threw his bag into the back seat and try as he might; John was unable to draw him into conversation. Watching him now, he noticed the trembling had stopped only to be replaced by hunched shoulders and a scowl worthy of a Greek God.

"You know I wouldn't have left my occupied bed for anyone else right?" John asked.

"Yeah." Paul sat up straighter and looked at his Uncle "Sorry I dragged you into this. If I had known you were on a promise I'd have waited."

"But you would still have dragged me into it?" John replied with an amused smile "Don't worry about it kid, like I've told you before, I'm on your side and I'm more than capable of handling my sister." He swallowed the last of his surprisingly good coffee "Let's hit the road."

A few hours later, the drifted to a stop outside a rundown house in a ramshackle estate, neither of them making a move to leave the car.

"Not exactly what I'd pictured." Paul spoke, he shifted in his seat and reached for his bag.

"It's hardly up market is it?" John replied "But then perhaps we are snobs and far too used to the finer things in life."

"Now we really need to sell that house. Carmen can't bring the baby back here."

"It's probably better once you get inside." John suggested hopefully only to receive a baleful look from his nephew "Ok so that's wishful thinking. I'll crack on with the house first thing tomorrow." He promised.

"Thanks for everything John." Paul reached for the door handle.

"No problem. Listen, call me if you need anything ok?" He asked, Paul nodded "Do you have money?"

A smile then "Of course."

"Ok, make sure you call Monica, just let her know you are alright."

"I will." He answered as he stepped out of the car and into the freezing night air.

A security light snapped on as he approached the door, temporarily blinding him. While he waited for the door to be answered, he glanced around the facade of the house in the glare of the light and noticed that it was in a sorry state of repair making him even more determined to get Carmen out of here.

"You'd better come in."

The voice had startled him, he turned from his appraisal of the house to see and painfully thin blond woman staring at him.

"Helen?" he asked.

"Of course." She stepped aside and allowed him inside the shabby but clean house. She recognised him from the pictures in the papers and had to admit they hadn't done him justice.

Paul hovered as Helen closed and locked the door then gestured for him to follow her through to the kitchen where they found Carmen trying to tempt Helen's robustly protesting son to eat his dinner a task quickly forgotten when she saw him.

As she came to her feet, Paul took in the large bump of her abdomen and the increased size of her breasts through the tight fitting top and experienced the simultaneous squeeze of his heart and tightening of his groin "Carmen" his voice barely above a whisper as he shortened the gap between them, ignoring Helen's loud cluck of disapproval when he wrapped his arms around her and pulled her into a long awaited kiss.

Finally loosening his grip, Paul held her at arm's length as he drank in the delicious site of her voluptuous body. Hesitantly, he reached out to lay the open palm of his hand over the mound of her stomach, a smile playing on his lips.

Carmen watched the growing wonder in his eyes as she felt his warm hand on her, she couldn't help it when she swayed towards him, the physical draw of him was too much for her, with hormones flooding her body, his presence only serving to heighten them, all she wanted right now was him, naked beneath her, she didn't want to talk, she didn't want explanations and excuses, she wanted to dig her nails into his flesh and make him groan.

"God. Would you two come and sit down, if it isn't hard enough getting him to eat anyway, you are causing far too much distraction." Helen cut into their thoughts, they started guiltily and hastily sat. "So, Paul," she began whilst deftly shoving a spoon into her sons' mouth "Is there any particular reason you chose to show your face now?"

Carmen cut in before he could reply "Helen, leave him alone, he's just got here, we can tackle his reasons tomorrow."

"Fine." Helen answered alternating her glare between her friend and the teenager at her table "You'd better find him somewhere to stay then hadn't you."

"He's staying here" Carmen replied.

"Oh, I beg to differ. I'm more than happy for you to stay here but putting him up is an entirely different matter. Our lives are disrupted enough by the constant streams of reporters and photographers trying to get a glimpse of you without the added attraction of him coming and going."

"There's no press outside now." Paul commented.

"Then it would be a good time for you to leave." Helen answered "Besides, it's so cold outside at the moment that they tend to disappear when the sun goes down."

"It's not much warmer in here," he told her, wishing the instant the jibe came out of his mouth that he'd bitten his tongue.

"I take it you remember the way to the door?" Helen snarled at him.

Paul stood, his long confinement at home and the fraught evening had served to fuel his temper and he bit back the stinging retort bouncing around his head "If I could just make use of your facilities, I'll be happy to leave." He said tightly.

The venomous hissed argument that took place while he was in the bathroom had the desired effect and by the time he returned to the kitchen to say goodbye, he was told he could stay but that he would under no circumstances be allowed into Carmen's room and he was sleeping on the sofa. When Helen took Luke upstairs to bath him and read him a bedtime story, Carmen snuggled close to Paul on the sofa, explaining to him that Helen slept like she was dead and she would come and get him when the coast was clear. He made mild protestations at this deception but once Carmen laid her hand over his groin and whispered in no uncertain terms what she wanted to do to him, he was one hundred percent behind the idea.

He was dozing in between fits of shivering as the house was horribly cold when Carmen came for him, silently leading him up the stairs and to her room, closing the door, perching on the bed and beckoning him forward. Leaning down to kiss her, he could feel her hands all over him, opening his jeans, prying off the layers of clothing over his torso, finally standing naked in front of her, goose bumps rising on his skin.

"Why is it so cold in here?" He asked, the freezing air distracting him from her mouth lapping at him.

"Helen doesn't like to leave the heating on for too long, she's afraid she won't be able to afford the bill." Carmen explained. She kissed his abs, licking where she had just kissed while her hands massaged him to erection, or at least tried. "What's wrong?" She asked, gently squeezing him before looking up into his eyes.

Observing his goose pimpled flesh and his still soft manhood, Paul was less than impressed with himself, "I'm freezing," he shivered "And as much as I would love to stand here and let you blow me, I think I'd rather be under the covers warming up right now."

"I'm sorry; I guess I've got used to being cold," she shuffled back across the bed and pulled back the covers, laying her head on his shoulder as he wrapped his arms around her, letting her hand drift once again to his groin.

"It doesn't help that the windows rattle every time there's a breeze" He complained half heartedly, her naked body and expert hands were beginning the have the desired effect.

"Perhaps you could do something about that while you are here, it would thaw Helen out towards you I'm sure. Kiss me."

With the bump of his baby pressing into him, Paul found it difficult to get as close as he wanted to her without angling his body away, his hand caressed the bump as his tongue played with hers, he felt movement under the skin and broke the kiss moving down to her swollen stomach, he pressed his lips to it, softly covering it with kisses, the baby kicked again.

"You aren't going to make this easy are you baby?" he spoke quietly to his child "Fair's fair little one, you've had her for months, now it's my turn."

"Stop it." She laughed, her hand in his hair.

"You are even more beautiful with the bump." He told her "I want you so badly but I have no idea how we are going to do this."

Carmen sat up and pulled him into another kiss, then, turning her back on him, she lowered herself onto her left side, guiding him behind her, her hand reaching backwards for him, smiling when she felt the warmth of his body pressed into her back and his hardness probing for entry.

"This isn't working," Paul whispered a few moments later "I can't feel anything," he withdrew and balanced on his knees, encouraging her on to all fours "Is this ok for you?" He asked.

"Yes, what are you waiting for?" she replied over her shoulder.

Paul wasted no time in ramming into her; she was ready for him, bracing her hands on the mattress, pushing back against him, smiling behind the veil of her hair when the long low groan escaped through his lips. His fingers were digging into her hips as he repeatedly powered into her, altering the speed and angle constantly making the experience more pleasurable for both of them. Although it lasted only moments, Paul was panting for breath and certainly warmer when it was over. He settled down happily, Carmen wrapped in his arms as they began to discuss everything that had happened over the months of their separation.

"Have you been with anyone else since we've been apart?" Carmen asked.

"No." He answered truthfully.

"You haven't learnt any new skills then?" She smiled in the darkness, knowing from his tone that he wasn't lying.

"You'd hate me if I had." He answered.

"True. Would you tell me if you had?"

"Probably not." Again the truth.

"Oh."

"Not because I wanted to lie," he explained "But because I wouldn't want to hurt you."

"I see." She answered.

"I have learned that if I have a wank with my left hand it feels like someone else is doing it," he admitted and heard her soft laugh "I also learned that getting blind drunk and announcing to your entire family during your parents anniversary dinner that you have got your girlfriend pregnant probably isn't the best way to inform them."

"You didn't?" she gasped, she hauled herself into a sitting position and switched on the bedside light, looking over at him, as he stretched out on the far side of the bed.

"I did."

"What happened?"

"My Dad went nuts or so I've been told, I was drunk, I don't remember saying anything, I apparently told him he should show me some respect, bad move." He shrugged.

"Did he hit you?"

"Yep. His first blow knocked me out, I didn't feel the others but the bruises let me know how much of a beating I got."

"You should stand up to him."

"There's no point, it only makes things worse."

"You are big enough to defend yourself though." Carmen countered.

"Yes." He agreed "And I know I can take him and that my temper is every bit as bad as his but I won't hit him, that would mean bringing myself down to his level and I won't stoop that low."

"You really have given this a lot of thought haven't you?"

"Uhuh. What scares me though is that one day he'll push me too far and I will lash out."

"It'll be no more than he deserves." Carmen countered.

"I know, but what if I take a swing at him and I can't stop? I'll kill him. I have it in me; I can feel it every time he has a go at me."

"You won't, you have far too much self control for that."

"I'm glad someone thinks that. I'm not so sure." He admitted. "Enough of that now, tell me more about Helen, I'm getting a serious man hater vibe off of her."

As they snuggled closer, warming each other with their body heat, Carmen explained that she and Helen had been friends since nursery school and were extremely close. Helen had married in her late teens, the boy in question had been her sweetheart all through secondary school and they had a close loving and faultless relationship right up until Luke was born whereon, Helen focused all of her attention on her baby, alienating her husband which in turn made him leave.

Initially concerned when her husband failed to return from his cigarette finding expedition, Helen contacted the police and reported him missing, it was a week later when the police tracked him down and he confirmed who he was and that he wouldn't be going home. The police duly informed her that the case was closed; her husband was alive and well and had no intention of returning home. Helen coped well with the news, consoling herself with the rearing of her son; she fell apart later that month when the divorce papers arrived.

Helen hadn't had the foresight to have herself either on the mortgage or deeds of the quaint two bedroom bungalow they lived in, resulting in her husband taking everything in an awful, drawn out divorce. He graciously gave her enough money to buy another property after the bungalow was sold along with a lump sum payment for child support before he disappeared from her life for good.

Carmen had taken leave of absence from college and cared for Luke whilst her friend slowly but surely pulled herself together. When the money ran out, Helen went into panic mode and would be forever grateful to Carmen for the shopping she brought and the clothing she provided for both her and her baby. Helen survived on a day to day basis on the small wage she received from her part time job but there was nothing left over for luxuries and she often went without food in order to feed her quickly growing child.

When he woke the following morning, the first thing Paul noticed again was how cold it was. His bare chest and shoulders were protruding from the covers and he shivered as he rescued the duvet and tuned to press his cold torso into Carmen's naked back.

Carmen shrugged him off. Covered entirely by the duvet, she was snugly warm and resented the intrusion of his cold skin against hers. Sighing, Paul left the bed and hastily donned his clothing before creeping down the stairs to the kitchen.

Opening the door, his heart dropped when he heard Helen cajoling her son to eat his breakfast but he couldn't help but smile at the robust blond child as he entered the room for the boys face and hair was smeared with cereal and he was slapping his hands happily in the spillage contained by the tray attached to his high chair.

"You didn't stay on the couch for long." Helen accused, accosting her son and cleaning him up.

"Er, yeah, sorry." He mumbled .

"Carmen's bed creaks," she continued, to her surprise, Paul blushed and she felt her steely resolve towards him softening "It's ok; it gets cold downstairs, just try to keep the noise down."

"Sorry." He repeated.

"Do you know how long you will be here?" She asked, Luke was holding his arms up to her, his protests getting louder as she ignored him.

"Not yet, that will depend on Carmen."

"Oh, ok. Do you want something to drink?" She asked, she heaved the wriggling child out of his high chair and set him on the floor where on his chubby legs promptly carried him to Paul.

"Tea thanks," Paul replied, hating the awkwardness "Helen, I do appreciate you letting me stay here."

"It's ok." She shrugged, not turning to look at him.

"I know it's been difficult for you having the press hanging around here, I'll sort it so that they leave you alone."

"You don't have to do that, they'll get bored eventually, some big story will hit sooner or later and you won't be flavour of the month anymore."

"Ok whatever, look Helen, please don't think I'm being condescending or trying to belittle you in way at all......"

"But," Helen prompted when he faltered.

"I've noticed a few things that I could help with around the house," he blurted. "Pretty much all of the windows need new putty and repainting at the very least and you are only single glazed, it's what I do, what I'm good at. I can put them right while I'm here."

"I know the house is a mess but I can't afford to do the repairs."

"No, no, I'd like to do it, call it a gift from me to you for looking after Carmen, besides, there's only so much she and I can talk about, it'll keep me busy and have the end result of warming the house up a bit, I just need someone to take me into town so that I can get everything I need."

"That's very kind of you, it would be a great help. Are you sure you don't mind?"

"Not at all" he smiled then and even she had to catch her breath "I'll get some money out of the bank while I'm there, it'll help towards the added bills you must have while Carmen's here."

"I don't want your money," she answered "He wants you to pick him up." She gestured to her son who was standing, arms raised by Paul's feet.

Paul stooped and swung the child into his arms, looking into the huge brown eyes, he smiled again "Hey bud," he crooned at the child "I just want to help you both out and I'm not boasting when I say I can afford it. Your friendship means a lot to Carmen and while I know you don't approve of our relationship, it makes it all the more poignant that you have helped her regardless of that. It's time I gave something back." He winced as the boy pulled his hair.

"Luke," Helen warned and stepped close enough to disentangle his hand from Paul's hair, she made the mistake of looking into the young man's face. She had to admit to herself that he was beautiful, and kind. "Do you love her?" She asked, this close, she would see if he hesitated or lied.

"Yes. I want what's best for her." He answered.

Satisfied that he had spoken the truth, she removed Luke from his arms and stepped away "I can see why she likes you so much." She put her toddler back on the floor "And it would be nice not to hear the windows rattle every time there is a slight breeze." She backhandedly accepted his help.

"Cool, can I have a pen and some paper, I'll make a list."

For the following week, Paul worked hard, fixing all of the windows throughout the house, even buying temporary double glazing and doing a general bit of decorating as well as plying both Helen and Carmen with vast amounts of money to stop both women worrying about forthcoming bills. Helen secretly admitted to herself that it was good to have a man about the house, outwardly; she admitted to Carmen that although Paul was still only a teenager in years, in attitude, he was very much a man and she completely understood what she saw in him.

Back in the Jensen house, all hell broke loose when Monica discovered Paul's absence. Having calmed Michael over the revelations in the papers, she had gone in search of her son only to find the bedroom empty. When Matt came out of the shower, he was questioned over his brothers' whereabouts; she became irate when Matt couldn't give her any information, positive that this son was lying to her. She cursed herself for taking Paul's phone from him, at least she would have had some line of communication even if, as she suspected, he didn't answer her calls immediately.

Chapter Fifteen

Coming up empty handed at home, her next port of call was her parent's house, again, they had no information for her but suggested that she try her brother as Paul and John had a close relationship and if Paul had run anywhere, it would have been to his Uncle. She received no reply from John's home phone; she drove to his flat only to be told by a scantily clad woman that John had left after a phone call earlier that evening. Barging past the woman, Monica told her that she would wait until her brother returned, suggesting to her that she dress properly and leave.

John saw Monica's BMW parked on the road shortly before pulling into his allotted parking space and sighed, his sister was obviously on the war path. Letting himself into his flat, he glanced into the bedroom, noticing his empty bed before going through to the lounge to find Monica sitting, stiff backed on his most comfortable armchair.

"Hello Mon." He said quietly, choosing to sit opposite her.

"Where is he?"

"He needs some space." John started "I think you should give it to him."

"I'm not here to play twenty questions with you. You can be as irresponsible with your own life as you like but I will not allow you to encourage my son into the same lifestyle now tell me where he is."

"I took him to Gloucester." John admitted.

"Take me there" She demanded.

"It's late Monica, I've had a six hour drive and I'm shattered, can we talk again tomorrow?"

"No we can't. I cannot believe that you would take him on a whim into the arms of that dreadful woman."

"For starters, it wasn't a whim, he's where he needs to be right now, you don't know if she's a dreadful woman or not, she obviously has some redeeming qualities or Paul wouldn't still be with her and he certainly wouldn't jeopardise his relationship with you over her, he thinks the world of you Monica but you are being too hard on him right now." He held up a hand to stop her from speaking "He may be your son but at the moment, I know him better than you do, let him be. He said he'd call you and let you know he was safe so just leave it at that for now. I'm tired, I'm going to bed, and we can talk some more in the morning. You are more than welcome to stay if you want but if you decide to go, make sure the door is closed properly behind you." He left her standing in the middle of the living room.

Sweeping Carmen into his arms, Paul danced her around the kitchen much to the delight of Luke who began screaming and clapping in delight while Carmen laughed and allowed Paul to guide her. As Helen came into the room to find out what all the noise was about, Paul switched from Carmen to her, pulling her against him as they completed a circuit of the kitchen, making her aware of the hard muscles across his chest where her hand rested and she felt the first stirrings of desire. Dropping his hands from Helen's miniscule waist, Paul scooped Luke into his arms whereon the little boy bounced up and down in his grip and squealed with delight at his spin around the kitchen. They were all laughing when Paul dropped into a chair, still holding Luke.

"What was all that about?" Carmen stifled another laugh.

"It was a good song," he inclined his head towards the radio "I felt the need to dance."

"I'll hand it to you Paul, you certainly liven the place up." Helen added "Come on Luke." She reached for her son "Is it still ok if I borrow your car?" she asked Carmen.

"Yeah, sure." Carmen confirmed, she was looking forward to having Paul all to herself for a couple of hours.

"What are you up to?" Paul asked.

"I'm taking Luke swimming." Helen answered.

"Can we come?" He asked, looking at Helen, he missed Carmen's frown.

"Er, if you really want to." Helen hesitated.

"You don't have any trunks with you." Carmen interjected.

"That's not a problem; I'll buy some on the way there." He stood up "Come on, I read in one of those baby books that swimming is good for pregnant ladies and I haven't worked out since I got here, I could use the exercise." He told her.

Carmen scowled after him as he left them to retrieve his towel. "You could have put him off." She snapped at Helen.

"Why? He obviously wants to come and he's right with what he said about swimming in pregnancy."

"I was hoping I could have a few hours alone with him." Carmen hissed "You knew that."

"You'd better keep your pregnancy hormones in check when you are talking to me." Helen replied, "From the sounds emanating from your bedroom, I'd say it's time to give it a rest for a couple of hours."

Since Paul had had a few quite words with the local newshounds who insisted in staking out Helen's house, they had been able to go about their business relatively unhindered and their arrival at the swimming pool went unnoticed.

Paul was already in the pool by the time the ladies and Luke eased themselves into the shallow end. Swimming the length of the pool, he came to his feet by Helen's side as Carmen busied herself with tying back her long hair. The water came to his knees, Helen, on her knees in the water, clutching her son, found her gaze on a level with his groin and quickly looked up to his face; her gaze couldn't fail to notice the ripped abs and hard Pecs on his otherwise slim and superbly toned body.

"Oh my god," she thought as she gasped at the sight of him, he was the epitome of beautiful, his body could have been carved from marble, it was absolutely flawlessly perfect.

"Are you ok?" He asked as he sunk to his knees, he had heard her gasp and he knew the reason for it, "Huh, not such a cold bitch after all." He thought.

"Water's cold," she covered her confusion.

"It is a little chilly." He agreed then wrapped an arm around Carmen's shoulders as she sank down beside him "If you two want to have a swim, I'll take care of Luke." He offered.

"Oh, I don't know." She hesitated.

"Come on Helen, God, it's been years since we have done this. Luke will be perfectly safe with Paul."

Swimming breaststroke and chatting amiably, it took some time for either of them to notice that Paul and Luke were surrounded by women in the shallow end.

"What the hell?" Carmen asked as she caught sight of Paul, broad grin and all, in the shallow end of the pool.

"He's an attractive boy," Helen lengthened her reach to keep up with Carmen. "And he has a baby in his arms, it's kind of an irresistible draw."

"He's flirting." Carmen answered.

"From what I've seen so far, that's just him, it doesn't mean anything, please don't make a scene." She pleaded.

"What a cute baby, is he yours?" A luscious brunette asked, pretending to get Luke's attention while edging closer to Paul, her bouncing breasts, barely concealed by two tiny triangles of material definitely had his attention.

"Er, no." He smiled and looked into her eyes, thinking "Wow, she's pretty."

"Oh, so are you just looking after him?" Another female voice from one of the seven women around him.

"Yeah, his Mum's having a swim and a few moments to herself."

The conversation continued, the girls getting bolder until he found he was completely surrounded by firm young flesh and smiling faces, his natural charisma took over and he had the girls giggling and blushing as he talked to them.

"Paul?" Carmen's voice at which he started guiltily "Excuse me!" She waded through the water and surrounding women to his side.

He stood, handing Luke back to his mother who promptly left the pool. He placed his hand on her swollen abdomen and announced to the waiting females "This is my baby." Before swiftly wrapping an arm around Carmen "And this is the love of my life." He finished, his actions alone should have been enough to appease her.

Carmen heard gasps of "Oh" and "Yuk, she's so old." And "What a waste of a decent piece of man, he's a granny lover" as he guided her away.

The ensuing argument lasted for hours when they got home making Paul for the first time, regret his decision to visit her. From whatever angle he found to apologise from, she found fault with. He was remarkably calm and accepted her rebuke until she started in on what a bad mother Monica was and then he lost his temper.

From the living room, Helen was initially surprised at the low level of the argument, she could clearly hear Carmen but Paul's replies were just low mumbles and she was glad that he seemed to be able to let her friend rant and not rise to the bait. Within moments of her thinking that she had underestimated Paul, his voice rose to a roar and she heard every single word as he barked at Carmen exactly what he thought of her and her opinion of his mother. She heard rapid footsteps on the stairs and the front door slammed then silence.

"You handled that well." Helen remarked as Carmen came into the room.

"Shut up Helen." Carmen snapped.

"What did you say to make him lose his rag?"

"I gave him a few home truths about his not so perfect mother." She replied "He just can't see that she's still trying to smother him." She explained.

"I take it that is a sore point with him?"

"It doesn't matter what she does, what punishment she doles out to him, he takes it without question, it makes me sick."

Paul walked to the nearest coffee shop, bought a drink and sat in a window seat, chain smoking and trying to cool his temper. He hated it when she took cheap shots at his mother; he couldn't just let them go but was his own worst enemy. Carmen knew that it was the quickest way to wind him up and she used it to her full advantage, knowing that it was like lighting the fuse on a bomb. Thinking of Monica, he knew he really should phone her and let her know he was ok but the thought of having yet another argument with her so soon after the one with Carmen left a sour taste in his mouth and he decided to leave it for a few more days.

He hadn't realised how hungry he was until he stepped into the house, the smell of a roast dinner permeated the house and saliva rushed into his mouth and his stomach growled. He peeled off his coat and sweatshirt, the heat from the oven and the fact that he had paid the heating bill meant that the heating was on full pelt making the house tropically hot.

"Hey," he spoke quietly on entering the kitchen, both women and the boy were seated at the table, food in front of them.

"You decided to come back then?" Carmen stated the obvious.

"Yeah", he hovered in the doorway, uncertain.

Helen got out of her chair "Sit down Paul; I kept your dinner warm."

He slid into the seat next to Luke's highchair, the youngster holding out a gravy covered hand towards him, opening it to reveal a smashed roast potato before smushing the same hand against his open mouth making Paul chuckle at the child's obvious enjoyment.

"If Luke is anything to go by, it looks tasty." He watched as the child started in on a carrot, thanking Helen as she put the plate in front of him.

"Aren't you going to apologise?" Carmen asked.

"It doesn't seem to make the slightest bit of difference if I do, you still niggle at it." He told her. "This is fantastic." He addressed Helen.

"You are unbelievable." Carmen hissed.

"I think we owe each other an apology. I shouldn't have shouted at you or flirted with those girls and you have to stop taking pot shots at my Mum."

"That seems reasonable." Helen commented, "you need to meet each other half way."

"I don't see why I should make allowances for your Mother." Carmen persisted.

"Give it a rest Carmen" Paul sighed "We were both wrong, I'm more than willing to accept responsibility for my part in it, can we just put this behind us and start again?"

"I suppose." She conceded.

With the meal finished and Luke eventually cleaned up from being gravy coloured, Paul offered to tackle the washing up. Talking to both the ladies over his shoulder as he supported Luke on the chair in front of the sink while the youngster proceeded to soak both of them in his attempts to help.

"I'll start painting the upstairs windows if it doesn't rain tomorrow." He said, he took the small side plate from Luke.

"That'll be great. I really do appreciate all your hard work." Helen replied.

"It's ok, I enjoy doing it and you have to admit, the house is warmer with the fresh putty in the panes and the double glazing" he answered, then "Shit." As the plate slipped from his hand and smashed on the floor "Sorry Helen."

"It's fine." Helen jumped to her feet and grabbed the dustpan and brush "Just keep Luke up on the chair."

"For God's sake Paul, cant you be more careful and watch what you are doing?" Carmen barked at him.

"I didn't do on purpose." He protested.

"We're on a budget you know, one that doesn't cover the cost of replacing dishes." She snapped.

"I broke one plate."

"Leave him alone Carmen, he didn't actually throw the bloody thing on the floor, it was an accident." Helen tipped the shards into the bin "Don't worry about it Paul."

"You are such an inconsiderate piece of shit." She seethed "You shouldn't stick up for him." She told Helen.

"Wind your neck in." Helen spat "It's no big deal and you are making mountains out of molehills."

Carmen stormed from the room, slamming the door, leaving a stunned silence behind her.

"I have no idea what just happened." Paul broke the silence.

"You have to understand, she's overly emotional and hormonal at the moment, she doesn't mean half of what she says, just try and tread carefully with her."

"I don't know who she is anymore, she's a totally different person to the one I fell in love with."

"Huh. Just you wait until she's had the baby."

"Sounds ominous." He looked at her.

"You'll see." She smiled "Come on, let's get this finished then you can go and make yet another apology for something you didn't do."

Although the following day was crisp, there was a weak winter sun which brightened the day and allowed Paul to make a start on painting the outside window frames. Standing at the top of the ladder, he shivered as he painted but his concentration soon consumed him enough to let him forget about the cold. Carmen bought tea and sandwiches out to him at regular intervals, although neither of them had apologised, they had made up but things between then were still a little awkward.

The house was situated on a busy through road and Paul took no notice of the constant traffic noise of car horns, slamming doors, squeaking brakes, loud stereos and air brakes and so he was taken completely unaware when a familiar voice called his name making the cold fingers of dread wrap around his gut. He looked down from his lofty position to see his mother and Uncle looking up at him expectantly.

"Crap, shit, fuck, bollocks." Paul murmured to himself during his decent "Hello Mum" he said, not quite meeting her gaze as his feet hit terra firma.

"It's nice to see you are alive and well."

Annoyed with himself for being a coward and not phoning her and irked by her tone, Paul opened his mouth before engaging his brain "I'm hardly likely to be anything else am I?" he snapped, then stepped back, his hand covering the cheek that received her slap.

"Do not take that attitude with me young man," she hissed "What the hell were you thinking running off in the middle of the night?"

"I was thinking that home was the last place I wanted to be." He replied, his arms folding defensively across his chest,

"All you've done by running away is provoke the press and further inflame your fathers' temper. I was in the process of reasoning with him on your behalf and was winning the battle when you upped and left, now he's baying for blood, I don't know if I will be able to restrain him when I get you home."

"Oh, like you've done a stellar job of keeping him off me so far," he flung his arms wide in frustration, raking his fingers through his hair and pacing. "And what makes you think I'm going home?" He turned towards her again, his brows drawn together in a frown.

Helen looked up from the game she was playing with her son when she heard raised voices outside to see Paul pacing and snarling at a dark haired woman who appeared to be holding her own against him and a tall, equally dark haired man who stood quietly on the sidelines.

"Who's Paul talking to?" she called to Carmen.

Walking from the kitchen and through the living room to stand by the window, Carmen watched the exchange between Paul and his mother, knowing she couldn't be seen thanks to the heavy net curtains.

"That's Paul's Mum." She stated.

"Is that his Dad?" Helen asked, standing beside her.

"No, I don't know who that is." Both women flinched when Monica lashed out at Paul and were equally astounded when Paul rounded on her and continued his diatribe. "She'll make him go home." She finished.

"You don't know that, perhaps you should go out there and intervene."

Paul caught sight of Carmen as she stepped out of the house and frowned at her, shaking his head, willing her with a look to go back into the house. Carmen held his gaze steadily as she walked towards him and slipped her arm through his, together they faced Monica.

"Good morning Mrs Jensen" she greeted the older woman.

"What reason do you have for keeping my son here?" Monica attacked.

"I'm not keeping him here, he can leave any time he pleases and he seems quite content to stay." Her tone had become sharper and she felt Paul tense beside her.

"Mum, I'll come home when I'm ready." He interjected.

"You will come home today, it isn't open for discussion." Monica glared at her son before turning back to Carmen "You and I need to talk, you are after all, carrying my Grandchild and there are arrangements that need to be made both financial and visitation."

"Very well, would you care to come in?" Carmen stepped aside and gestured to the house.

"No, we can go somewhere neutral." Monica refused.

"Alright, when would suit you?"

"Now would suit me, I have no intention of leaving here without my son. Paul, Miss Scott and I will return shortly, you stay here with John."

"But...." Paul started.

"It's ok" Carmen turned to him "We knew this day would come, I'll see you later."

Standing beside his Uncle, Paul watched as his Mother and lover drove away in Monica's car "That is such a bad idea" he murmured.

"Yep, I agree but you know what your Mum is like when she gets the bit between her teeth, it's best just to let her get on with it."

"Hmm. You'd better come inside." He preceded John into the house and offered him something hot to drink, meeting Helen as they reached the kitchen "Helen, this is my Uncle John, John, this is Carmen's friend Helen."

"Nice to meet you." John held out his hand, a warm smile lightening his grave expression

Helen looked into the honey brown eyes boring into hers, set in a ruggedly handsome face surrounded by neatly cut, naturally waving hair and realised that genetically, it was impossible for Paul not to have inherited some of his Uncles looks through his mother and his lips were almost a perfect copy of the older man's.'"

"Likewise." Helen returned the smile, it was impossible not to "Please excuse the mess, Luke and I are just finishing our artwork."

John turned and saw the chubby boy sitting in his high chair, he couldn't help the laugh that escaped his lips, the child had paint everywhere but on the paper in front of him and was himself multi coloured "What an adorable child." He breathed "May I?" he asked as he reached for the boy.

"Just let me clean him up or he'll get you covered." Helen jumped closer with a cloth.

"It's no bother." John answered and hauled him from the chair, setting him on the floor and promptly coming down to his level and happily babbling away while he took the cloth from Helen and cleaned away the paint.

Helen stood back and watched her son interact with this relative stranger, amazed at the man's reaction to her son. She glanced up at Paul who was busying himself making tea and sandwiches for them all, she had noticed a similar reaction to Luke in the boy who stood beside her and wondered if it was a family trait as Paul had displayed natural, nurturing behaviour towards Luke from their very first meeting.

Placing the sandwiches on the table, Paul turned back for the mugs of tea and noticed Helen watching his Uncle, an indulgent smile playing on her lips.

"We're Spanish, it's inbred that we love children." He said as he grabbed the mugs, "John was just like that with me."

"What do you mean was?" John asked as he clambered into his chair and heaved the robust youngster onto his lap "I still bounce you on my knee and read you bedtime stories." He laughed "The house is looking nice." He addressed his nephew.

"Paul has been fantastic." Helen gushed "I couldn't ask for a better house guest. I'll be sorry to see him leave."

"I'm not leaving." Paul said, his mouth set in a determined line.

"If I didn't know better I'd say that you were the one he was having the affair with." John smiled at her but he was watching Paul from the corner of his eye "You are after all, more to his taste as far as I'm aware, my nephew prefers blondes and make no mistake Paul," he turned his attention fully on him "You are going home today."

The silence was uncomfortable while they waited for their drinks, neither woman making the effort to speak but regarding each other closely, sizing up the enemy.

"I understand why you are angry." Carmen broke the ice.

"I wonder if you do." Monica replied.

"I've taken your son from you."

"You've done more than that. I know Paul wasn't sweet and innocent before he met you but he had never lied to me or kept secrets until he got involved with you, my son has become distant from me and that's all because of you. What were you thinking when you agreed to be with him?"

"I suppose I wasn't thinking clearly. I was highly flattered, Paul is a very attractive young man, he could and did pick up absolutely anyone he wanted and he chose me. I shouldn't have let it continue, I know that. He is a very hard habit to break." Carmen tried to explain

"You should have sent him home when he turned up here. I was worried sick but you won't understand that feeling until God forbid, something happens to your child, I don't expect you to understand the relationship between a mother and her son yet, perhaps if you have a boy you will in time fully comprehend what it is that you have put me and my son through. I don't like you, I suspect I never will, as far as I'm concerned, you molested my child and now you hold him to you with the child you carry. Paul could go far, he's intelligent and determined and level headed for the most part, I want my son back to the focused boy he was before he met you, I want him home and taking care of his business. How much can I offer you to make you go away and disappear from his life?" Monica surprised herself with her last question but she knew then that there was nothing she wouldn't do for the boy.

Carmen, momentarily stunned by Monica's last comment, took her time to mull over what the other woman had said before letting rip, "How dare you try to buy me off?" she seethed "I tried to break it off with Paul on several occasions, I didn't even tell him I was pregnant, he worked that out for himself. Nothing is going to keep me from being with him; the age gap makes no difference to me what so ever. He may be your son but he is my lover and I will not give him up on the whim of an over protective mother. Whatever problems you and Paul have are for you to sort out, my main concerns are having him in my life and having a father for my child, he has no problem with supporting me, he hasn't shied away from any of his responsibilities. I would have thought any Mother would be proud of that, whatever the circumstances."

"Do you honestly think Paul will remain faithful to you?" Monica questioned "Whether or not what he actually feels for you is love, he is after all, a sixteen year old boy, his groin rules his head and heart right now and when he comes to his senses he'll drop you like a brick. He has already made a name for himself amongst the girls and young women who travel in the same circles as him, one of them will catch him and as soon as that happens, he will turn his back on you and walk away then it will be me who has to make sure that you and my grandchild are cared for as I guarantee he will begin to question it's parentage once he is involved with someone new."

"That simply won't happen, Paul may be many things but he is well aware of his responsibilities to this child whatever happens between us. If it kills me, I will make sure he is a good father to this baby."

"At last, something we agree on." Monica conceded, she firmly believed in making her son do the right thing.

At his Uncle's insistence, Paul packed his things and waited for his Mother to return, his sullen mood returned as he slumped on the sofa with Luke sprawled across his lap having finally succumbed to his afternoon nap.

"How is he?" Monica asked her brother after greeting Helen and thanking her for putting up her son.

"Brooding." John replied "Are sure this is the right thing to do?"

"No." Monica answered "I want him home but whether or not it's the right thing to do for any of us is another matter, he seems to excel in causing trouble when he is unhappy and the last thing I need is him facing off with Michael."

"Then leave him here, he's not doing any harm, if anything, he's doing a stellar job of taking care of these two ladies and the boy."

"So it would seem but he has a business to run and there is only so long those men will organise themselves, they are fine with the contracted jobs but the day to day maintenance and gardening is suffering, Paul needs to come home." Her resolve hardened.

"Do you want me to wake him?"

"Yes, I'll wait in the car."

Paul didn't speak to either of them during the long journey home, not even when they stopped for fuel and something to eat. He sat up straighter in the back seat as they pulled up outside John's apartment building.

"Keep your head down mate." John told him "If it all kicks off Mon, he can come and stay with me."

Monica thanked her brother and drove off, glancing in the rear view mirror she noted Paul returning her gaze levelly and her heart dropped, he was plotting, she just knew it, Paul was far easier to deal with when he was ranting, his brooding silence and seeming calm acceptance of things was a sure sign of trouble.

"You should unpack, then perhaps you should let your staff know you are home" Monica told him as they entered the kitchen, he didn't reply, he simply turned his back on her and headed for the stairs "Once you've done that, we should talk." She raised her voice so that he would hear her.

"I have nothing to say to you." He answered from the foot of the stairs.

"That's fine." Monica came into the hall "I have plenty I want to say to you."

"You can say what you like; I'm done listening to you." He shot back.

"We'll see, I think you will find my will is far stronger than yours."

"Huh, whatever." He took the stairs two at a time and on reaching the top, turned towards his room, the door was open and he stood for a while on the threshold, blood seething through his veins, anger pulsing in his head. He hefted his bag and with a roar of frustration, threw it across the room, it hit the wall above his bed, cracking the paint before landing on his pillows, the zip of the bag bursting open and spilling the contents.

Hearing the bang, Monica rushed up the stairs to find her son gathering up his clothes by the armful, the broken bag now discarded in the corner of the room where he had kicked it, the crack in the paint and dent in the wall more than evident.

"You aren't going to make this easy are you?" she asked.

"Nope." He eased by her and dumped most of his clothing in the dirty linen bin inside the bathroom door. "I want my phone back."

"Sorry. No."

"Fine, I'll just go and buy another one."

"Look Paul, sit down and talk to me, then I will give you back your phone." She cajoled, sitting on his bed.

"Ok, but this time, I have some conditions of my own, I'm open to compromise but if you want me to stay here, there will be certain things I want to be able to do."

Keeping her voice calm and level, Monica told him of all her fears and worries for him, often harking back to his childhood and touching on his time at boarding school which had him absent mindedly touching the scars on his right arm, that simple movement flooding her with guilt.

248

By the end of the conversation, she had him in tears, huge racking sobs shook his body as he responded to her gentle questioning with a long overdue outpouring of emotion from the loving, sensitive boy she knew him to be. No-one would ever know the content of their conversation but it would serve to cement the relationship between Mother and son making an unbreakable bond between them.

Paul threw himself back into the day to day running of his business and was welcomed warmly by his staff when he arrived on site on Monday morning, each and every one of them stopping to watch him saunter towards them, breaking into a chorus of "Why was he born so beautiful?" As he got closer making the serious young face break out into a smile followed by his contagious laugh.

"Cut it out guys," he laughed as he joined them "It's good to be back." He finished amongst massive amounts of back slapping.

As Monica had returned his phone, he was able to speak to Carmen several times every day and was doing just that when he returned home that evening and began going through the ritual of stripping off his dirty clothes in the utility room, bidding her goodbye and hanging up as he hurried through the kitchen and into the hall which is when he heard Michael bellow and Monica's placating reply.

Indecision froze him to the spot, he wondered if he should knock on the study door as the argument was invariably about him or if he should simply stay out of the way until summoned. The door handle to the study moved making him jump, he decided to wait and quickly bolted up the stairs and into the shower.

After showering and putting on clean clothes, he crept to the top of the stairs; the argument was still in full swing so he returned to his room. He stood for a while looking at the crack in the wall above his bed and thought perhaps he should do something about it. Moving silently on bare feet, he made it, unnoticed to the garage and gathered the tools he would need, noticing for the first time since arriving home that there was nothing cooking in the kitchen signifying that the row had indeed been going on for quite some time as Monica would never leave starting the dinner this late.

Tessa found him in his room, music playing quietly while he worked, humming along with the song, his bed pushed into the middle of the room so that he could reach and repair the wall.

"What did you do now?" She asked, her hip pressed to his chest of drawers.

Turning from the wall, he replied "Nothing as far as I'm aware although I guess every breath I take is a crime in Dad's eyes." He turned back to his work.

"Come on Paul, they wouldn't be arguing if it wasn't for you." She persisted.

"Agreed," he answered over his shoulder "They were at it when I got home, I honestly don't know why; I just thought it would be a good idea for me to stay out of the way."

"Hmm, sounds reasonable. I'm going out, see you later."

Within moments of Tessa leaving, Monica and Matt appeared in the room.

"I'm starving Mum, what's for dinner?" Matt asked as he threw himself on his bed.

"We're getting take away, my discussion with your father took longer than expected." She replied.

"That doesn't sound good, what did you do now?" He threw his pillow at Paul.

"Why does everything have to be my fault?" Paul asked.

"We were discussing you but there was nothing wrong darling, we were just talking," Monica stepped in scowling at Matt and smiling at Paul "Do you think you could spare us a few moments?" she asked him.

Paul glanced back at the wall; he had nearly finished filling the crack "Can I just finish this? It'll take a couple of minutes max."

"Alright, we will wait for you in the study." She shot him another reassuring smile before she left.

"You're in the shit." Matt stated.

"I don't know, she didn't seem too pissed off." Paul shrugged "Not that it matters, I seem to be in the shit on a permanent basis right now, I may as well get used to it."

Paul was subjected to an intimidating question and answer session by Michael, not once did he meet his father's eyes and was only slightly comforted by Monica's hand resting on his shoulder.

Chapter Sixteen

He was informed in no uncertain terms of the type of behaviour expected of him and in return for that behaviour he would be allowed to socialise with his friends and granted all the freedom he had before his scandalous relationship. It had been decided and wasn't open for negotiation, that he would join Michael and his siblings for two days each week in the Jensen office to start learning the business from the ground up. Although he didn't formally acknowledge the boy as a true Jensen, Michael did recognise that he had a quick mind and could prove useful around the office.

Pauls protests were stilled by a gentle squeeze on his shoulder and he resigned himself to working for his father every Thursday and Friday starting the following week therefore allowing him the time needed to get his own business in order and arrange the work schedules of his staff for his days in the office, it meant he would be working a six day week, only having Sunday to himself.

Three weeks into his new schedule and enduring yet another day at the office, Paul looked up from the stack of files he was set to destroy when his Grandfather greeted him.

"Hi Grandpa," he smiled at the older man and stood to shake his hand/

"I heard rumours that you were here, I just had to come and see for myself if they were true." Charles greeted his grandson "How are you getting on?"

"I hate it." Paul stated "But I have been promoted to destroying files instead of correlating them so I guess I should be thankful for small mercies."

Charles laughed "Tow the line boy and you'll be out of here quicker than you can blink."

"Here's hoping." Paul pushed his hair out of his eyes "Honestly though, I don't mind being here, it makes a change from gardening in the freezing cold but it would be nice to have something to do that would get my mind working, a trained monkey could do this."

"I'll have words. Don't you own a suit?" Charles asked, he had instigated a strict dress code at Jensen Incorporated and Paul's faded black jeans and grey t-shirt was a total debasement of that code.

"I do, it doesn't fit me anymore, it would seem that doing physical work has filled me out a bit and my shirts and jackets don't fit across my chest." He shrugged "Besides, all the time I'm doing this kind of work is it really necessary to me to wear a suit?"

"Rules are rules boy and while I am aware of your fondness for breaking them, this is one that you will adhere to." Charles tried his best to frown.

"Ok, I'll see if I can sort it." Paul turned back to his work.

Michael hated it when his father arrived at the office unannounced, the man was supposed to be retired. He soon got wind of his arrival as his staff began fluttering around the office in a high state of agitation as they passed the knowledge of Charles' presence from one section of the office to another. Closing the open files on his desk so that Charles wouldn't be able to casually peruse his work, Michael sat back in the large leather chair that his father had once occupied and awaited his arrival.

Glancing quickly around his former office, Charles tutted in disapproval at the box files piled in the corners before greeting his son, noting with a little satisfaction the irked expression on the face that was a younger version of his own.

"Father, this is a surprise." Michael's lips pulled into a smile that didn't quite reach his eyes.

"So I gather given the state of your office." Charles replied, he helped himself to a coffee from Michael's filter machine, an improvement that he did approve of before seating himself in the client chair "I do hope you don't bring clients in here."

"No Father, I conduct all of my meetings in the board room, I prefer to keep my office private." Michael answered tersely "Is there any particular reason for your visit?"

"Not really, Mother and I are in town to see a show so I thought I'd drop by while she is cleaning out Harrods. How is business?"

Within moments Michael found himself justifying some of the decisions he had made over the last couple of months, each and every one of which Charles questioned and picked holes in. Inevitably, the conversation turned to Paul as Michael knew it would.

"Do you think Paul's attire is entirely suited to the office environment?" Charles questioned.

"As he is doing menial work I see no reason why he shouldn't dress as he pleases." Michael replied.

"Ah yes, about that, you wouldn't dream of making Tessa or Matthew do the kind of work you have set Paul so why on earth is he scrabbling around on his hands and knees destroying files?"

"He is here as a punishment Father, a fact of which you are well aware, he doesn't deserve the privileges the other two get."

"Think about it Michael," Charles countered "Paul runs his own extremely successful business and has proved time and again that he can manage that and his staff with ease, I appreciate that he has a natural talent for causing problems and getting himself into trouble but the boy is bright, he has a quick mind and all you will succeed in doing by putting him to menial tasks is destroy his spirit."

"That was sort of the point." Michael admitted "To destroy his spirit, he has far too much of it and needs to be curtailed into behaving, if that means breaking him, then so be it."

"Do you honestly think he will sit back and let that happen? He will simply run off again and I seriously doubt that you will get him back again. I expect that prospect fills you with joy, you never did bond with him but think of your wife, estrangement from Paul would destroy her."

Michael had to admit that Charles was right, he sighed, pressing his fingers together and resting them on his pursed lips as he regarded his father "You are right," he eventually spoke "Paul leaving would do a great deal of harm to Monica and I won't allow that to happen. What do I do with him though? I don't want him disturbing Matthew or Tessa nor do I want him involved in the day to day running of the office, he is intelligent enough to be able to bring this place to a standstill if he chooses."

"I've been thinking about that ever since I heard he was here. Why don't you put him with Satchell?" Charles asked referring to the mole of a man who resided in one of the tiny front offices, sifting out customers who were potentials for bankruptcy.

"Of course, it would keep him out of the way and give him something to occupy his mind." Michael beamed.

"And Satchell always seems to have an overflowing in tray, he could teach Paul to take over from him when he retires." Charles added.

"Father, you are brilliant, I will call Satchell in this afternoon and let him know what's expected of Paul. Thank you."

"My pleasure but before Paul can go into Satchel's office, he needs a suit."

"Yes, of course, I will take him to buy one in the morning." Michael relayed his conversation with his father to Monica that evening as they were preparing for bed, adding "I think it's time I had a new suit, I think I'll get measured while we are there."

The following morning, after a brief visit to the office, Paul accompanied Michael on his very first suit buying expedition.

"I'm getting my suit handmade," Michael told him as they entered the store, "Tessa's friend Joanne, Maureen or someone..."

"Suzanne." Paul corrected.

"Yes that's right Suzanne, she works here and I believe she deals with off the rack clothing, go and find her and get sorted out with a decent suit."

Paul grinned as he walked away; his father had just given him permission to seek out his lover, it had been a while since he'd seen her and he was looking forward to it immensely.

Ten minutes later he finally tracked her down. He stopped halfway across the floor space of the jewellery department to take in the delicious sight of her tight pencil skirt stretched across her pert bottom as she leant over one of the glass display cabinets. His eyes travelled from her behind down her legs, noticing the clasps of her suspenders pressing against the fabric of her skirt, her dark stockings clung to her shapely legs; her nicely turned ankles drifted into tiny feet and obscenely high heeled black shoes. As he watched, she came up onto tip toe, stretching the fabric of her skirt further as she leant the weight of her upper body on her arms to get a better look at something in the glass display stand beneath her chest.

Standing beside her, he too leant over the cabinet to see what had grabbed her interest, she smelled heavenly and the tight white blouse didn't detract from her delightful breasts of which he had a lovely view as they pushed against the open neck line.

She caught his scent before she noticed his face reflected in the glass below her, she glanced into his eyes via the glass and smiled before standing straighter, her hands on the counter as she turned her head towards him.

"Can I help you?" She asked, her eyes twinkling as he tore his gaze from her breasts.

"I sincerely hope so." He answered, biting back on the huge grin that threatened to burst onto his face.

She laughed "What are you doing here?" She asked.

"I have to get a suit." He shrugged "What were you looking at that gave me the fantastic view as I walked over?" He asked, glancing down at the cabinet.

Stretching her arm out, Suzanne placed the tip of her index finger on the glass above the diamond tennis bracelet "That. I love it but I'll be drawing my pension before I can afford it."

Leaning closer to get a better look, Paul smiled; he liked the look of the bracelet and thought it would suit her very well. "I'll get it for you one day." He said.

"Uhuh, of course you wil.l" She mocked.

"I promise," he placed his hand over his heart "Now that's out of the way, are you going to help me find a suit?"

"Follow me." She beckoned him, knowing he would watch the sway of her hips for a couple of paces before he followed.

"Gladly."

He stood patiently as she cajoled the male assistant to lend her his tape measure under protestations that measuring customers was his job. Batting her eyelids and adjusting her breasts, drawing the man's gaze, she assured him that she was more than capable and as this man was a friend and his family valuable customers, it was part of her job to give him preferential treatment, she did all this whilst escorting him out of the department and insisting he take his lunch break while she took care of the customer.

"Nicely done." Paul commended her.

"Thank you, do you know what size neck you are?" She asked.

"Not a clue but I can give you my other measurements." He grinned.

"I am well aware of the size of your dick." Her professional veneer cracked "Stand still while I measure you."

He complied while she measured his shoulders, chest, sleeve length and waist but he stepped out of her reach as she went down on her knees, the tape measure pressed into his groin. His hand covered hers and removed it,

"Suzie, I can't in good conscience let you do that part."

"Why not?" She looked up at him from her knees "I do need your inside leg measurement."

"I understand that but the last time you were on your knees in front of me you were sucking me off, it's been a while and I only have so much self control."

She smiled and pressed the tape measure into his hand "Fine. You hold that end and I'll take the measurement."

Once she had completed this task she told him to go into the changing room while she selected shirts, suits, ties and shoes and arrived while he was undressing with four very nice off the rack suits, two pairs of shoes, a selection of ties and shirts in varying shades.

He hated the first two suits and try as she might not to laugh at the faces he was pulling in the mirror, she had to agree that something wasn't quite right with them, he returned to the dressing room with an additional shirt she had found, had taken off the offending suit and was buttoning the newest shirt when she stepped into the room. With no preamble what so ever, she swayed up to him and pressed her lips to his, her high heels giving her the height she needed so that she didn't have to stand on the tips of her toes to reach his mouth, her hands flying over the recently fastened buttons of the shirt.

Breaking the kiss, he watched her hands roaming his chest, swiftly followed by her mouth, "This shirt appears to be faulty, I thought I had just buttoned it up and yet it looks as though they've come undone again."

"Shut up. I've missed you. I want you. NOW." She pressed her chest to his.

"Oh God!" He groaned, instantly aroused "Suzie, I can't, I'm seeing someone and it's pretty serious."

"I know all about the teacher and the baby and I don't give a flying fuck." She wriggled her skirt up over her hips, revealing her suspenders and the creamy skin above her stocking tops before hooking a leg around his hip and grinding her mound into his groin "Admit it, you want me" her tongue teased his lips and she clung to him as he grabbed her and kissed her.

Letting his shoulders rest against the wall of the changing room, he thrust his hips. outwards as she hooked her other leg over his hip, her hands gripping his shoulders, leaving it to him to free his erection, move her underwear aside and lower her down onto him, she was so aroused and wet that she accommodated him easily, he shuddered as he sank into her, his full length disappearing with ease.

"We have to be quick lover" She breathed.

"I seriously doubt that will be a problem." He gasped as she wrapped her arms firmly around his neck and began to ride him, "I love how wet you get, it's beautiful, fuck, Suzie, I'm nearly there."

"Wait." She hissed "Me first," she knew he would hold back, she knew exactly how to play him, she placed one heeled foot on the floor and wrapped the other leg further around him, grinding her mound into his pubic bone, capturing his mouth to drown out the groan of their combined orgasm. Feeling him subside, she let her other leg fall to the floor and kissed him while adjusting her underwear before stepping back and easing her skirt over her hips. "Thank you Mr. Jensen that was just what the doctor ordered."

"Boyfriend not doing it for you?" He asked, his underwear back in place, he once again buttoned the shirt and reached for the trousers.

"Not like you do." She admitted.

"Then dump him and date me." He glanced at her as he reached for the jacket.

"No, I like him and he'll get there in the disgusting sex stakes besides, didn't you say you were serious about the teacher?"

"Hmm," he mumbled "So serious that I've just fucked you in a dressing room."

"Proving my point that you aren't ready for a serious relationship. That looks great." She smoothed the lapels on the jacket. "Come outside and have a look in the bigger mirrors."

Michael was sitting in the waiting area, a coffee on the table beside him as they left the dressing room and entered the department the sight of him making Paul do a quick recap of what had just happened, hoping that neither of them had voiced their pleasure as Michael would be sure to mention it at some point during the day.

"Hello Mr. Jensen, we won't keep you long." She beamed at him "Yes, I think this is definitely the one." She smiled at Paul "What do you think?"

"I like it." He agreed.

"Hmm, there's something missing, let me see, erm I know, cufflinks." She eased the cuffs of the shirt out of the jacket to make sure it didn't have buttons before whirling away only to return moments later with the cufflinks, fastening them to the shirt, she told him to remove his jacket and have a hard look at the fit of the trousers and shirt, their eyes meeting in the mirror and both smiling, the end effect was dazzling, his frame carried a suit perfectly. "Will this be suitable?" she turned to Michael.

"That will do nicely." Michael nodded "Please remove the tags, he can keep it on, we are returning to the office."

Once in the car on the way to the office, Paul glanced at his father, one hand playing with the lapel of his new jacket "Thanks Dad." Those two words being the most he had said to the older man in weeks.

"I didn't do it out of the kindness of my heart." Michael gruffed "You will soon be meeting clients, the suit is a necessity." He didn't see eye to eye with this boy but he was pleased his manners appeared to be intact.

PRODIGAL SON

By then end of Saturday, Paul was exhausted and pleased to find his brother was nowhere to be found when he stepped out of the shower. Dressing in an old sweatshirt and loose fitting jogging bottoms, he joined the rest of his family for an early evening meal, stifling yawns repeatedly throughout before retiring to his room.

"Hey Paul, wake up" Matt shook his sleeping sibling again.

"What?" Paul gruffed, he felt as though he had only just closed his eyes "It can't be morning already?" he mumbled, rolling away from Matt's persistent shaking.

"Nah man, it's Saturday night, why are you in bed? It's time to partay." Matt grinned dancing to the imaginary beat in his head "Come on, get up."

"Matt, I'm knackered, I'm gonna stay in tonight." Paul brushed his hair out of his eyes, frowning at his brother but he couldn't help smiling when Matt began to dance.

"Paul, it's two for one night at Jokers, we have to go."

"Well, if you'd said we were going to Jokers, I'd be dressed already." He sat up, grinning at his brother "Give me ten minutes."

Jokers, hardly a premier night spot but the Jensen twins loved it, if they were to be found anywhere on any given Friday and Saturday night, it would be there. The club was run down to say the least, the furnishings were shabby, the dance floor worse but the booze was cheap and the music jumping, this coupled with the fake ID's the boys had got their hands on and a sizeable donation to the scarily large doorman guaranteed them entry to the club each and every time they arrived at the door, Jokers was indeed the venue of choice for them.

The Jensen boys were well known at the club and were a draw in themselves, both being outstanding in the looks department and with physiques to die for, no sooner would they step into the club than they would be surrounded by the people they knew there, all much older than them and mainly of the female persuasion.

Sending Paul to the bar, Matt headed for the dance floor and gyrated his way into a delightful smelling group of ladies who were dancing around their handbags, within seconds he was up close and personal with the girl he had selected from the group, her bottom pressed to his groin, grinding hard to the beat.

Paul fought his way to the packed bar and amusing bar staff, all of whom were either lithe, scantily clad women or handsome, built men who would further encourage the deviant behaviour at the club by dancing so close that they could be mating and openly kissing and fondling each other as well as flirting outrageously with the patrons.

As was the norm when Paul approached the bar, the manager appeared in front of him, not needing to ask what he wanted; the two had an established rapport and the man had, on several occasions, offered Paul a bar job to which Paul would smile and come up with a feasible excuse as to why he couldn't take the job up until the day the bar manager had cottoned on that he was not only too young to serve behind the bar but also too young to actually be in the club in the first place. After, taking Paul to one side and telling him he knew both the boys were underage; he smiled and then told him that he was prepared to turn a blind eye to that fact provided they didn't cause any trouble.

By half two on Sunday afternoon, both boys had surfaced, Paul sitting at the breakfast bar nursing a cup of tea along with a pile of chocolate digestives while trying to get his banging head around that week's staff schedules, a pen in one hand, a largely un-smoked cigarette in the other, he stared, uncomprehending at the paper in front of him.

Matt, having risen mere moments before his brother had made it as far as the bottom of the stairs before his spinning head succeeded in getting the message through to his bubbling stomach that it needed to void its contents and quickly. Bolting for the downstairs cloakroom and managing to angle his head over the bowl milliseconds before the acidic contents of his stomach flowed into the toilet. Trying not heave in time with his brother, Paul made a hasty retreat to the kitchen which is where Monica found him.

"You look dreadful."

"I feel worse." Paul mumbled "Is Matt still throwing up?"

"Yes" she confirmed noticing that her youngest son made a tremendous effort not to dry heave at the thought, "Can I get you something a little more substantial than biscuits?"

"No thanks Mum; it's about all I can manage right now. I'll be fine once my head stops pounding."

Monica put a packet of paracetemol and a glass of water in front of him, adding another glass when Matt stumbled into the kitchen and took the stool next to Paul.

"I am never drinking again." He declared as he downed two tablets and sunk the glass of water.

"Ah, the morning after lament" Monica quipped.

"I don't know why you bother drinking when you inevitably end up puking most of it down the toilet." Paul commented, he tentatively managed to stretch his tight muscles, the large glass of water and pain killers were slowly taking effect.

"One way or another it all ends up down the bog." Matt told him "Whoa, whoever gave you that sure had a big mouth." He finished having caught sight of the dark red love bite on Paul's neck.

Sliding off his stool, Paul approached the mirror at the far end of the kitchen "Shit" he muttered "How the hell did I get that?" he asked no one in particular as he re-took his stool

"Don't know why you bother drinking if you can't remember anything." Matt shot a sideways glance at him.

"Very fucking funny." Paul lashed out, landing a playful punch on Matt's hugely muscled arm "Did you see me with anyone last night?" he asked, all the while painfully aware that although Monica seemed occupied with the dinner preparations, she was listening intently to her sons.

"I saw you with several someone's last night but you didn't seem to be that close to any of them, you did disappear for about half an hour though and I did see a couple of ladies coming in from the compound straightening their clothes, it wasn't long after they hit the dance floor that you appeared."

"Crap. I really shouldn't drink." Paul put his head in his hands; Matt's description was prodding memories and did also explain why he'd woken up still wearing a condom.

"Paul, I thought you were a one woman man and that you were in love with Carmen?" Monica stepped into the conversation.

"I do love Carmen; I'm having a hard time with the one woman bit." He sighed "I've been with Suzanne this week as well as whomever that was at the club."

"You old dog." Matt chuckled.

"I suppose I'm hoping in vain that you were safe?" Monica asked.

"I know I was last night if only for the fact that I was still wearing my protection this morning." He cringed.

"Oh, that right there is just plain wrong" Matt shuddered "Ergh."

Monica suppressed a smile at the horrified expressions both of the boys wore "Don't you think you would be better off with Suzanne, she is at least more your age."

"She won't have me, she says I'm not ready to be with her on a permanent basis yet and she's right but I can't get enough of her."

"And where does Carmen figure in all this, remember her, the one carrying your baby?" she prodded.

"I love Carmen, I really do but I'm in love with Suzanne, it's hard to explain." He shrugged.

"Try." Monica put her hands on her hips.

"Well," he paused, searching for words, running his fingers through his hair "If I were an artist I would say she's my muse, the one I want to capture, she's my soul mate, I can tell her anything and everything and none of it phases her, she's the only one besides you who truly knows me."

"And the girl or girls last night?"

"Drunken fumbles." He admitted "Something which I hope won't be repeated but who knows?"

Later that evening, after a lengthy phone call to Carmen which revealed that not only was she experiencing increasingly regular Braxton Hicks contractions but also that her house had finally been sold and she was actively looking for somewhere to live.

Paul silently thanked his Uncle for purchasing the house while he made plans to step up his work load and make a lot of money in as short a space of time as possible.

He began to rise earlier in the mornings and was already well into the day's work when his staff arrived on site and on the days where he had to work for his Father, he would put in a few hours gardening work before going to the office, often working by the light of the spotlights he had hired to extend the winter working day and washing and changing into his suit in the men's bathroom's at Jensen Incorporated only to return to site when the office closed and put in a few more hours before going home.

His commitment to his job and staff had the desired effect of making them work harder and he encouraged them to make decisions and take responsibility for their own sections of the job. It gave him immense pleasure to tell them that they were ahead of schedule and the Council were prepared to pay a sizable bonus amount if they managed to complete the job one month earlier than planned.

He kept up his routine for six weeks before it began to take its toll. Working six days a week, partying Friday and Saturday nights and spending most of his Sunday's working out in the gym left him permanently tired. Each day he found it harder to wake up and staying awake during office hours was a mammoth task even though he now found the work interesting thanks to Alan Satchell but as Monica kept telling him, something had to give, she expressed her concerns for his health on a daily basis but he would simply smile and tell her he was fine.

Returning home from the gym the following Sunday, Monica found her son in the kitchen at his favourite stool by the breakfast bar. He had made himself something to eat and was glancing through his staff rotas while chasing the food around his plate with his fork, he greeted her with a weary smile and she watched him as she peeled potatoes. Paul began to sway in his seat, almost asleep over his plate of food. Monica removed the plate from him, closed his diary and ignored his protests as she told him he had done enough for the time being and he should go and take a nap.

Within the hour, the phone rang, Monica answered and listened to the woman on the other end speak, hanging up, she climbed the stairs, entered her son's darkened room and crossed to the bed shaking Paul's shoulder and saying his name, he didn't stir on any of the four occasions in which she tried to wake him and, taking note of the dark circles under his eyes and the way his deep breathing didn't alter, she knew further attempts at waking him would be futile, he was utterly exhausted and in a dead sleep, she returned downstairs, leaving her son to his dreams.

End

PRODIGAL SON

So, what happens next?

Book 2 that's what! Father & Son should be with you around Easter 2013 and I hope to release book 3 this year too.

Just in case you can't wait, the prologue to Father & Son is below:

There are many things I hope to achieve with my life and some that I have already accomplished. I own my own business; I have fathered a child, I am successful in my own right but I have yet to capture the woman of my dreams, I will get her, mark my words.

I have accepted that I am not ready to settle down at this particular moment in time just as I have come to terms with the fact that I will never and I do mean absolutely, positively, never achieve anything which would cause my Father to tell me he is proud of me, I can live with that. I sometimes feel it would be nice to be acknowledged as his son but those moments are very few and far between.

My aim right now? To retire by the time I am thirty. Yeah, right, as if I could leave the running of anything I own to another for any length of time, it just isn't going to happen. Perhaps I should lower my expectations and say instead that I plan to be a millionaire by the time I hit twenty five, that's certainly achievable, I am well on my way although I do keep my finances a closely guarded secret.

I am beginning to find that I like the finer things in life. I like my cars fast and my women faster, the faster the better as it means they don't stick around too long. I like made to measure clothes and the revel in the fact that at this point in my life, I can afford pretty much anything that takes my fancy. I take great pleasure in treating my Mother, the woman who gave me life and continues to support me in all of my endeavours. From trinkets to holidays, whenever I feel the urge to splurge, she is at the forefront of my thoughts and that first purchase will always be something for her.

I work hard, play harder and I try to be a good father, I am a terrible boyfriend by my own and everyone else's admission. Women are my weakness; they have been for a very long time and probably will be for a long time to come.

I take pride in my success even though it sometimes makes me sacrifice time with my child. I have worked hard, sweated, bled and cried for every penny I have earned. It's added another layer to my personality and has got me noticed. Yes, I do still play up to the media, I freely admit that I love the attention but I'm building an empire here and empire's need a paparazzi boost every now and then, I recognised that fact at an early age and use it to my full advantage at every available opportunity.

I am your tall, dark and handsome guide of Prodigal Son, this is the continuing story of my life and those who come and go through it. It is intertwined with that of the mother of my child and the people in her life too, from the good times and the bad as I try to become something that resembles a decent human being and a good parent and role model as I go about my daily business making sure everything is as it should be and laying the foundations to my future fortune.

I am a young man on the precipice of greatness. I intend to fulfil the goals I have set for myself and I'm aware I will have to tread on a few toes, stab a few backs and break a few hearts to get there.

I am Paul Jensen